J. F. STRAKER

GOODBYE, AUNT CHARLOTTE!

Complete and Unabridged

LINFORD
Leicester

First published in Great Britain in 1958

First Linford Edition
published 2004

British Library CIP Data

Straker, J. F. (John Foster)
Goodbye, Aunt Charlotte!.—Large print ed.—
Linford mystery library
1. Detective and mystery stories
2. Large type books
I. Title
823.9′14 [F]

ISBN 1–84395–387–0

Published by
F. A. Thorpe (Publishing)
Anstey, Leicestershire

Set by Words & Graphics Ltd.
Anstey, Leicestershire
Printed and bound in Great Britain by
T. J. International Ltd., Padstow, Cornwall

This book is printed on acid-free paper

GOODBYE, AUNT CHARLOTTE!

Nobody had a good word for Aunt Charlotte, not even her niece, Elizabeth. When the rich, old lady arranged a trip to London, Elizabeth's friends thought it would be a joke to hoax people into believing that Aunt Charlotte had disappeared. Fake telegrams were sent, telephone calls made, clues laid — and then Aunt Charlotte was found dead. Inspector Pitt discovered that several of the practical jokers might have had a motive for the crime, but it was a complicated business separating the false clues from the real ones . . .

Books by J. F. Straker
in the Linford Mystery Library:

A CHOICE OF VICTIMS
SWALLOW THEM UP
DEATH ON A SUNDAY MORNING
A LETTER FOR OBI
COUNTERSNATCH
ARTHUR'S NIGHT
A PITY IT WASN'T GEORGE
THE GOAT
DEATH OF A GOOD WOMAN
MISCARRIAGE OF MURDER
SIN AND JOHNNY INCH
TIGHT CIRCLE
A MAN WHO CANNOT KILL
ANOTHER MAN'S POISON
THE SHAPE OF MURDER
A COIL OF ROPE
MURDER FOR MISS EMILY

1

What's Wrong with Murder?

Michael Lane stood with his back to the room, the lean fingers of both hands drumming rhythmically on the window sill. Below him the forecourt of the Tower Hotel provided an oasis of light in the dark countryside, but the cars parked on it were few. Milford Cross was a quiet village on a quiet road, with little through traffic.

'Be your age, Michael,' said Elizabeth. 'Stop sulking.'

The drumming fingers stilled abruptly.

'I'm not sulking,' he said petulantly, turning to face them. A lock of dark hair flopped over his forehead, and he flicked it back with a quick, mechanical movement of his head. His dark eyes, set beneath long, curling lashes in an olive-skinned face, brooded on his audience of four. 'I'm just fed to the teeth with the way you crab everything I suggest. What's wrong with murder, I'd like to know?'

'It's agin the law,' Alan Torreck informed him kindly.

'Very funny. Your trouble is that you lack imagination. You say you want something on the grand scale, something original, but you go all lily-livered when I suggest it.' He shook his head sorrowfully. 'I don't know what's come over you fellows. You used not to be this way.'

He had spoken to the men, but his eyes were on the girl — Elizabeth Messager, his cousin. A girl with red hair and a trim figure, but with little claim to facial beauty. A girl with large grey eyes and a wide gash of a mouth, and a pointed elfin face that could switch from gloom to gaiety and back as swiftly as an English summer. *She* was what had come over them. He had been a fool to introduce her into their hitherto masculine circle. Before she had cast her subtle feminine net over the others they had been a carefree, happy bunch, with no inhibitions and with an aptitude for practical joking which it had pleased them to indulge. Now — well, they took their cue from her, approving where she approved, frowning where she frowned. Or Bruce and Alan did. He wasn't sure about Desmond.

He was suddenly aware of her steady gaze, and he smiled at her, exerting all his charm. If he could win her support . . .

'Murder isn't original,' Alan said. 'It's as old as the hills.'

'And one's got to observe the decencies,' Bruce Poulton said. He was a fair, heavily built young man, lacking a sense of humour. The others had never ceased to be surprised that Bruce should be one of their number; a taste for practical joking was not what one would have expected in so stolid a being. 'Personally, I don't see murder as a proper subject for joking.'

You wouldn't, thought Michael. You're in love with that blasted red-head, and you see it the way you think she sees it. Yet only a few months back . . .

'Neither do I,' Alan Torreck said, slightly surprised at finding himself in agreement with Bruce. 'It's a cheap suggestion, Michael. What's more, it's impracticable. Murder demands a corpse, and that's something we don't happen to possess right now.'

'What, no corpse?' Desmond Farrel, who had been lying on the bed blowing smoke rings at the ceiling, raised himself on one elbow and stared gravely at his friend. 'Ought we not to do something about that, Alan? It would be rather embarrassing, don't you think, to have to admit that we lacked a corpse? If some one asked, I mean. So — well, so inefficient.'

Alan threw a cushion at him, and he flopped back on the bed. It was his bed, and his room. In a sense it was also his hotel; his father, the Hon. George Victor Farrel, owned and managed it.

Elizabeth, perched at the foot of the bed, caught the cushion. She placed it on her lap, smoothing it with a slim hand.

'Lots of people haven't got corpses, Desmond,' she said. Her voice was deep, almost masculine; it had a vibrant warmth that fascinated. 'You mustn't let it upset you.'

'It's just that I'm sensitive about these things,' he murmured.

'We'll give you one for Christmas.' Alan picked up his tankard, found it empty, and replaced it reluctantly. 'Well, now. Having disposed of murder — what next?'

Bruce Poulton, his brow furrowed, shook his head. His strength lay not in ideas but in a husky body and a thoroughness of execution; his almost fanatical attention to detail was as Teutonic as his blondness. Elizabeth continued to smile — a withdrawn and secret smile, as though her thoughts and not her companions formed the substance of her amusement. Michael Lane shrugged his slim shoulders and turned again to the window, piqued at their refusal to consider his suggestion.

'Inspiration appears to be lacking,' Desmond said lazily, still at full stretch. 'We need lubrication. Whose round is it?'

'Mine,' Bruce said.

He stood up and flexed his knees. It was Desmond's round really; he knew that. He suspected that Desmond knew it too. But he had sat for too long, and it was stuffy in the bedroom, and he welcomed the opportunity to leave it for a while. It also flattered his vanity to usurp a responsibility, however paltry, that should have been shouldered by the man on the bed. He had no particular regard for Desmond Farrel; he disliked him as a person, hated his unconscious air of superiority, and was deeply suspicious of his interest in Elizabeth. But he could not forget that Desmond was the grandson of an earl — and that he, Bruce Poulton, was the son of the local butcher. It was snobbishness, not regard, that prompted him now.

When he had gone Elizabeth left her perch on the bed for the armchair he had vacated. She stretched delicately, wriggling her body into a comfortable niche among the cushions. 'Have you always suffered from a paucity of ideas?' she asked. 'Or are you losing interest? Speaking as a newly elected associate member, I wouldn't say that you strike me as being a vigorous, go-ahead society. What's wrong?'

You, Michael wanted to say, whirling to face her. Instead he said, failing to keep the resentment from his voice, 'They've got cold feet. They're fine at impersonating Eastern potentates or fiddling with the hall piano, but anything more grandiose or imaginative unnerves them. They're as dull as this blasted village.'

'Don't malign the village. It's no duller than most,' Elizabeth told him. 'And you and Bruce are out of it all day. Desmond and Alan might reasonably yearn for more excitement, but I don't see why you should.'

'Too true.' Desmond sat up and swung his long legs, encased in stove-pipe trousers, to the floor. 'And who says my tiny feet are frozen? That most definitely is *not* true. It's just that right now I lack imagination.'

Through half-closed eyes Elizabeth regarded his slightly dishevelled appearance. She did not want him to know that she was watching him — yet watching him was one of her delights. How attractive he was! It was an attractiveness that did not depend on facial beauty (as did Michael's) or on the magnificent physique that was Bruce's. It had something of both of these, yet so much more. Desmond looked well in any company, in any guise. He had the poise and assurance that go with fine breeding.

And what fun he was. Michael and Alan could be fun too; but Michael had the Latin temperament of his looks, he was volatile and moody, and Alan's brand of humour verged on the schoolboy's. An evening with Michael depended for its success on his present humour; with Alan, on hers; with Bruce, on the excellence of the entertainment provided. But with Desmond it never failed. His charm was effortless, his timing perfect.

'We must be circumspect,' Desmond was saying. 'That above all. Our somewhat unusual tuning of the hall piano has raised suspicion in the paternal bosom, and I would hate for him to rumble me right now. I am, as it were, delicately poised.'

'How come?' asked Alan.

'Between ruin and solvency. I look to

the old man to declare for solvency, bless him.'

He was always broke, thought Elizabeth. That was why she had refused to marry him. That — and Aunt Charlotte. There was always Aunt Charlotte. Yet even so she had hesitated over her refusal. She wasn't in love with him — but still . . .

'Maybe we ought to lie low for a while, then,' Alan said. 'I prefer you solvent. You have a habit of borrowing when broke.'

'Good Lord, no!' Abruptly he shed the languid pose he delighted in assuming. 'But nothing crude, nothing obvious. Anything that shrieks of practical joking is out. It has to look genuine.'

'Such as murder,' Michael said, seizing his opportunity. 'Nobody ever faked a murder, did they? Your father wouldn't connect you with that. Or would he?'

'Ah! You have a point there,' Desmond conceded.

Bruce returned with a tray of drinks. He looked hot and flushed, and Desmond eyed him curiously.

'Dulcie,' he diagnosed. 'That's what

delayed you. Either Dulcie or a new barrel.'

'She wanted to know about the film at the Regal.' Bruce's cheeks turned even pinker, and he glanced anxiously at Elizabeth. 'She's thinking of going to see it.'

'With you?'

'No.'

He spoke curtly. Had Elizabeth not been present he would have been smugly complacent at the suggestion that the blonde hotel receptionist was trying to date him, but in Elizabeth's hearing it was most unwelcome. To divert attention from himself he said, 'How's it coming? Any bright ideas?'

'Only a repeat of Michael on murder. It's becoming an obsession with him. Maybe his ancestral background should be investigated.'

Michael laughed. It was no use letting himself be rattled, he would not gain his point that way. And he wanted to gain it. He had thrown murder at them at random, with no plan behind it and no thought that it would be accepted. But he had expected that it would at least be discussed before being discarded. Its immediate and somewhat contemptuous rejection had nettled him. It had also made him ponder the idea more seriously himself, so that now the nucleus of a plan had begun to form in his mind.

'I can take it,' he said. 'But we don't have to have a corpse, if that is what is holding you back. All that's needed is for one of us to disappear. Drop a few not too subtle clues around, and the village will lap it up.'

Alan's pale eyes narrowed. They were a watery blue, and gave an impression of weakness; yet for all his easy good nature, his willingness to go with the crowd, he could be stubborn. It needed tact to shift him; Michael's direct methods had little or no chance of doing so. And he could have been shifted then. He had not been so set against the suggestion as his words implied; it had a crudeness about it that appealed to the schoolboy in him.

But he would not be bludgeoned into agreement. 'Cut it out, Michael,' he said.

'You've had your murder. Don't keep harping on it.'

'He's got a one-track mind. He doesn't appreciate that 'no' means 'no,'' Bruce said. Michael glared at him; he would take criticism from the others that he would not take from Bruce. Aware of this, and that he might be considered to have spoken out of turn, Bruce added quickly, 'It wouldn't work, Michael. For one thing, which of us could take time off from work to disappear for a few days? I know I couldn't. Could you?'

Michael did not answer.

'I couldn't,' Alan said curtly. 'And I wouldn't if I could.'

'That would leave me, then,' Desmond said. 'Yes, I suppose I could manage it; the old man is used to my itinerant habits. But naturally I should expect to disappear in style. No mouldering in a morgue for *this* corpse.' He grinned at Michael. 'Did I mention that I'm broke? If you insist on murder, Michael, it could be expensive.'

'Then I'm even more against it,' Alan told him. 'I'm not subscribing to a plan which lets you loose with any of *my* money. I know your tastes in living, and I can't afford them.'

'My tastes in dying are even more expensive.'

'I suppose it doesn't have to be one of us,' Michael said. 'Anyone in the village would do, provided he or she went off without too much fuss.'

Elizabeth had taken no part in this discussion. She had been shocked at Michael's proposal, and would have vehemently declared against it had the others not done so. But she was relieved that their veto absolved her from interfering. She disliked quarrelling with her cousin, and to have inveighed against an otherwise unanimous decision would have made them regret her presence.

Aware that the discussion was now a hypothetical one, from which no decision would emerge, she allowed her thoughts to wander from Desmond, on which they had been centred, to Aunt Charlotte. Would Aunt Charlotte, despite her objection to any talk of her niece's marriage, object quite as strongly if

Desmond were the prospective husband? Was there enough of the snob in her? And if there was did she, Elizabeth, really want to marry him?

Elizabeth feared she knew the answer to the first query; she was less sure of the second. But thought of Aunt Charlotte had reminded her of an event to which she was looking forward with some pleasure, and she said, without motive, not realizing the implication of her words, 'Aunt Charlotte is going to spend a few days in London next week with a friend.'

They stared at her. She was looking at Desmond as she spoke; his easy smile became a broad grin, and he winked. Even Alan Torreck showed interest.

'What's the matter?' she asked, surprised.

'Aunt Charlotte!' Michael spoke the name softly, savouring it. 'Thank you, Elizabeth. If that isn't manna from heaven then I don't know what is.'

'The perfect murderee,' Desmond agreed. 'It could be fate, you know, Elizabeth. I hate to speak ill of any relative of yours, but you must admit that, if some one in Milford Cross has to come to a sticky end, no one deserves it more richly than does your dear Aunt Charlotte.'

'Good Lord!' Memory of their conversation returned to her, and she caught the drift of their thoughts. 'So that's what you're getting at, is it? Well, you can drop that idea right now. As for what you said about a sticky end, Desmond — well, I know she isn't popular, but I'm quite sure no one in the village dislikes her sufficiently to murder her.'

'Don't they?' Desmond looked hard in turn at each of the other three men in the room, and then back at the girl. He was about to expand that remark, but changed his mind. 'Well, maybe they don't. But I guarantee none of them would shed a tear if they heard that some one had done it for them. Would you, after the way she's treated you?'

Elizabeth flushed. Her dislike of her aunt — though not the full reason for it, thank goodness — was too well known for her to deny it now, but it troubled her conscience to hear it so bluntly expressed.

Nor had she failed to interpret the significance of the look Desmond had given the other three. They all had good cause to hate Aunt Charlotte. Aunt Charlotte had done her best to ruin Alan and his father, she had ensured that Michael and his parents did not benefit from her husband's will and had cut them out of her own, she had insulted Bruce almost beyond belief. Elizabeth thought she would never forget the one and only occasion on which Bruce had called at The Elms to see her. 'The butcher's boy is here, Elizabeth,' Aunt Charlotte, who had opened the door to him, had called out, in that soft, purring voice of hers that could so quickly turn as raucous as a fishwife's. 'Get rid of him, will you? And tell him to use the back door in future. I won't have the tradesmen calling at the front.'

Bruce — 'the butcher's boy '! Poor, snobbish Bruce, who was so proud of his job at the bank, who hated any reference to his father's business.

He had never called at the house again.

'Yes, I would,' she said curtly. 'Disliking

a person doesn't necessarily mean you wish them ill. And if you're suggesting that Michael's stupid plan should operate with Aunt Charlotte as the victim you can think again. I won't have it.'

'Don't agitate yourself,' Desmond told her, smiling. 'Nothing will come of it. It was only a beautiful dream.'

'But something *must* come of it!' Michael's eyes were gleaming. 'It's too good an opportunity to waste, damn it! Cut out murder if you must, but let's make use of it somehow.'

'How?' asked Alan.

'Well — make out she has disappeared, and that we don't know what has happened to her. We could hint at abduction, robbery, loss of memory; anything you like. Even an elopement.'

That got a laugh. It also did more to sway them to his way of thinking than all his previous pleading. Even Elizabeth, cross with her cousin as she was, could not repress a smile at that last suggestion.

'Maybe you've got something there,' Alan conceded. 'Who else knows about her visit, Elizabeth?'

'The Greens, I suppose.' She was surprised that Alan, who had been, as it were, the leader of the opposition, should so suddenly have been won over. It threw her momentarily off balance, so that she answered mechanically while pondering on the reason for his *volte-face*. True, murder was no longer the hook on which the joke was to be hung; but did that make so much difference? Perhaps. She did not know. 'They are moving in for that week; Aunt Charlotte doesn't like leaving me alone in the house.' (Only Aunt Charlotte hadn't put it as pleasantly as that. 'I don't trust you, my dear,' Aunt Charlotte had said. 'I've a suspicion you won't give me a thought once my back is turned; you're getting too fond of the men. So I'm having the Greens move in to keep an eye on you. I'll not have the place turned into a bawdy house during my absence.') She turned to Michael. 'I don't know why you should pretend to be so surprised at the news. I told you last week that she was going away.'

He scowled. 'Did you? I don't remember.'

'Is Green the gardener?' asked Alan.

'Yes. And Mrs Green comes in twice a week to help with the housework. But, Alan, I don't think we ought — '

'Now don't start being difficult, Elizabeth,' Desmond said. 'Nobody is going to hurt Aunt Charlotte. She will probably never even know that she was reported missing. Who's to tell her? Not the folks who were fooled. Besides, she doesn't mix with the village — you know that. And, anyway, what does it matter if she does get to hear of it? It would probably appeal to her sense of humour. If she has one, that is.'

'Oh, yes, she has one,' Michael said. 'But it doesn't function the same as other people's. She — ' He paused, his dark eyes considering them. 'Couldn't we include murder as one of the possibilities?' he pleaded. 'One among many?'

Elizabeth shivered. It was only a joke he was planning — but would he have been so insistent if the proposed victim had been other than Aunt Charlotte? Did his dislike of her embellish the plan with a vicarious and macabre excitement? Like sticking pins into an image?

'No,' she said sharply. 'You cannot. I won't have it.'

She looked to Alan for support, and he nodded. But he no longer displayed annoyance at Michael's insistence. 'When is she off, Elizabeth?' he asked.

'Thursday,' she said reluctantly. 'I heard her telephoning for a taxi this afternoon. She's catching the six forty-five that evening from Tanbury.'

'Did she order the taxi from Herring?'

'I shouldn't think so. More likely from a garage in Tanbury or Wendingham. She doesn't like Herring; she says he's rude and discourteous.'

That was so much like the pot calling the kettle back that they laughed. All except Bruce. Since Aunt Charlotte's name had been mentioned Bruce had not spoken, had appeared to take no interest in their planning. He sat hunched forward in his chair, staring fixedly at the tankard cupped in his two hands.

'Fine,' Alan said. 'It will be dark at six forty-five, and if she's using a foreign taxi no one in the village will know that she's gone. You're right, Michael — this is an opportunity not to be missed. Though murder is out, of course,' he added, catching the girl's eye.

'There's the Greens,' Michael reminded him, delighted at this unexpected ally. 'When are they moving in, Elizabeth?'

They were all on Michael's side now, she thought; Alan and Desmond openly, Bruce tacitly. Yet they were normal, kindly young men; was she stupid and unnecessarily sensitive to oppose them? They meant no harm, least of all to Aunt Charlotte. No one would suffer. Those who had been taken in by the hoax might feel rather foolish, but that wouldn't harm them.

'That morning,' she said. At least she would go a little way with them. If the idea got out of hand she could always put the brake on later. 'But they'll be out for most of the day. Young Willie Green broke his leg last week, and they're going to visit him in hospital that afternoon. Aunt Charlotte said it would be all right. They won't be back until nine or ten, because afterwards they're going on to their married daughter.'

'For the first time in my life,' Desmond said, 'I am beginning to think well of Aunt Charlotte. You'd think she was on our side, wouldn't you, the way she's got it all taped? It seems almost a shame to take advantage of the old so-and-so. However, this is no time for sentiment. What is to be the *modus operandi*, Alan? Any ideas?'

It was strange, thought Elizabeth, that they should look to Alan for leadership. She had thought it would be Desmond — or Michael, since he had originated the plan. Alan had been so familiar a figure in the days when she was a schoolgirl that she had come to take him for granted. She had not seen so much of him lately, but she still thought of him in a minor key. The others, apparently, did not, and she looked at him now with a new respect. Yet he did not look any different. He stood by the fireplace gazing at a photograph of Desmond's grandfather, the late Earl of Hemmingway, his blue eyes thoughtful, his stocky figure looking almost squat beside the tall grace of Michael and Desmond. His small moustache was neatly clipped, his curly hair was practically white in its blondness. Remembering the many times she had twined those curls round her fingers in the past — and the occasional tugs of exasperation — Elizabeth smiled to herself.

'The first thing would be to establish the fact that she's missing,' he said. 'We could do that by means of a telegram purporting to come from this friend of hers (fancy Aunt Charlotte having a friend!) to say she hasn't arrived. That would set the ball rolling. If the postmistress doesn't talk the Greens will; Mrs Green is reputed to be one of the biggest nosy parkers in the village. You could leave the telegram lying around, Elizabeth; somewhere where she's bound to see it.' He frowned. 'To give it the authentic touch I suppose it ought to be sent off from London, or wherever it is Aunt Charlotte's staying.'

'Purley,' said Elizabeth.

'Fine.' Desmond rubbed his hands

gleefully. 'I'll be the sender-offer. I could do with a night out in Town.'

Michael stared at him. 'I thought you said you were broke.'

'Well, you know how it is.' Desmond shrugged. 'One can usually raise the little extra when one must.'

'And what do I do when the telegram arrives?' asked the girl. 'Nothing?'

Michael frowned. It was just like Elizabeth to throw spanners right at the start. But he could not answer her question, and that annoyed him further.

The others were equally at a loss. To ignore the telegram would reflect discreditably on Elizabeth; Mrs Green would see to that, for Aunt Charlotte's unpopularity had inevitably caused the village to regard her niece with some distrust. Yet to take the action she might be supposed to take — to follow up the telegram with suitable inquiries — would quickly establish the fact that it was bogus.

'We'll sort that one out later,' Alan said eventually. 'But there's something else that concerns you, Elizabeth. It would be better if you were out of the house when

Aunt Charlotte leaves, so that you can truthfully plead ignorance about her departure if questioned. Could you manage that?'

She shook her head.

'No. She'd expect me to be there to see her off, and there'd be an almighty row if I didn't.'

'You ought to be used to rows by now,' Michael said, with some impatience. This solicitude for Elizabeth was bogging them down. 'What's the next item? Blood? Some good hefty dollops of red paint would be a nice touch. Or why not the real thing? There must be buckets of the stuff swilling around your father's shop, Bruce.' For the first time he and the other men realized that Bruce had so far added nothing to the discussion, and they looked at him, heedless of the girl's horrified gasp. Bruce flushed under their gaze, but said nothing.

'That okay by you, Bruce?'

'Yes, if you want it. But I thought murder was out.'

It was hesitantly said. For a brief moment Michael continued to stare at him. 'You don't seem mad keen,' he said slowly. 'Still with us?'

It was Elizabeth who answered.

'I don't know about Bruce, but I do know that I most certainly am *not* with you. Send a telegram if you must — I can't see much harm in that — but when it comes to blood . . . ' She shivered. 'What's more, it's quite obvious that you're harking back to your original plan. Once and for all, Michael, murder is out. You may think it amusing, but I don't; I think it's horrible. And no blood; it's my home, not yours, and I prefer it bloodless.' She paused, staring at them in turn. 'And there's another aspect of it that you don't seem to have considered: any hint that Aunt Charlotte may have been murdered, and it's I who will be suspected, not you. And though normally I don't give a hoot for village opinion, I refuse to be branded as a murderess. It may be your idea of fun, but it isn't mine.'

Michael broke into loud protests, ridiculing her argument. But Alan cut him short.

'You never learn, do you, Michael? Why

can't you leave well alone? Elizabeth's absolutely right. She's on the spot, and she's Aunt Charlotte's heir. Add to that the way the old girl treats her, and she makes a cut-and-dried suspect for the village to pounce on.' He turned to the girl. 'Don't worry, Elizabeth. We'll see you're not involved.'

Elizabeth looked at him askance. It sounded fine — but could she trust him? Was he speaking with his tongue in his cheek?

'What damned rubbish!' Michael jumped up and began to pace the room with short, nervous steps strangely at variance with his height. He kicked petulantly at a cushion that had slipped to the floor. 'You and I, Alan, will be just as suspect as Elizabeth. And what about my father? And yours? Every one knows what *they* think of Aunt Charlotte. Why, practically everybody in Milford must have come up against her at one time or another. The place is lousy with suspects. So why should they pick on Elizabeth?'

Elizabeth breathed a sigh of relief at the

direction of his anger. Alan had spoken of her as Aunt Charlotte's heir, and it always embarrassed her when that happened in front of Michael. It was not her fault that her aunt had cut him and his father out of her will, but she could not entirely subdue a feeling of guilt.

'I can't claim to stand as high on the list of suspects as the rest of you,' Desmond said, 'but I do feel that my old man at least deserves an honourable mention. He and Aunt Charlotte have been at loggerheads over that strip of land at the back ever since we came here. I can't have you leaving him out.'

And Bruce? thought Elizabeth, wondering why he kept quiet. Bruce probably hates Aunt Charlotte more than any of them. But then the others wouldn't know about that. Perhaps that accounted for his silence.

Alan gave a slight bow. 'I beg your father's pardon, Desmond,' he said gravely. 'I assure you that no discourtesy was intended in his omission. But the fact remains that none of us will be at The Elms when Aunt Charlotte leaves. And that seems to put the baby right into Elizabeth's lap.' And, as Michael once more started to protest, he added, 'We can send the telegram, however. As Elizabeth says, there wouldn't be any harm in that.'

'But what use is the telegram unless we follow it up?' Michael demanded. 'Where does it get us? Leave out the blood, if Elizabeth feels squeamish, but let's have something a bit more ominous than just a ruddy telegram.'

'Such as what?'

'Well, we might arrange for an anonymous letter to arrive the next morning. If we worded it so that it appeared to link up with the telegram it would help to create the right atmosphere. Or we could leave something belonging to the old girl down by the river. Anything to give the impression that all was not well with her.'

Alan looked doubtful; but Elizabeth, having won her point, was inclined to relent. She felt kindly towards them — perhaps because they were young and good-looking, or because she had drunk more that evening than was usual with her — and wanted to add to the comradeship to which they had admitted her. It had also suddenly occurred to her that she had been making considerable fuss about nothing. If they went too far, if the situation got out of hand, the remedy lay with her. She had only to contact Aunt Charlotte, and the bubble would burst.

'I don't mind that,' she said, smiling at Michael. She was always outwardly sweeter to him than her feelings warranted, because of the money; and it was Michael who had been the most upset by her previous objections. 'But couldn't you lay conflicting clues, so that they don't point to any particular solution? Apart from making it easier for me, that would really puzzle the village. They wouldn't know what to believe.'

Desmond gazed at her in admiration.

'How very right,' he said. 'Murder here, suicide there, abduction somewhere else. Also flight, elopement, loss of memory, accident, and robbery — with or without violence. The more the merrier.'

The girl laughed. 'Not murder, please.

Remember? You're as bad as Michael. And I don't think I like suicide or violence. But you can take your pick of the rest.'

'Elopement for me,' Alan said. 'It's so unlikely. A love note dropped on the floor of her bedroom, say, for Mrs Green to see.'

'Robbery,' Michael said thoughtfully. This had possibilities. 'We might make it look as though some one had tried to force the safe in that little room she uses as a study. It's a tinpot affair; anyone could open it, I imagine, given a screwdriver and a little patience.'

Elizabeth grimaced. 'I know. I'm always terrified its limitations may become too well known, and that one night we'll have burglars. And it's usually bulging with money.'

'Really?' said Alan. 'How much money?'

'I couldn't say. But she likes to have plenty on the premises. Uncle Edward kept a tight hold on the purse strings while he was alive, and now she's making up for lost opportunities.' She turned to

Bruce. 'You'll see her at the bank early next week. She's going on a shopping spree while she's away, and she always pays cash.'

'That sounds promising,' Desmond said. 'Find out what she draws, Bruce, and let us know. We might be able to make use of it.'

This time there was no hesitation. 'I shall do nothing of the sort,' Bruce said stiffly. 'It would be most improper.'

'What's a little impropriety among friends? However, have it your own way.' Desmond turned to the girl. 'I suppose she'll take it all with her?'

'Most of it. But not all. She likes to leave a hundred or so in the safe against emergencies.'

But who would use it, she wondered, while her aunt was away? Would she be given the necessary cash to run the house, or would it be entrusted to Mrs Green? Aunt Charlotte had been generous in buying things for her, but she had never entrusted her with money to spend the way she wanted to spend it.

'Full or empty, I don't really see how

we can make the safe look as though it has been tampered with,' Alan said. 'Mrs Green would be the only witness to it, and she isn't likely to notice a few finger-prints or scratches. What kind of safe is it? It's so long — ' He had intended to say, 'since I was in the house.' But that might have embarrassed Elizabeth, and he cut short the sentence, his cheeks tinged with red.

Elizabeth noticed the flush, and guessed the reason for it. I've inherited guilt towards Alan too, she thought ruefully.

'It's a wall safe,' she said quickly. 'Shielded from the public gaze by a large portrait of Aunt Charlotte.'

'Take the portrait down, then,' Michael suggested. 'That would attract Mrs Green's attention. A few scratches round the edges would do the rest.'

'Who? Me?'

'Yes. Why not?'

Why not, indeed? It would give her the greatest pleasure to remove that photograph and put it somewhere where she need never look at it again. She could tell

Mrs Green that the wire had broken or the hook had come away from the wall. But that would defeat their object — or, if Mrs Green did not believe her, brand her as a would be thief.

When she put this to the others Desmond and Alan agreed with her, Bruce gave a half-hearted nod of assent, and Michael interpreted it as yet another attempt to foil them. But he was howled down when he said so.

'I'm all for not taking Elizabeth into our confidence unless we have to,' Alan said. 'Then she can be completely surprised at everything that happens. That will make it look more convincing — and it will be easier for her, too. As for rigging the safe, one of us can see to that after Aunt Charlotte has gone. If I were to call round that evening with a *billet doux* for Aunt Charlotte, Elizabeth, you could go upstairs and drop it conspicuously in her room while I get busy in the study. Okay?'

'I suppose so. But if you are going to keep me in the dark for goodness' sake don't do anything that might upset Aunt Charlotte on her return. I have to live with her; you don't. And now I'm going home. It's after ten.'

She looked at Bruce, who nodded and gulped down the rest of his beer.

'I'll take you in the car,' Desmond said.

'No, thanks. I'm walking back with Bruce.'

'What, in this rain? Don't be childish, Elizabeth. Bruce can come with us, and we'll drop him off on the way.'

It was warm and snug in the room. The uncurtained panes were misted, and she had not thought of the rain. She looked questioningly at Bruce, reluctant to break her promise to him, but hopeful that he would agree with Desmond. But Bruce was not in an agreeable mood; he shrugged his shoulders and turned away, his back as eloquent of ill-humour as any words.

While she hesitated Desmond took her arm and led her to wards the door. Oh, well, thought Elizabeth, acquiescing; if Bruce is annoyed it's not my fault. He can't really expect me to walk when I can ride. Not on a wet evening.

Dulcie Rivers was in the lounge when

they passed through. Dulcie was blonde and cute and curvaceous, and Elizabeth suspected that she was the magnet for many of the men who frequented the Tower Hotel — her own escort of four not excluded. She saw the gleam in Michael's eyes as he caught sight of the girl, and remembered Bruce's long absence from the room that evening, and his guilty look when Desmond had chaffed him about Dulcie. And the other two? Alan, she decided, would be a tough nut for any girl to crack, and Desmond wasn't the type to fall without a struggle. But Dulcie lived in, and that made Desmond an easier target for her wiles.

I'm being a cat, Elizabeth thought. But then both Bruce and Desmond have protested their love for me, and although I don't mind about Bruce I do mind about Desmond. Even if I decide not to marry him I wouldn't like Dulcie to get him. He's too good for her.

Or perhaps I'm not a cat. Just a dog in the manger.

'Good night, Elizabeth,' said Dulcie. 'Good night, boys.'

The second goodnight was on a more seductive note than the first. She blew them a kiss.

Bruce declined the proffered lift; he would walk, he said. They passed him later striding angrily through the rain, and the girl felt a twinge of remorse. Certainly he was behaving like a spoiled child; but she *had* promised to let him see her home, and there hadn't been any 'ifs' or 'buts' attached to the promise. Then she remembered Dulcie, and her self-esteem was partially restored. He deserved a rebuff for flirting with Dulcie; he couldn't have it both ways.

She was still thinking of Dulcie when the car stopped outside her aunt's house. When she made to get out Desmond stopped her.

'You're not terribly keen on this lark we're planning, are you?' he asked.

No, she wanted to say, I'm dead against it. But she was young, and they were her friends, and the rôle of spoil-sport was not a pleasant or an easy one to adopt. So she said, swallowing her misgivings, 'I don't mind. Not so long as you keep off blood and murder and things like that.'

'We will. But let us know if you change your mind. She's your aunt.'

'And Michael's,' she reminded him.

'True. Maybe it was that sobering thought that gave him the murder bug.'

They were silent for a while. Elizabeth waited for him to put his arm round her shoulders and kiss her goodnight, but he made no move. With his hands still on the steering-wheel he sat staring thoughtfully through the rain-spattered windscreen at the small area of light thrown by the side-lamps.

Well, thought the girl, it's not for me to suggest it. 'Good night, Desmond,' she said. 'Thanks for the lift.'

He stopped her again, a hand placed quickly on her arm. But he did not change his position or turn his head.

'There's that other little matter I mentioned a week or so back.' He sounded unusually diffident. 'About getting married. Remember?'

Elizabeth turned towards him, glad of the darkness that enveloped them. It made it easier to say what she had to say.

'Yes, I remember. In fact, I've thought about it a lot. Only — well, for one thing I don't think I'm in love with you. Not madly, head over heels, in love, anyway.'

'I might grow on you,' he suggested. 'Why not try it and see? Or is there some one else?'

'Oh, no.' She squeezed his arm gently. 'You're streets ahead of all rivals. So far ahead, in fact, that I'd probably say 'yes' if it were not for Aunt Charlotte.'

'Marry me — marry anyone — and bang goes a tidy little fortune. Is that what you mean?'

'No,' she said sharply. But she did not blame him. That was what they all thought; not only her friends, but the whole village. Every one believed that she only put up with her aunt for the inheritance that would one day be hers. Had she Aunt Charlotte to thank for that belief? It was the kind of malicious story that Aunt Charlotte would delight in spreading. 'Oh, I'm not saying the money isn't attractive; I wouldn't be human if I didn't think about it sometimes, and it helps to tide me over some of the more difficult moments. But the all-important reason is that I promised Uncle Edward I'd stay with her; and I don't like breaking a promise.'

He was all contrition. 'I shouldn't have said it. I'm sorry, darling.'

'It's all right. I've got used to it now; everybody says it — or thinks it. But if they only knew how gladly I would give up all thought of the money for a chance to get away from her — go out and earn a living, be independent. It would be marvellous.'

'Or get married, perhaps?' he suggested.

'Yes. Or get married.' He had spoken lightly, but her voice was serious. 'That's why I don't think I'm in love with you, Desmond.'

That took some working out.

'You mean that, if you were in love with me, the promise to your uncle wouldn't seem so binding? Is that it?'

'Yes. At least — oh, I don't know what I mean. It isn't only Uncle Edward, you see; there's Aunt Charlotte herself. She couldn't live alone with that heart of hers

— and who else would stay with her?'

'There wouldn't be a rush for the job,' he agreed. 'But why shouldn't we get married and have her to live with us?'

'She'd never agree.' But she could not tell him why; that was something she would never willingly confide to anyone. They all knew that Aunt Charlotte was difficult; but they didn't know just how difficult or in what way, and she hoped they never would. 'She doesn't want me to get married at all, you see. She's threatened to disinherit me if I do.'

A match flared in the dark. He lit two cigarettes, handing one to her.

'I wouldn't want to come between you and affluence,' he said slowly, 'but I do want to marry you. You wouldn't care for a secret wedding, I suppose?'

Elizabeth's heart beat a little faster. A secret wedding! How romantic that sounded, and what a happy jewel to hug to herself in the drab unpleasantness of life with Aunt Charlotte! She said, trying to keep the flutter from her voice, 'How would that help? Anyway, Aunt Charlotte would get to hear of it eventually. You know how people talk.'

'I do indeed. But I meant secret from every one, not just from Aunt Charlotte. As for how it would help — well, that's debatable, I suppose. It would help me because I love you. To know that you really belong to me, that no one could step in and whisk you away — that would be more than something.' He sighed. 'I'm not very good at this, am I? Maybe I should have put in a spot of practice first.'

'You're doing all right for a beginner.' Elizabeth no longer tried to keep the tenderness from her voice; it was wonderful to be loved, even if she could not love him in return. And if his phrasing was not in the vein of the great lovers there was sincerity in his voice. 'If I don't fall for it it's because I'm not sure of myself.' She gave a nervous laugh. 'I'm not completely sure of you. I'm no *femme fatale*; it could be Aunt Charlotte's money that attracts you.'

He groped for and found her hand, pressing it gently.

'Why not put me to the test? Marry me openly, and to hell with the money. It's you who are hesitating, darling, not me.'

That was true. But even if no money was involved she could not do as he asked. There was still her promise to Uncle Edward.

'I didn't really mean it,' she said, returning the pressure of his hand.

'Money comes in handy,' he said, 'but it isn't everything. You are — to me. As for not being a *femme fatale* — who'd want to marry one of those?' He let go of her hand and put his arm round her shoulders, pulling her towards him. 'I've a feeling I've handled this badly. I should have been more demonstrative — swept you into my arms with bags of ardour. You might have said 'yes' then. But if you marry me the risks are all yours, darling, and I wanted to be fair. Keep your big hands to yourself, I told myself, and talk it over dispassionately first. The rest will follow — I hope.'

He kissed her gently. Her cheeks were cold. 'Can one be dispassionate about love?' she asked wistfully.

The rain had ceased, but it still dripped in untidy splodges of sound on to the roof of the car from the tall elms that partially concealed the house from the lane. As a child Elizabeth had been fascinated by the old rambling building, with its buttresses and gables, its soft grey stone walls almost hidden by wistaria, its windows askew and its roof sagging. The garden was a large, untidy wilderness that stretched from the main road to the river, with a gravel drive debouching into the narrow lane that led down to a disused ford and nowhere else. It was a house of character, a house of memories — memories of which the youthful Elizabeth had known nothing, but about which she had never ceased to wonder.

That was in the past. Now, though the house had not changed, it seemed to Elizabeth more of a prison than a home. For her Aunt Charlotte had warped its character, destroyed its memories.

She rubbed the mist away from the car window. No light shone from the house. 'She must be in the kitchen,' she said. 'She can't have gone to bed; she knows I haven't a key.'

'Does it mean a row?'

'Not exactly a row. Just a full-scale ticking off. You can't have a row, can you, when all the noise is on one side?'

Her voice was bitter. The grip on her shoulder tightened.

'Is it worth it?' he asked. 'When you made that promise to your uncle you didn't know what you were letting yourself in for. Do you have to go on?'

'She's ill,' Elizabeth said, begging the question. 'She looks healthy enough, apart from her high colour; but her heart's dicky, and she doesn't give it any rest. She drives herself almost as hard as she drives me.' That was a lie, but it was what she wanted him to believe. She reached for the door handle. 'I must go, Desmond. It really is late.'

'And you won't marry me? Not even in secret?'

'I don't know. Perhaps. Don't press me for an answer tonight, my dear. Let me sleep on it.'

'Of course.' He leaned forward to stub out his cigarette in the ashtray, and then turned to put both arms round her. Elizabeth responded only mechanically to his kiss; already her thoughts had strayed into the house and were pondering on the unpleasantness that lay ahead. 'But don't let it slip your memory, darling. To me it's important.'

'It might be important to me too,' she said.

2

An Accumulation of Straw

I'm afraid It's rather late,' Elizabeth said. 'I'm sorry.' The apology was not entirely mechanical. She had snatched at liberty that evening without first seeking permission from her aunt, and she felt some contrition at her part, however small, in the plot that had just been hatched. But the expression on her aunt's face told her that the apology would not be accepted, and had there been the slightest chance of escaping from the wrath to come she would have taken it. Mrs Lane, however, was not easily eluded. Although short, she was buxom. She stood squarely in the narrow hallway, seeming to the girl to swell with indignation until her elbows almost touched the walls.

'Is that all you have to say?' the woman said softly.

Elizabeth closed her mind to all the

other things she would have liked to say, and nodded.

'Nearly midnight. It surprises me that you bothered to come home at all.' The voice had lost its purr, was becoming shriller. 'Perhaps the rain interfered with your — pleasure?' Aunt Charlotte hesitated over the word, stressing it. 'Or maybe he wasn't sufficiently generous?' She shot out an arm and snatched at the startled girl's handbag. Her podgy hands shook as they fumbled with the clasp. 'Let me see.'

Elizabeth's face went white, and she clenched her fists in an agony of restraint. It had never been like this before. Tears, reproaches, rage, invective — she had imagined that by now she knew all the forms in which her aunt's jealousy was likely to express itself. But this was something new, something she did not know how to handle. There had been scantily veiled hints of the menace that was man, warnings that Aunt Charlotte would oppose any male interest in her niece's life. There had even been accusations that such an interest existed. But this crude suggestion that Elizabeth . . .

'I — I don't understand,' the girl said. She felt cold, her body was trembling.

'Oh, yes, you do.' Unable to find what she sought, the woman let the handbag fall to the floor, its contents spilling. 'You've been with a man, haven't you?'

'Only with Michael and — '

'Michael!' She spat the name venomously. 'That good-for-nothing cadger! Very flattering, I'm sure, to know that you prefer his company to mine. Who else was with you?'

'Some of his friends.' No names, thought Elizabeth. Mention of Alan and Bruce would only infuriate her further, and she didn't want to bring Desmond into such a scene. Desmond was a possible way of escape; Desmond must not be allowed to come under suspicion.

'Friends of Michael's, eh? I can imagine what *they'd* be like.' She took a step forward, peering suspiciously up at the girl. Although she was short-sighted, vanity forbade the wearing of spectacles. 'Which of 'em brought you home? Not Michael — he hasn't a car.'

Elizabeth looked with distaste at the too heavily powdered face, the faded eyes under the mascara-ed lashes, the plucked and pencilled eyebrows, the cracked red lips, the thinning grey hair freshly waved and set. Revulsion rose in her, as it did when ever her aunt came too close. The cloying scent with which the older woman was wont to drench herself made her feel sick, and she drew back involuntarily, aware that the movement would only increase her aunt's anger, but unable to prevent it.

'Well?' Aunt Charlotte demanded.

The girl shut her eyes, straining the lids against the cheekbones. 'Go away from me, you horrid old woman,' she wanted to scream. 'Go away — before I put my hands round your fat neck and strangle the life out of you. I can't stand any more, do you hear? I can't stand any more.'

Instead she said evenly, 'No, it wasn't Michael. One of his friends had a car. It was raining, and he offered to run me home.'

'Very kind of him. No doubt he was suitably rewarded. Or did you merely discuss the weather while you were sitting out there in the lane?' The shrill voice faltered, a plump, bejewelled hand clutched the girl's arm. She went on, not waiting for an answer, 'Why can't you find your pleasures at home, Elizabeth? Here, with me? Aren't I good to you? Don't I look after you better than your mother ever did — feed you, clothe you, give you all the pretty things you want? Isn't that enough for you?'

No, it isn't enough, thought Elizabeth. You give me all that, but you don't give me freedom. You're a rapacious maw trying to swallow me up, to make me so much a part of you that I'll no longer have a will or a life of my own. I have to fight for every moment away from you, lie and trick and deceive in order to gain what every human being has a right to enjoy. And when I come home . . .

Home!

She opened her eyes. Fat tears were on the woman's cheeks, ploughing their crazy way through the powder. Elizabeth sighed. Now we are back to normal, she thought, uncertain whether to be glad or sorry. Now she will tell me how much she loves me, that I'm all her life, that . . .

'You wouldn't understand,' she said. 'Need we discuss it any more to-night, Aunt? I'm tired.'

'Tired!' The tears were coming fast now, the voice was a little shriller. 'Do you never think of anyone but yourself, Elizabeth? You walk out of the house without a word of explanation, leaving me to fret myself silly with anxiety, wondering where you are and what you are doing, imagining all the terrible things that might be happening to you, and me unable to lift a finger to help. *You're* tired! How do you think *I* feel?' Another step nearer, another sigh welling up from her well-filled stomach. 'Oh, Elizabeth, how can you be so heartless, so cruel, to the one person in the world who loves you just for yourself alone? Do you think Michael feels that way about you? Or the others? Of course they don't. They're selfish, like all men. *They* wouldn't be content just to sit and look at you, to talk to you; you're not all that beautiful, my dear, and it's no use pretending you are.

You're young, and your figure is good, but that's not enough to hold a man's attention for long.' A sly look came into the weak eyes. 'It wouldn't be your money they're after, I suppose?'

'I haven't got any money,' Elizabeth said.

'Not now. But you will have when I'm gone. And they know that, don't they? Every one knows it. But that man who brought you home — did you tell him he's wasting his time, that you won't have a penny, never, if you leave me or marry before I die? He might not be quite so attentive if he knew that.'

'We didn't discuss it,' Elizabeth lied.

The reproaches went on, but the girl gave them little heed. She was thinking of Desmond. It was true that she was not beautiful. It was also true that by marrying now she would impoverish both herself and her husband. But Desmond knew that — and still wanted to marry her. What makes a man fall in love, she wondered, with one particular girl — with some one like me, for instance, who has so little to offer? Can it be . . .

Her aunt's next words jerked her back to the present.

'For some time, Elizabeth, I've been doubting the wisdom of leaving you on your own, and this confirms my doubts. I shall write to Ethel and tell her I can't come. It's a pity — I've been looking forward to my visit — but it cannot be helped. You're not to be trusted, Elizabeth. That is a terrible thing to say of a person one loves, but unfortunately it happens to be true.'

The thought of losing her precious days of freedom, so eagerly anticipated, seemed to the girl like a major catastrophe. What a fool she had been not to consider this possibility before walking out so recklessly that evening!

Somehow she must rectify that stupid blunder.

'I shan't be alone,' she said. 'The Greens will be here.'

'The Greens won't be able to exercise the control over you that I can.' The tears had ceased, though their ravages remained. Mrs Lane was feeling better. 'Mrs Green will do her best — I fancy she knows on which side her bread is buttered — but she cannot insist on your staying at home in the evenings. I shall hear all about it later, of course; but by then the harm will have been done.'

'But there won't *be* any harm,' Elizabeth protested, forcing herself not to appear too eager, too willing to please. 'I'm sorry about this evening; it was thoughtless of me to go out without letting you know, and I can see now why you were upset. But I wasn't doing anything wrong. We just sat and talked over a drink or two, and it was the rain that made me late. I was waiting for it to stop. I didn't know one of them had a car; he hadn't mentioned it before.'

'Who was he?'

'Oh, just one of Michael's friends,' Elizabeth said hurriedly. That was not a topic to be pursued. With feigned pathos she added, 'If only you were not so willing to think ill of me, Aunt Charlotte, we could be a lot happier together.'

Charlotte Lane said nothing. Sentiment was as necessary to her as oxygen, but she was still suspicious. The moment of forgiveness was precious and not to be missed, but it was not yet due.

'Of course I like to go out,' Elizabeth went on. 'Every girl does. And Michael and his friends are the only young people I know. I haven't any girl friends — except Valerie, and she's right out at Cosmeston. Besides, Anthony takes up most of her time.'

'*I* don't want to go out of an evening,' her aunt said, her voice once more a purr. 'I'm perfectly happy to stay at home with you.'

Elizabeth knew she was about to be forgiven. Relief was tempered with dismay, for forgiveness would bring with it a further and more unpleasant ordeal. But she had to go on.

You're not a girl, she wanted to say. You're not young. You may ape youth, but you no longer possess it. You're not young, and you're not normal. Instead she said, 'I'm happy too, Aunt Charlotte. But every one needs a change. I know I do. It makes me appreciate — ' She hesitated. She had been about to say 'you,' but the word stuck in her throat.

‘ — home more. And you need a change yourself. That’s why I think it would be such a pity to give up your visit to Mrs Donelly. You really must go.’

It was impossible to keep the anxiety, the hope, out of her voice. But Mrs Lane misinterpreted the emotion in her niece’s pleading to suit her own emotion.

‘It is encouraging to know you occasionally consider my interests,’ she said, angling for yet further proofs. ‘But I still wonder — ’

‘Oh, Aunt, you’re impossible!’ And then, impetuously, ‘If it will make your mind easier I’ll give you my word of honour not to go out at all in the evenings while you are away.’ It was a school-girl trick to salve her honour, this use of the future tense; the ‘word’ would never actually be given. It was a measure of her desperation that she resorted to it now. ‘There! Will that persuade you?’

Charlotte Lane’s eyes were moist — with happiness this time.

‘Yes, dear. But I shall miss you. I’d never have even contemplated leaving you if I hadn’t needed some new clothes. You know I like to look smart for you — though goodness knows why I bother; I might as well go about in a sack for all the notice you take of what I'm wearing.' She moved closer to tuck an arm inside the girl's. Elizabeth shuddered inwardly at the contact. 'Will you read to me for a little while, dear? It helps me to relax before bed, and I've had a trying evening.'

It was nearly an hour later when Elizabeth escaped to her room. She loathed those reading sessions; the two of them on a small settee, her aunt's heavy body leaning against her own taut, upright one. And always the same trashy books. Occasionally Elizabeth had tried to introduce a choice of her own, but Aunt Charlotte would have none of it. 'This one, dear,' she would say, producing yet another volume of sickly sentiment. Where does she get them from? wondered the girl. The supply seemed inexhaustible.

But if the reading sessions were bad the moments immediately succeeding them were worse. That pause at the foot of the stairs for the final 'goodnight' — that was a ritual she could not escape, yet which seemed to the girl the most degrading of all. Sometimes, humiliated and disgusted, she would break away and run up the stairs to her own room, heedless of the pleas from below, to lean, nerve-racked and hysterical, against the door, swearing to herself that never again would she allow it to happen, that no promise could be considered binding against such provocation.

That was at night. Yet doubt, if not contrition, returned with the morning. Aunt Charlotte was her only relative, and a sick woman. Aunt Charlotte had given her a home, had educated and provided for her, was even contemplating making her, Elizabeth, her heir. Under those circumstances, hadn't she a duty to stay? How else could she repay the debt?

So she stayed. But each day the duty became harder, the debt more oppressive — until lately she had begun to wonder whether, if nothing happened to rescue her (and by that she had meant her aunt's demise, though even to herself she had hesitated to express the thought fully), she might not eventually become as warped and as twisted as Aunt Charlotte herself.

Perhaps it was the sharp contrast between Desmond's and her aunt's expressions of affection that made her decide that night that she had reached the breaking point. To-morrow it *will* be different, she promised herself, as she scrubbed vigorously at her cheeks in the nightly effort to feel clean. *She* will think it's the same — but she'll be wrong. There won't just be her and me, there'll be Desmond as well. I'll keep my promise to Uncle Edward — but I shan't feel so alone, so desperate, if I'm married to Desmond. And I *will* marry him; I must, if I'm to stay here and remain sane. Desmond's love is healthy and right, it will give me back my self-respect, make me feel clean again. To-morrow morning she'll go off to the shops as usual, and I'll ring him up and tell him it's all right, that I'll marry him just as soon as he can fix it. And then . . .

Oh, God, she prayed, as she climbed into bed, let us be happy together, Desmond and me!

The sheets were cold, and for some time she lay there shivering, keyed up and unable to sleep. Her thoughts drifted away from the future to the past. It had all been so different when Uncle Edward was alive. Aunt Charlotte had bullied or ignored her; but her uncle had given her more love, had shown her more kindness, than her own father, harassed by continuous financial failures and an inability to hold down any job for long, had ever done.

And then Uncle Edward had died. To Elizabeth it had seemed a disaster even more tragic than the accident which had made her an orphan. Bewildered and sad, drowned in a sense of loss from which she could envisage no recovery, she had given him her promise. It was the only thing he had ever asked of her, the only thing she had to give; and she gave it willingly, fervently, happy to be able in this small way (it had seemed small to her then) to express her love for him.

For the first year after his death Aunt Charlotte had been too engrossed in the new delight of spending money to pay much attention to her niece; it was not until she was seventeen, and had left school, that Elizabeth had noticed a difference in her aunt's attitude towards her. At first she had welcomed the change, although she knew she could never reciprocate the affection. (She knew this with a sense of guilt, for it seemed ungrateful to dislike some one to whom she owed so much materially.) Her dislike grew with the ever-increasing demands made on her — grew to disgust, and loathing, and occasional revolt, so that there was seldom any peace between them, and Aunt Charlotte came to represent all that was obscene and degrading in human relationship.

Elizabeth shuddered. It was not pleasant to dwell on. Think about to-morrow, she told herself. Think about Desmond.

She thought about Desmond. But when she screwed up her eyes against the dark and tried to picture him the image would not come. The faces of Bruce and Alan and Michael slid in turn across the screen of her mind, but not Desmond's. Is that because I don't really love him?

she wondered. But then I don't love the others either.

How would Bruce react to her marriage when he came to hear of it? He had told her many times that he loved her, that he wanted to marry her. I wouldn't like Bruce to feel that I've cheated, she thought uneasily. But why should he? I've never singled him out for attention, I've never given him any reason to suppose that one day I might marry him. He'd have no right to reproach me,

And yet Bruce was a man of unpredictable moods and temper. Sometimes he blazed, sometimes he smouldered. Nor did he forgive easily, as his unremitting hatred of her aunt proved. By marrying Desmond she too would be wounding Bruce's pride. Would he forgive that?

The moon shone fitfully through racing clouds. Unable to sleep, Elizabeth turned, pulling the blankets over her head. If trouble with Bruce was inevitable, at least it would not be yet. Not until she and Desmond could announce their marriage to the world. And when would that be?

Not until Aunt Charlotte was dead, presumably.

Desmond.

Oh, God, she prayed again, let us be happy together!

* * *

'That's enough,' gasped Elizabeth, freeing herself, albeit with some reluctance. 'Be sensible, Desmond. There's so much to discuss, and it may be ages before we have another opportunity.'

'I don't feel sensible,' he told her, smiling. 'I'm walking on air, and my head's spinning round and round among the clouds. I'm in the sixth heaven.'

'Oh? Why not the seventh?'

'Why not, indeed?' he said, and reached for her.

It was the next morning. They were down by the ford, whither Desmond had come hurrying on receipt of her telephone call. She had not expected such a prompt response, and at first doubted its wisdom; the desire to see him, to hear him say what he could not say over the telephone, was tempered with the fear that Aunt Charlotte might discover them. But Aunt Charlotte was out, and at that time of the year the river was deserted. The copse at the bottom of the garden shielded them from the house and the lane. Their meeting could not have been more private.

'When do we get married, darling?' she asked. She felt warm and content inside. She no longer doubted his love, was even beginning to wonder if she had not minimized her own.

'What maidenly immodesty!' Desmond said. And then, becoming serious, 'Aunt Charlotte goes on Thursday, doesn't she? Let's make it the day after, then. The Friday. It'll be easier with her out of the way.'

'Nearly a whole week to go.' Elizabeth sighed. Friday seemed æons away, and having made a momentous decision she was impatient to implement it. 'I doubt if I can wait that long.'

'Say, what *is* this? You don't *have* to get married, do you?' He laughed at her angry protest. 'Okay, okay; I believe you.

But a week isn't long, darling, and a wedding can't be fixed up overnight. I'm not sure how long it takes to get a licence, but I imagine you can't just walk into the office, plonk your money on the counter, and depart fully equipped for marriage. And you ought to have a ring. You won't be able to wear it publicly, I suppose, but you'll need one for the ceremony.'

'Yes.' She smiled up at him happily. 'Don't worry, darling — I'll wait months if necessary. But I hope it won't be. After last night — '

She paused. Last night was best forgotten.

'I meant to ask you about that,' he said. 'What happened when you got in? More aunt trouble?'

'Yes. On the same lines as usual, but more intense, more — more unpleasant. Or perhaps it was just an accumulation of straw.' She put her arm through his, unwilling to discuss it. Desmond believed — they all believed — that it was Aunt Charlotte's anger, not her affection, that was the trouble between them. She did not want to disillusion him now. 'Where will we be married?'

'Well, I had thought of Tanbury Cathedral, with Aunt Charlotte as the principal bridesmaid. No? It will have to be a registry office, then.'

'In Tanbury?'

'Yes.'

Arm in arm, they walked slowly along the river bank. Elizabeth was pondering on what she should wear for the wedding. At least she had a decent wardrobe; Aunt Charlotte had not been mean over clothes, although she always insisted on a say in their selection. Should it be the grey costume or the green? The grey suited her better, she thought; but Desmond had seen her in that, she had worn it only the previous evening. As for undies . . .

Elizabeth found herself blushing. She squeezed Desmond's arm.

'We shan't be able to have a proper honeymoon,' she said, 'but at least we shan't have to share it with Aunt Charlotte. Only the Greens.'

'A cheering thought.' Suddenly he stopped. 'I say, how about that little plot we were hatching last night? Is it all right to go ahead with it? This doesn't change anything?'

'Why should it?' She was so happy herself that it would have seemed mean to curb the fun of others. 'Only don't expect me to take much interest in it; I've other things to think about now. And for goodness' sake don't let it get out of hand, Desmond. You know what Michael is.'

'I'll keep an eye on him,' he promised. 'When I remember, that is. I too have other interests.'

'Such as what?'

He showed her. Presently Elizabeth came up for air and looked at her watch. 'I'd better get back,' she said. 'Aunt Charlotte will be home soon. Help me over the fence, darling, and I'll go up through the garden. I don't want Green to see us together; I think she's paying him and his wife to spy on me.'

'And when do we two meet again?' he asked, kissing her.

'I don't know. I'll phone you, shall I? But I'm not taking any risks between now and Thursday. I shan't feel safe until I've seen her into that taxi and I know she really has gone.'

As she emerged from the copse at the bottom of the garden she saw Green, bent over his spade on one of the beds bordering the path up to the house. He straightened when he saw her, and stood watching her approach.

'Good morning.' Elizabeth tried to sound casual and friendly. She disliked the man — he was often surly, and treated her with scant respect; perhaps he despised her for letting her aunt tyrannize over her — but since he and his wife were to be her gaolers she had no wish to fall out with him. 'The undergrowth is terribly thick down there. I've laddered both my stockings.'

The man nodded.

'I'll get around to it,' he said, unsmiling. 'This here garden's too big for one man to keep ship-shape. And what for would you be walking there, anyways? Ain't nothing to see.'

'I know. Stupid of me.'

It had not been a happy remark, she

realized. She began to admire the chrysanthemums, hoping to please him. But he did not respond to her friendliness. He looked at her suspiciously, as though mistrusting her praise — as well he might, thought Elizabeth, for they did not deserve it.

A black Wolseley saloon came up the lane from the river. Green followed it with his eyes until it disappeared behind the house. 'That's young Mr Farrel's car,' he said, turning to look at her. 'What would he be doing down by the ford at this time o' year, I wonder?'

Elizabeth shrugged her shoulders, inwardly cursing Desmond for being so precipitate in his departure.

'Goodness knows,' she said lightly. 'Fishing, perhaps.'

'Fishing? Fishing for what, miss?'

'Fish,' she felt tempted to reply. But she mistrusted the tone of his voice and the look on his face. It was time to close the conversation, she decided.

But when she turned away he stopped her. 'Me and the missus will be moving into the house next Thursday,' he said.

'While your aunt's away. You know about that?'

'Yes. I hope it won't be too inconvenient for you both.'

'We'll manage.' Once more he turned to stare in the direction in which the car had vanished. 'But there's things we'd fixed to do. I was wondering how it'd be if we was to take a few afternoons off. And evenings, maybe.'

Elizabeth stared at his back. Blackmail, she thought; he knows I was with Desmond. Did he see us, or did he just guess?

'I think that could be arranged,' she said slowly. It was hateful to let him get away with it, but at least it would suit her own plans. The less she saw of the Greens the better.

'Thank you, miss. I — er — well, it didn't seem necessary to mention it to your aunt, seeing as she won't be here.'

'No, of course. I quite understand.'

A faint and fleeting smile appeared on the man's face.

'I thought you would, miss,' he said.

3

Goodbye, Aunt Charlotte!

The door-bell rang as Valerie was putting her four-year-old son to bed. She swiftly tucked in the bedclothes, looked in the mirror to ensure that her hair was tidy, applied lipstick and powder, and, with a promise to Anthony that Mummy would be back in a few minutes, ran down the stairs. She was not expecting a visitor. Her next-door neighbour, a childless widow, often called around that time to join in the happy ritual of putting Anthony to bed. But never on a Thursday. Thursday was reserved for visiting her married sister.

A look of pleased surprise appeared on Valerie's face as she opened the front door.

'Elizabeth!' she exclaimed, drawing her visitor into the hall and embracing her warmly. 'What a lovely surprise! I don't know what happy chance brought you out here, my dear, but I'm delighted to see you.'

Elizabeth returned the embrace. She seemed confused.

'I don't understand,' she said. 'Didn't you send for me?'

'Send for you?' They were in the sitting-room now. 'No. Why should I?'

'I don't know. But I had a phone call saying you wanted to see me, that it was desperately important. So I came.'

'You would, bless you.' Valerie busied herself with a gin bottle. 'But what an extraordinary thing! I always want to see you, Elizabeth, you know that; but I certainly didn't ask you to come this evening. Who was it phoned?'

'I don't know. She didn't say.'

'It was a woman, then?'

'Well, I thought so. But you know how odd some people's voices sound on the phone. It certainly wasn't a voice I recognized.'

Valerie handed her a drink.

'You must need that. I'm terribly sorry, my dear, that you should have been dragged out here on a false alarm. I assure you I had nothing to do with it. Did this person say why I wanted to see you?'

'No. Just that I was to come at once.' Elizabeth sipped the gin and tonic appreciatively. 'I thought perhaps Joe might have turned up again — drunk, perhaps, and pestering you to take him back — and that you needed my moral support. I couldn't think of anything else. I knew you'd get Mrs Sillett in if you or Anthony were ill.'

Valerie shook her head.

'Joe won't bother me again; he knows I'm finished with him for good. Right now I think he's in Australia. But this mysterious phone call worries me. It could be just a hoax — though a pretty dirty one, if you ask me — or it could be serious. I think we ought to tell the police.'

'No,' Elizabeth said. 'We won't do that. It must have been a hoax.'

'But you can't be sure.'

'I think I can.' She smiled faintly.

'Oh! Well, in that case you must know who it was.'

'Not for certain. But I've a pretty shrewd idea.'

'Well, if you're satisfied . . . ' Valerie said doubtfully, after a pause for an explanation that did not materialize. She finished her drink. 'How is Aunt Charlotte? Did she kick up rough when you told her you were coming out to see me this evening?'

Elizabeth grimaced, nodding. 'She certainly did. It so happens she's off to London this evening to stay with a friend, and naturally she expected me to be there to see her off.' She levered herself out of the chair and began to wander restlessly about the tiny sitting-room. 'The fur fairly flew. It was still flying when I dashed off to catch my bus. Honestly, Val, you're about the only person I'd have left home for to-night. I've been looking forward to these few days of freedom, and now I'm terrified that she'll still be there when I get back. It would be just like her to cancel or postpone her visit; she has already threatened to do so once.'

'Don't worry, my dear. She's a selfish old bitch; she'll go if she wants to. But it beats me how you manage to put up with her tantrums. I know I wouldn't. How long will she be away?'

'About a week, I think. I wish it were longer.'

'Won't you be nervous in that big house by yourself? It's very isolated. No one within screaming distance.'

'I don't mind that. But unfortunately I shan't be alone. Aunt Charlotte has arranged for the gardener and his wife to move in while she's away. Thank goodness, they don't look like taking their duties as gaolers very seriously. They cleared off after lunch to-day — their first day there — and they won't be back until ten or eleven to-night.'

'Fine. That means you don't have to hurry back. I know you've never been allowed a latch-key, so you won't be able to get into the house until they return.'

'I've got one now,' Elizabeth said. 'Aunt Charlotte gave it to me this afternoon.'

Valerie looked astonished.

'How very odd! In the middle of the big scene?'

'Oh, no. Before it started.'

‘Well, key or no key, you can still stay to supper. Now come up and say goodnight to Anthony. The poor child will think I’ve forgotten him.’

Elizabeth stayed. But as the evening wore on Valerie became worried and puzzled. Elizabeth wasn’t herself, she thought; she seemed keyed up, as though some momentous event in her life had just taken place — or was about to take place, perhaps. She could not concentrate for long on any topic, and least of all on the one — Aunt Charlotte — that most intrigued Valerie.

‘Can’t we forget her for this evening, Val?’ she said eventually. ‘You may find her amusing, but I don’t.’

Valerie wondered if the mysterious telephone call had disturbed her friend more than she cared to admit. If there’s anything wrong, she thought, I wish she’d tell me. We’ve never had any secrets from each other before.

By eight-thirty Elizabeth had already begun to watch the clock, and ten minutes later she said it was time for her to leave. Her bus passed the end of the road at five minutes to the hour.

Valerie did not seek to detain her. 'I don't like leaving Anthony alone in the house,' she said, as she helped her friend on with her coat, 'or I'd walk to the bus with you. It's a dark night to be out alone.'

Elizabeth assured her that she wasn't at all nervous; it wasn't far, and there was a street lamp by the bus stop. But she felt less assured when the front door had shut behind her and she was alone in the street. Valerie had been right, it *was* a dark night. Heavy clouds obscured the moon; there was no rain, but a chill and blustering wind fought her every step of the way. It blew even harder at the bus stop. The street lamp was some comfort to her nerves, but it offered no protection from the wind.

Elizabeth shivered, turned her back on the wind, and pulled her coat tighter about her.

The headlights of a car turned the corner and came towards her, but as the vehicle began to slow she saw it was not the bus, and lost interest. She expected it to turn down the street she had just left. Instead it pulled over to her side of the road and stopped.

A man's face, grey-haired and weather-beaten, peered out at her.

'Good evening, Miss Messager. Can I give you a lift? I'm on my way back to Milford.'

It was Alan Torreck's father.

He used to call me Elizabeth, she thought, as she thanked him and climbed in beside him. But that was before he quarrelled with Aunt Charlotte. He has hardly spoken to me since.

Knowing his antipathy to her aunt, she felt awkward in his company. She had even hesitated before accepting his offer of a lift. Yet she knew it was foolish to think that way. In the old days she had been fond of him, had called him Uncle Henry. There was no quarrel between them. Only the shadow of Aunt Charlotte.

She found difficulty in making conversation during the twenty minutes' journey, and Henry Torreck was no more talkative. The weather and the few items of local interest were soon exhausted, and after that they were mostly silent. As they neared Milford Cross Elizabeth asked what Alan had been doing that evening, but Torreck could not tell her.

'He had talked about going in to Wendingham,' he said, 'but I don't know if he went. I haven't seen him since half-past five. Why? Did he cut a date?'

'Oh, no,' Elizabeth said. 'I just wondered.'

The Elms was in darkness when they reached it. Henry Torreck got out quickly to help her from the car, and for a moment they stood together in the lane staring up at the dark mass of the house. Elizabeth wondered what thoughts possessed him; in Uncle Edward's time The Elms had been almost as familiar to him as his own home. She knew from Alan that the bitterness had not left him, but surely there must be nostalgia too?

'Thank you,' she said. 'Not only for the lift, but for saving me from that long walk up from the village. It's rather spooky in the dark.'

He was still staring at the house. 'Is

there anyone at home?' he asked abruptly, as though he had not heard her thanks.

'There shouldn't be.' The question surprised her. 'I'm on my own for a few days. Aunt Charlotte went up to London this evening to stay with a friend.' Once more she found herself explaining about the Greens, though in less detail. 'They'll be back shortly. They've gone to — '

'Listen!'

He gripped her arm. Elizabeth jumped, startled by the sudden command and the unexpected touch of his hand. She stood silent and motionless, wondering what had alarmed him, what she was supposed to listen for. There was only the wind in the trees and the sad creaking of tossing branches.

'I can't hear anything,' she said, her voice low. 'What was it?'

'Some one moving on the path,' he said. 'Not this path, the one down to the river.' He felt her shiver, and loosed her arm to grope inside the car for a torch. 'I'll walk up to the house with you. Maybe I was mistaken — maybe there wasn't anyone there — but I'll feel easier in my mind if I see you safely inside before I go.'

Elizabeth hesitated. For a brief moment she had shared his alarm, but now she remembered. If there *was* some one in the garden she had a shrewd idea who it might be. And the boys wouldn't welcome Henry Torreck as a visitor.

'There's no need for you to bother,' she protested. She fumbled in her bag, producing torch and key. 'You wait here, and I'll give you a shout when I've opened the front door.'

'I wasn't proposing to come in,' he said stiffly.

Oh, dear, she thought; now I've offended him. 'You know I didn't mean it that way,' she said. 'Walk up with me by all means. I just didn't want to be a nuisance.'

As they went he kept flashing his powerful torch from side to side. Elizabeth was alarmed lest it should light on a crouching figure, and that he would recognize the prowler and demand an explanation. But they reached the house without seeing anyone. She asked him to come in for a drink, feeling she owed him that; but he declined.

'I'm late,' he said. 'Alan will be wondering what I'm up to.' For the first time that evening she saw him smile. 'I wonder what he'd say if I told him I'd been seeing a pretty girl home.'

Elizabeth laughed. He's a dear, she thought. Why did Aunt Charlotte have to be so beastly to him?

'He wouldn't believe you,' she said. 'But thank you for the compliment.'

She stood in the dark hall and watched the light from his torch as it moved down the path to the lane. Only when the car had turned and disappeared did she switch on the electric light.

The house was very quiet. This is the first time, she thought, that I have come home and not been met by Aunt Charlotte. In all these years there has always been Aunt Charlotte waiting to scold or to fawn.

It seemed odd and slightly disturbing without her.

She went through to the kitchen, opened a window wide, and leaned out.

'Bruce!' she called softly. And then louder, knowing there was no one else to hear, 'Alan? Michael? Anyone there?' There was no answer.

Uncle Henry must have been mistaken, she thought. She shut the window and put a kettleful of water on the stove; the Greens would want a cup of tea when they returned, and she could do with one herself. Then she went back to the hall and telephoned the Tower Hotel.

It was Desmond's father who answered; he wasn't sure, but he thought Desmond was in his room. He had certainly been in to dinner. Did she particularly wish to speak to him, or would she leave a message?

Elizabeth summoned up her courage. She was somewhat in awe of the Honourable George, and over the telephone he sounded particularly aloof. 'I'd like to speak to him, Mr Farrel, if it isn't too much trouble,' she said diffidently.

'Hold on. I'll send for him.'

What would he have said, Elizabeth wondered as she waited, if I had told him I am marrying his son to-morrow?

A clicking noise at the other end of the

wire puzzled her momentarily. Then she heard Desmond's voice, and realized he had been announcing himself with a synthetic kiss.

'The real thing to-morrow,' he said gaily. 'And to-morrow and to-morrow. Has she gone?'

'Yes.'

'Hurray! Goodbye, Aunt Charlotte. Don't hurry back.' Another click. 'Pretty crowded here to-night, I'm afraid.' She interpreted this as a warning that others were within earshot, preventing intimacy in their conversation. 'Where did you get to this evening? You foxed us all. What blew?'

'That's what I wanted to tell you,' she said. 'Somebody rang me just after half-past four to say that a friend of mine out at Cosmeston wanted to see me as soon as possible. Valerie French — you must have heard me speak of her. So I went. Aunt Charlotte was furious, of course, but I couldn't let Valerie down. I caught the five-twenty bus. And then, when I got there, I found that Valerie knew nothing at all about it. The call was a hoax.'

'Good Lord! Any idea who the joker was?'

'I thought it was you,' she said.

'Me? Why me?'

'I don't mean you personally. But one of the gang. I thought it was a ruse to get me out of the way, so that I wouldn't be involved in whatever tricks you were playing on Aunt Charlotte. Some one — I think it was Alan — suggested last week it would be better if I was out of the house when she left. Remember?'

'Vaguely. Well, it wasn't me. Alan, more likely, or Michael. Whoever it was, he messed up our arrangements; we wanted you there so that we could lay our respective clues. Any good if I come round now?'

'I don't think you'd better. I'm sorry — I'd like to see you for other reasons, darling — but the Greens should be back any minute now. Have you seen the others this evening?'

'Only Bruce. Oh, by the way! Michael is dealing with the telly to-morrow. Get me?'

'Television?' she asked, puzzled.

'No, gram. Originally it was my job, but I've asked Michael to take over. At the back of my mind there's an idea that I'm booked for something else to-morrow. Can't remember what — but I expect it will come to me in time.'

'So will the kitchen sink,' Elizabeth threatened. 'Any more talk like that and it's off.'

'Impossible. I've sunk my all in this venture. I'll be calling for you at eleven sharp. Feeling nervous?'

There were voices in the kitchen; the Greens were back. She had wanted to tell him about the nocturnal prowler, but it was too late now. The Greens would certainly be listening.

Hastily she bade him goodnight and rang off.

'I've put the kettle on,' she said brightly as she entered the kitchen. 'I thought you'd be glad of a cuppa. I'd like one myself.'

Mrs Green nodded. She was a meagre little woman, all skin and bone, with sunken cheeks and eyes and thin lips that drooped disapprovingly at the corners.

Her conversation was stilted, and seldom cheerful. Only a juicy morsel of gossip or scandal had the power to put a sparkle into her voice and eyes.

They're a dismal couple, Elizabeth thought, looking at them. If I'm to be confined to this house with them for a week even Aunt Charlotte would be welcome. But then Aunt Charlotte . . .

'Your aunt go off all right?' asked the woman, busying herself with the teapot. Her husband had gone out again. He had not spoken to the girl, or acknowledged her presence.

'Yes.' It was the easier answer. 'I hope you will be comfortable here. It was kind of you both to come.'

'It's a draughty house,' Mrs Green said. 'Very draughty. These old houses always are. You been out this evening, miss?'

'Yes. Why?'

'You left the back door unlocked.' The woman handed her a cup of tea. 'You want to be more careful, miss. It's lonely here. And dark. All them trees.'

Elizabeth stared at her. The back door unlocked? But she hadn't used the back door. She had opened the window to call to Bruce . . . or Michael . . . or . . .

Or whom?

She sipped the tea thoughtfully, suddenly glad of its warmth.

* * *

The telegram came at ten o'clock the next morning. Mrs Green took the message over the phone and brought it up to Elizabeth's room, where the girl was dressing. Elizabeth seldom hurried over her toilet; it was usually time well spent, for it was time away from Aunt Charlotte. But that Friday morning she had an even stronger reason for taking pains over her appearance.

The telegram was much as she had anticipated it would be. 'Expected you yesterday,' she read slowly, unravelling Mrs Green's spidery, spineless handwriting. 'Please wire explanation and E.T.A.' It was signed 'Donelly.'

Elizabeth smiled. They had got the name right, but E.T.A. was an expression unlikely to be used by an elderly female.

Michael had not used his imagination.

Then she stopped smiling, aware that Mrs Green was watching her.

'I wonder what's gone wrong,' she said gravely. 'Perhaps Aunt Charlotte changed her mind at the last minute and stayed in Town for the night. She couldn't have missed the train, or she'd have come back.'

'It's not that,' the woman said. Her voice was shrill. From her apron pocket she produced yet another slip of paper and thrust it fiercely at the girl. 'I found that under the mat when I was sweeping the hall. I was on my way up with it when the phone rang.'

It was a startling note, written in ungainly block capitals. 'Pay up by Thursday or take what's coming to you,' it ran. There was no signature.

The girl considered it, amused. Whose pretty touch was that? Michael's, probably. Perhaps it accounted for the footsteps Uncle Henry had heard the previous night. Yet if it was Michael — or any of them, for that matter — why hadn't he answered when she had called out to him? Was he already out of earshot? Or was it because . . .

'Shall you be ringing Williams, miss?' asked Mrs Green.

Should she? Was that what the boys expected her to do? It was certainly what Mrs Green expected of her. But to call in the police now would mean delay in meeting Desmond. It might even involve postponing their marriage, for Williams, the village constable, was an eager and tenacious young man.

'I don't think so,' she said, putting the note down on the dressing-table as she turned again to the mirror. She was not really interested in their plotting, and if they had wanted her to follow any particular course of action they should have warned her in advance. 'Somebody is pulling our legs, I imagine. We'll let Aunt Charlotte deal with it when she returns.'

The woman said nothing. Elizabeth settled herself on the stool, picked up a lipstick, and leaned forward to complete the adornment of her face. She suspected that she had shocked Mrs Green by her apparent callousness, but she wasn't going to risk the postponement of her wedding. Once it had seemed to her the most unlikely of events; now it had become all-important.

But Mrs Green made no move to go, and her continued and silent presence began to unnerve the girl. Without looking round, she said irritably, 'What's the matter? Don't you agree with me?'

'No, miss, I don't. And I'm surprised, I must say, that you can treat it so lightly. Thursday, it says on that piece of paper, doesn't it? And Thursday was yesterday, the day your aunt left. But it seems she never got to her friend's. Why, miss? Because something's happened to her, that's why!'

'An accident, you mean?'

'Not an accident, miss. Murder.' She rolled the word out with macabre delight, noting with grim satisfaction the shock it occasioned her listener. 'It's my belief whoever wrote that note has done what he said he'd do.'

'It doesn't mention murder,' Elizabeth said. 'You're letting your imagination run away with you, Mrs Green. Aunt Charlotte didn't leave because of that note; she had planned this visit weeks ago.'

Mrs Green had no reply to this. But she had not yet finished. For a few moments she watched the girl, her thin lips pressed into an even tighter line, her sharply pointed nose seeming to sniff the air suspiciously, face and body uncompromisingly stiff. Then she said, 'Did you see the taxi-man?'

'No. I was out at the time.'

'Ah!' This was triumph. 'Last night you said as how you'd seen her leave.'

'Did I? No, I don't think so.' Elizabeth tried to sound indifferent. 'All I said was that she'd gone. And so she has, hasn't she?'

'Yes, miss. But how did she go? And where? That's what I'd like to know.'

'To London, by train and taxi,' Elizabeth said lightly. Time was running short; Aunt Charlotte was no longer there, but it seemed that she could still impede and frustrate. She stood up, twisting and turning in front of the mirror in a final critical appraisement. 'How do I look, Mrs Green?'

The woman frowned, resenting this attempt to disarm her. But her fast-vanishing femininity could not entirely ignore the appeal.

'All right,' she said grudgingly. 'I like the grey better.'

'So do I,' Elizabeth agreed. 'But it needs cleaning, and I see there's a button missing.' She sat down and began to put on her hat. 'Why don't you and Mr Green take the day off? You need not bother about me. I don't expect to be back until late.'

'Your aunt said as you wouldn't be going out of an evening.' It was more of an accusation than a reproof. 'She said you'd promised.'

Elizabeth made no reply. She wanted to tell the woman to mind her own business, but feared to antagonize her further. Mrs Green could be dangerous. She also resisted the temptation to point out that, if Aunt Charlotte had been murdered, it didn't much matter what she had promised.

'Well, I'm off.' She brushed a speck of powder from her skirt, picked up gloves and handbag, gave a last pat to her hair, and turned to go. 'Don't wait up for me. I've got a key.'

Mrs Green did not move. She eyed the girl malevolently, making no attempt to hide her suspicion. 'Seems like you don't want the police to know about your aunt,' she said.

'Well, really!' Elizabeth stared back at her indignantly, her fists clenching. 'I don't think you quite realize what you're saying, Mrs Green.'

The woman's eyes flickered, and she rubbed her hand nervously against her mouth. Her broad feet, hitherto planted firmly on the carpet, twisted slowly on to their edges and back again. But they did not shift their ground.

'That was the way it looked,' she mumbled sullenly.

If it was an apology it was a very meagre one. But Elizabeth decided to accept it. She could not keep Desmond waiting merely to satisfy her desire to put Mrs Green in her place.

'All right,' she said. 'We'll let it go at that. But I don't like people doubting my motives, Mrs Green. Nothing has happened to Aunt Charlotte — if it had we should have heard by now — and she wouldn't thank us if we asked the police to make inquiries about her. If you've set your heart on discussing it with Williams I can't stop you. But I advise you to be careful what you say.'

The woman nodded. She looked frail and small, but Elizabeth felt no pity for her. Mrs Green was a prying, mischief-making busybody. Yet she thought it wise to attempt some sort of a truce between them, however uneasy.

'You're all worked up over nothing,' she said, forcing a smile. 'Go out and forget it. It's a lovely day.'

'Yes, miss.' And then, as Elizabeth reached the door, 'What'll I do about the telegram?'

'Nothing. There's nothing you can do. I don't know Mrs Donelly's address, and she isn't on the phone.'

As she ran down the path Elizabeth knew that Mrs Green was watching her from the bedroom window. Damn the woman! she thought; she's made me late, and she's put me in a vile temper. And it is quite on the cards that she'll try to get her own back on me by talking to Williams.

Some of the uneasiness instilled in her by this last thought was dispelled as she turned into the lane and saw the Wolseley waiting at the corner. She even managed a wry smile as she realized how delighted Michael and the others would be at what they would no doubt consider a turn-up for the book. They had banked on Mrs Green to raise the alarm, but they could not have anticipated that she would make such a thorough job of it.

Nor could they have anticipated that, despite their precautions, murder would be Mrs Green's first thought.

* * *

Elizabeth was slightly disappointed by the wedding ceremony. It was all so business-like, so unromantic. The registrar was a scraggy little man with a cold and a sniff, the witnesses unprepossessing strangers picked up by Desmond. Even when they addressed her as 'Mrs Farrel' and wished her good luck she was not greatly moved. It just didn't seem real.

But I suppose the result is the same, she thought. And Desmond at least was real enough, and far from disappointing. He looked handsome and distinguished; and if the cut of his clothes was rather more Edwardian than Milford Cross was accustomed to, at least it suited him. I wouldn't have him any different, she told herself; and if I'm not in love with him I certainly ought to be. But maybe I am.

She squeezed his arm as they paused for a moment at the top of the wide steps that led down to Tanbury High Street. 'I suppose we're properly married,' she said. 'It doesn't feel like it, and I want to be sure.'

He grinned down at her.

'Positively no deception,' he assured her. 'We're stuck for life. Come on, let's eat. Getting married always gives me an appetite.'

They were half-way down the steps,

arms linked, when she stopped, holding him back.

'There's Bruce,' she whispered. 'See? Crossing the street. Oh, don't let him see us!'

She turned and ran back to the shelter of the hall. Desmond followed, amused by her panic but anxious to please her. From behind a stone pillar, with Elizabeth hovering anxiously in the shadows, he watched the large figure of Bruce Poulton dodging his way through the heavy traffic. Bruce seemed to be in a hurry, his progress causing more than one driver to brake sharply. Arrived on the pavement, he hesitated for a moment, gave a swift glance to where the two were hiding, and then, a frown on his face, walked quickly away.

Desmond watched him go. 'All clear,' he said at last, emerging from his post of concealment. 'I lost him in the crowd, but I'm pretty sure he's gone.'

'Do you think he saw us?' Elizabeth asked. She was still in the shadows.

'I doubt it. He'd have hailed us if he had.' He was not as confident as he sounded, but he did not want to alarm her. 'What does it matter, anyway?'

'He might guess why we're here. Our marriage wouldn't be a secret any longer.' She felt deflated, nervous. Bruce was in love with her, and had always been jealous of Desmond. How would Bruce react if he knew? 'What could he be doing in Tanbury, Desmond? Why isn't he at the bank?'

'Goodness knows. Probably been sent on a message to the branch here. Come on, darling, snap out of it. To hell with Bruce! The way I'm feeling even the sudden appearance of Aunt Charlotte in person couldn't perturb me. I'd probably invite her to the wedding feast.'

His gaiety cheered her slightly, but she had little appetite for the meal he ordered so carefully. She had suffered from Bruce's jealousy before; he could not bear her even to look at another man when she was with him. Or perhaps it wasn't jealousy, but pride; that stupid, unreasonable pride of his, that twisted harmless words and actions into unforgivable insults. It was the more frightening because it was unpredictable.

They drank champagne. Elizabeth felt better for it, and began to tell her husband of the events of that morning and the preceding evening. Occasionally he frowned, but mostly he laughed. He was particularly amused by Mrs Green's suspicions.

'Good old Mrs Green,' he said. 'Michael said she wouldn't fail us.'

'Well, I don't think it's at all funny,' Elizabeth said. 'I don't mind her spreading rumours that Aunt Charlotte has disappeared — that was what you wanted, wasn't it? But I hate this talk of murder. And what a nerve she has, actually daring to hint that I'm responsible. All right, you may laugh. But how would *you* like to be accused of murder?'

'Not much,' he agreed. 'But, after all, it's only Mrs Green. You don't have to worry about her, darling.'

'It's only Mrs Green so far. But it'll spread; she'll see to that.'

'But why should she pick on you? You told me you weren't even in the house when Aunt Charlotte left?'

'I wasn't — though I gather that doesn't impress Mrs Green favourably either. The point is, Desmond, that I've brushed off both the telegram and the note as unimportant, and I've refused to report either to the police. That's what has aroused her suspicions — and I can't altogether blame her. It does look bad, I can see that. Tell me — what *was* I supposed to do when that telegram arrived?'

'I don't know,' he admitted. 'We never got around to fixing that, did we?'

'If you did you omitted to inform me,' she said accusingly. 'Who slipped that unpleasant note under the front door?'

'I'm afraid I don't know that either.' He gave her a rather guilty smile. 'The truth is, darling, that I sort of lost interest in the plot after you told me I was about to become a husband. I just left it to the others to arrange, and did as I was told. But that note wasn't in the programme as outlined to me. It must have been Michael or Alan adding a last-minute touch, I imagine. It wouldn't be Bruce.'

No, it wouldn't be Bruce. Bruce wasn't

the type for inspired last-minute touches. 'What exactly *was* the programme?' she asked.

'Well, there was the telegram. Then Alan was going to call round and monkey with the safe, and I was supposed to collect something of Aunt Charlotte's and dump it near the river.'

'And did you?'

'You know I didn't. You foxed us all by going out last night. What's more, we couldn't leave that love-note for you to hide conspicuously in her room. And it was a beautiful note, too. I wrote it myself — dreaming-oh-my-darling-love-of-thee. Rather a bore having to waste it.'

With that sentiment Elizabeth concurred. A note hinting at an elopement would have headed Mrs Green away from murder. Its news value would have been greater.

When she told him of the unlocked back door, and the footsteps Henry Torreck had heard, he was as bewildered as she had been.

'Odd,' he agreed. 'Damned odd. Of course, the prowler could have been whoever it was pushed that note under the door; Michael or Alan, presumably. But why didn't he wait until Mr Torreck had gone, so that he could tell you what he'd been up to? But the back door —' He frowned. 'Could Aunt Charlotte have forgotten to lock it?'

'Perhaps.'

Elizabeth was suddenly impatient to be gone. This was her wedding day, but Aunt Charlotte was spoiling it for her as surely as she had spoilt so many other days. For as long as they sat at table the topic would continue to haunt them; there would be breaks, of course, but always they would return to it. Aunt Charlotte was as inevitable as — as death.

She stood up quickly. He had ordered coffee, but she could not sit there and wait for it. They must go — now, at once, before everything was ruined.

'Going some place?' Desmond asked, surprised. 'Can I lend you a penny?'

She switched on her most summery smile.

'A penny wouldn't be sufficient,' she said gaily. 'I was thinking of the South of

France. Isn't that a 'must' for a honeymoon?'

Instantly he switched his mood to hers. 'But of course,' he said gravely. 'Stupid of me not to think of it. I'll get the hall porter to call a 'plane. Or — you're sure you wouldn't prefer Purley? I'm told it's becoming fashionable. All the best people go there now.'

Elizabeth shuddered. Aunt Charlotte again!

'No, thank you. Any other suggestions?'

He came to stand beside her. Regardless of the curious stares of the other diners, he put an arm round her waist.

'The Tower Hotel,' he whispered. 'Have I ever shown you my etchings, Mrs Farrel?'

* * *

It was nearly eleven o'clock when they left the Tower Hotel. They walked sedately down the stairs and through the deserted lounge, not looking at each other, with Elizabeth humming a rather sad little tune they had heard over the radio earlier in the evening.

Dulcie was in the hall. She eyed them steadily, her face expressionless save for the slight frown that creased her pretty brows.

Elizabeth stopped humming. Do we look different? she wondered. Does being married show on one's face, in the way one walks and holds oneself? 'Good night, Dulcie,' she said. She felt brimful of good-will, even to Dulcie. 'Sorry if we've kept you up. I didn't realize it was so late.'

The other girl continued to stare at them, her eyes flickering from one to the other. Then, with a curt good night, she turned and walked away.

Perhaps she doesn't like me any more than I like her, thought Elizabeth — surprised, not at the fact, but that she had not realized it before.

Desmond drove her home, and for a while they sat in the car outside the house. It was hard, thought Elizabeth, to have to bid her husband farewell so soon after their marriage. She no longer had doubts about her love for him, or his for her. She was filled with gratitude towards him for having charged her life with excitement and purpose and future. Desmond had ceased to be a means to an end, he was the end itself.

When she eventually released herself from his embrace she got out of the car briskly, aware that if she allowed herself to linger separation would be all the harder.

'Good night, Mrs Farrel,' Desmond called to her softly as she opened the gate. 'Be seeing you some time.'

She watched him as he backed the car and turned. Then, with a wave of the hand, she ran up the path to the house.

There was a light in the hall; if the Greens had taken her advice and gone out for the day they were back now. She hoped they had gone to bed. Another dose of Mrs Green was more than she could bear.

But the Greens had not gone to bed. She could hear their voices in the kitchen, and as she tiptoed down the hall and began to climb the stairs the door opened behind her.

'We'd like to speak to you, please,

miss,' the woman said.

Reluctantly Elizabeth turned and descended the stairs, wondering at the 'we.' She suddenly felt tired and flat. Reaction setting in, I suppose, she told herself. It's been quite a day.

She slumped on to a hard kitchen chair, rested her arms on the table, and glanced inquiringly at the gardener and his wife. The man was at the far end of the table, biting the loose skin round the nails of his stubby, soil-stained fingers. He gave her a quick, speculative look, but said nothing.

Elizabeth turned to his wife. 'Well?' she asked. 'What is it?'

There was nothing speculative about Mrs Green's expression. It was one of triumph. There was triumph, too, in her voice when she answered.

'There's been another telegram,' she said. She leaned over and slapped the untidy piece of paper on to the table. Then she stood back, folded her arms across her meagre bosom, and nodded significantly. 'Read it, miss.'

Elizabeth picked it up with distaste. For

so many hours Aunt Charlotte had been forgotten. Now she was back.

'Worried at your non-arrival,' she read. 'Will telephone at eight o'clock to-night.' It was signed 'Ethel.'

She sat staring at it for so long that Mrs Green, who had anticipated instant panic, remorse, and apology, lost some of her poise and glanced with raised eyebrows at her husband. But Mr Green merely shrugged his shoulders. He had nothing to suggest.

Elizabeth sighed. Then she said, without looking up, 'When did this come?'

'Five o'clock,' Mrs Green said; and added (perhaps to impress on the girl that they, at least, were equipped with a sense of responsibility), 'We was just thinking of going to the pictures. But we couldn't, of course. Not after that.'

'And did Mrs Donelly ring?'

'Yes, miss, she did. She said as how she hadn't set eyes on your aunt. Nor she hadn't heard from her neither. The poor thing was terribly upset when I told her Mrs Lane wasn't here.' The note of malicious triumph was back in her voice.

'She said as how it was downright wicked of us not to have been to the police about it.'

Elizabeth nodded wearily. She had no fight left.

'I'm sorry, Mrs Green. I'll get on to them to-morrow. It's too late to do anything to-night.'

Green took his fingers from his mouth and coughed.

'We've took care of that, miss. You being out, I had a word with Ted Williams. He said to tell you he'd be up to see you about it in the morning.'

4

Not just a Rumour

Police constable Ted Williams was an intelligent young man, and it was his misfortune that he was more aware of this fact than were his superiors. Thus his approach to crime was not so much to prevent or uncover it as to use it to enhance his own reputation. This was not entirely a selfish attitude. He had not been long in the Force, but he considered that his own rapid promotion would be in the best interests of society.

He received the news of Charlotte Lane's mysterious disappearance with outward calm and inward excitement. However zealous in his attention to duty a policeman might be, drunks and speeding motorists were no stepping-stones to meteoric preferment. But this was different. If Walter Green's story were true — and he was careful to emphasize the 'if' — this could be his big chance.

He was briskly but courteously efficient when he called at The Elms the next morning. Though he had hoped first to check Green's statement with Mrs Green, he remained unperturbed when Elizabeth herself opened the door to him. She was out of breath, he noticed. She had probably watched for his arrival from an upper window, and had then hurried downstairs to forestall Mrs Green. She wouldn't want that old gossip making a mountain out of a molehill, thought Ted. If it was a molehill. Which he hoped it wasn't.

'There may be nothing to it, Miss Messager,' he said, when he had explained his errand. 'But the matter has been reported, and it is my duty to investigate.'

'Of course. Come in, please.' She led the way into her aunt's study, apologizing for its untidiness. 'How can I help you?'

He took his time over telling her, weighing his words carefully.

'As I understand it, miss, Mrs Lane left here on Thursday afternoon to stay with a friend in Purley. But it seems that she never arrived there. Now, why might that be?'

'I couldn't say. But the main purpose of her visit was to do some shopping in London. Perhaps she decided to stay in the West End for a day or so before going down to Purley.'

'In that case wouldn't she have advised her friend?'

'You'd think so, wouldn't you? But — well, you know my aunt, Mr Williams. She's not given to considering other people.'

It was weak and suspiciously forced reasoning, he thought. He gave the girl what was intended to be a searching look.

'You are not worried about her?' he asked.

'If you mean, do I think something terrible has happened to her — no, I don't. But I would like to know what she's up to.'

She smiled at him. But Ted Williams was not to be beguiled by a smile. He had often admitted to himself that there was something about the Messager girl that he found oddly attractive; her red hair, perhaps, or that deep voice of hers. But promotion was more attractive still, and her smile was out of place here. There might be more in Walter Green's dark suspicions than he had at first believed. If Miss Messager didn't actually murder the old girl she at least knew something she wasn't telling. He was sure of that.

'It was Walter Green told me of the telephone call from Mrs Lane's friend,' he said gravely. 'I expect you know that. He also said there was a note Mrs Green had found in the hall yesterday morning. Threatening, he said it was.'

'Oh, that.' She laughed. 'Don't take that too seriously, Mr Williams. It was only some one's idea of a joke. Aunt Charlotte was never in debt in her life.'

'You're sure of that, miss? About it being a joke?'

The girl hesitated. 'I can't prove it, of course, but — yes, I'm sure.'

'May I see it, please?'

'Certainly. It's up in my room. I'll get it for you.'

He was glad to be alone for a few moments; it gave him the opportunity to consider his next move. There was something wrong somewhere. If the girl knew neither where her aunt was nor what had happened to her it didn't make sense to pretend that everything was perfectly normal, that there was no need for police investigation. So she was putting on an act. But why? And was he handling her right? Should he frighten her by voicing his suspicions, or should he go along with her until she gave herself away by some unguarded statement?

How would the Inspector handle her? He wished he knew.

When Elizabeth returned with the note he took his time in reading it, puzzling over its possibilities. It had been found under the mat, the gardener had said. But when had it been put there?

'It wasn't there Thursday morning,' Elizabeth said, when asked. 'I swept the hall myself. *And* shook the mat.' She hesitated. 'I — er — I imagine the village is already full of rumours, isn't it?'

'There's talk,' he agreed. 'I'll keep this note, miss, if you don't mind. As you say, it may be a joke; but then again it may not. Mrs Lane would be able to tell us more about that, eh?'

'I doubt it. But keep it by all means.'

He was placing the note carefully in his wallet when he was visited by one of those moments of clear, deductive thought that had made him aware that nature had intended him to fill a rôle more exalted than that of village constable.

'Suppose this note means what it says?' he suggested. 'And suppose it made sense to your aunt? She could have been so frightened by the threat it contained that she decided to disappear. Mightn't that have been the way of it?'

'No,' the girl said firmly. 'This visit had been planned weeks ago. It wasn't a sudden decision.'

'Quite so, miss. But she hasn't gone where she'd planned to go, has she? She'd think, you see, that whoever was threatening her might know of her plans and would follow her. Instead, she just disappears.'

'No,' Elizabeth said again. 'In the first place, she wasn't frightened, she was perfectly normal. Ask Mrs Green if you don't believe me. Secondly, if she had read the note she would either have destroyed it or kept it; she certainly wouldn't have hidden it under the mat. And lastly, if she *had* been in trouble, and *had* decided to disappear, she would have confided in me.'

Yes, thought Ted Williams. And suppose she *did* confide in you? Didn't she also tell you to hold your tongue, to head off all inquiries? And isn't that what you're doing right now? As for the note — well, panic (if there had been panic) could account for it being left under the mat. In itself it didn't prove or disprove anything.

But he must not allow suspicion to cloud his judgment. He must be thorough, methodical. Not until he had all the facts would it be safe to consider possible solutions.

'I understand the Greens left the house shortly after lunch on Thursday,' he said. 'They weren't back until nigh on ten, Walter said, so Mrs Green wouldn't know much about your aunt's state of mind that afternoon, would she?' He paused. 'But you were here, I presume, when Mrs Lane left in the taxi?'

'No,' Elizabeth said. She was well aware that he presumed nothing of the sort; Mrs Green would not have omitted that piece of information. Reluctantly she told him of the bogus telephone call and of her visit to Valerie. No doubt he would seize on it with glee, dress it up in the most sinister garb; but to conceal it now, only to have it revealed later from some other source (Valerie, perhaps, if the police inquiries circulated that far), would be still more damaging.

He did seize on it. Seized on it and worried it until, by the time he had done, Elizabeth was both frightened and annoyed. Ted Williams was intelligent, but not intelligent or astute enough to conceal the drift of his thoughts. She didn't like the direction in which they were drifting.

'Well, that'll be all for now, miss,' he said, closing his notebook with regret. He had enjoyed the interview. 'I'll send in a report, and it will then be up to headquarters to decide what action is to be taken. Er — this friend of your aunt's, miss. I'm not sure I got the name right. Donly, is it?'

'Donelly. Mrs Ethel Donelly. I don't know the address, but it's somewhere in Purley.'

'Thank you, miss.' Pencil poised over the reopened notebook, he paused. 'Would you mind writing it down for me?' And, as she took the pencil and notebook from him, 'In capitals, please, so there won't be no mistake. Block capitals.'

Her face looked very pale under the auburn hair. But the flash of her eyes indicated more anger than fear as she answered, after a slight pause, 'Certainly. But don't waste your time comparing my writing with that on the note, Mr Williams. Any resemblance will be entirely coincidental. I assure you I didn't write *that*.'

She formed the letters with deliberate care, aware of his embarrassment but not of its cause. It was not, as she thought, because of the trick he had tried to play on her, but because the trick had been detected. It hurt his confidence in himself that this girl should have seen through the ruse so easily.

He was saved from comment by the entry of Mrs Green, carrying a tray on which were two cups of coffee. She glanced eagerly at the two young people, and was greatly cheered by the obvious signs of strain.

'Time for elevenses,' she said. 'Everything all right, miss?'

Elizabeth ignored her. 'Will that be all, Mr Williams?' she asked, handing back the notebook. Her tone was frosty. 'I have things to do.'

He took it from her mechanically. He had temporarily forgotten the girl. His eyes were fixed with interest on Mrs Green, who was staring open-mouthed at the wall. Following the direction of her gaze, he found he was looking at the circular door of a small wall safe.

'Anything wrong, Mrs Green?' he asked hopefully.

'Wrong? Her picture's gone, that's what's wrong. Mrs Lane's picture, that's always hung there.' She turned to the girl. 'Did *you* take it down, miss? It was there Thursday morning, I'd swear to that. You always said you didn't like it. Come to that, you didn't like her either, did you?'

There was no mistaking the malice in her voice. To Elizabeth, already overwrought by her interview with Constable Williams, it was the last straw. Unmindful of the policeman's presence, she whirled furiously, on this new tormentor.

'Get out!' she snapped. Her fury almost choked her, so that all the scathing words she wanted to utter seemed to stick in her throat. The skin was stretched tight over the knuckles of her clenched fists; if the woman had been nearer she would have struck her. 'Get out, damn you!'

Mrs Green drew herself up to her full five feet five.

'Well!' she exclaimed. '*Well!*'

As she stalked from the room Elizabeth collapsed on to a chair and burst into tears.

Ted Williams was embarrassed. But he had his duty to perform, and Mrs Green had introduced a new and mysterious twist to the puzzle. 'About this picture, miss,' he said, after a long pause. 'You can't say what has happened to it?'

She took her hands away from her face and, lacking a handkerchief, wiped the tears from her cheeks with slender fingers.

'No,' she said, and sniffed. 'It was there Thursday morning, as Mrs Green said. It used to hang in front of the safe.'

'Was it there yesterday?'

'I don't know. I haven't been in this room since my aunt left.'

'Have you had any visitors?'

She shook her head.

The constable was puzzled. In itself the picture could not be important; only the mystery surrounding its disappearance made it so. Who else but the occupants of the house could have moved it? And why? And where was it now?

When he put these questions to the girl she turned on him angrily. Her nerves were all to pieces, and she was in no mood to be reasonable.

'I don't know,' she said. 'You can search the house if you like — I don't care. All I know is that I haven't touched the beastly thing. And I didn't write that silly note . . . and . . . and I don't know what's happened to Aunt Charlotte . . . and . . . oh, leave me alone, can't you?'

With the tears again welling into her eyes, she ran from the room.

* * *

The Speckled Trout overlooked the Tan Valley from the top of a high hill; it stood on the site of a fifteenth-century inn, some of the original walls of which had been incorporated into the newer building. The long, low dining-room, all dark oak and whitewashed walls and gleaming copper, was on two levels; from it the diners had an uninterrupted view, down a wide ride of green fields and brown earth broken by hedges and lone trees and flanked by dark conifers, to where the river cut like a flashing blue and silver streak across the landscape. Cattle dotted the distant fields, thin plumes of smoke spouted lazily from farmhouse chimneys. A church spire peeped coyly from above a cluster of tree-screened cottages.

'It's just perfect,' Elizabeth said, and sighed. A toy train emerged from behind the right-hand bank of conifers, and she watched it dreamily until it had dawdled its way across the scene and disappeared. 'Why haven't I been here before?'

'You must have chosen the wrong meal tickets,' Desmond suggested. 'Cigarette?'

The lunch had been excellent; their stomachs were comfortably full. They sat in well-padded chairs on the lower level, coffee and liqueurs on a table between them. The sun shone; they could feel its warmth through the closed windows. Behind them the room was empty of diners, for they had lunched late; but lights glowed cosily in the bar. Waiters were clearing and re-laying tables, glasses tinkled as the bartender washed up.

'I wish now that I hadn't done it,' Elizabeth said, her mind returning to their previous conversation. 'Let off steam, I mean. It was stupid and undignified. But coming on top of Ted Williams' insinuations she — well, she got me down. I let fly at her regardless.' She puffed nervously at her cigarette. She was not a hardened smoker; Aunt Charlotte did not approve. 'I suppose they'll walk out on me now. Well, let them; I never wanted them there in the first place. There'll be hell to pay when Aunt Charlotte returns, but who cares?'

She shrugged her shoulders, and looked at him anxiously through the cigarette smoke.

But her husband could not entirely allay her fears. 'Rather a bore to be out of order with the police,' he said thoughtfully.

'Why?' She knew he was not being flippant; the most tragic and unwelcome event could be described by Desmond as a 'bore.' 'Who cares what that stupid young man thinks? I haven't done anything wrong, have I?'

'Of course not. But you made it look that way by pretending you weren't interested in what had happened to Aunt Charlotte. Two telegrams, a threatening note, the picture missing; you can't laugh that lot off and expect to get away with it.'

'I'm not expecting to get away with

anything,' she said sharply. 'Nothing has happened to Aunt Charlotte. You know that.'

'Do I?' He frowned. 'I'm not so sure. The note could have been left by Alan; I haven't seen him since that evening, I've been too busy seeing you. But the picture is a little more tricky. None of us could have liberated that; we couldn't get into the house. And since it is now certain that Aunt Charlotte never arrived at Mrs Thingummy's — well, where is she?'

Couldn't get into the house? But they could. The back door was open, Mrs Green had said.

Mrs Green had said!

'I don't know,' she said abstractedly.

'And it doesn't look too good your clearing off on Thursday afternoon,' Desmond went on. 'You say you had this mysterious telephone call, but — '

That shook her out of her reverie. 'Wait a minute!' she demanded. 'Are you suggesting I invented it?'

'Of course I'm not, darling. But the police may. If they suspect you of being responsible for Aunt Charlotte's disappearance it's the logical conclusion. They'll say you were trying to fake an alibi.' He paused. 'I suppose it must have been Alan who rang you.'

'Of course it was Alan.' Elizabeth nervously stubbed out her half-finished cigarette. 'If it wasn't you or Michael or Bruce who else could it have been? Anyway, it's not important.'

'It could be,' Desmond said seriously. 'The police may say — '

'Oh, for heaven's sake stop bleating about the police,' she said irritably, stressing the final word. 'You make it sound as though the whole of Scotland Yard is after me — whereas it's only Ted Williams poking his nose into a little dirt the Greens have obligingly stirred up for him. And there wouldn't even have been Ted Williams if Michael and the rest of you hadn't tried to be funny.'

'But you agreed to it at the time, darling. Be reasonable. It's not fair to blame us now.'

'I know. I'm sorry. But I ought to have had more sense.' She lifted the lid of the coffee-pot and peered into its depths. 'More coffee?'

He nodded, pushing his cup towards her.

'You know, darling, it isn't true to say that we're responsible for everything that's happened. We may have set the ball rolling, but that's all we did do. We didn't send that second telegram, we haven't liberated Aunt Charlotte, we — '

'Wait a minute, Desmond.' She put down the coffee-pot and gripped his outstretched arm. Her eyes were shining. 'What if we're not the only practical jokers in Milford? What if some one is hoaxing *us*? No, not us — me.'

'Eh?' He shook his head. 'I don't get it. Who?'

'The Greens,' Elizabeth said excitedly. 'It was Mrs Green who told me the back door had been left unlocked. But had it? Did she make that up? And that second telegram . . . and the phone call from Mrs Donelly . . . she could have invented those too, couldn't she? Yes, and no one but the Greens could have taken that picture down and hidden it,' she added triumphantly. 'Apart from me they're the only people who've been in the house.'

'Good Lord!' Desmond was startled and impressed. 'You may be right on the beam, darling. But why? What could be behind it?'

'Goodness knows. They only suffer Aunt Charlotte for what they can get out of her — they're that kind of people — and they certainly haven't any use for me. Mrs Green has made that perfectly clear. But there must be more to it than that, surely? You don't try to get people suspected of murder just because you dislike or despise them. Still, whatever the reason, it must have been Michael's telegram that gave them the idea. That and the note. Or perhaps they wrote the note too?'

'Why not? If Alan didn't they must have done. But what a turn-up, eh?' He grinned. 'What do we do now? Play up to them?'

'We can't do much else, can we, until we hear from Aunt Charlotte? But I'll ask Miss Webber at the post-office for confirmation of that second telegram. If she can't produce it we'll know I'm right.'

The thought of Mr and Mrs Green's probable discomfiture seemed to cheer her. But not for long. Whatever they talked about — and mostly they talked about themselves — Aunt Charlotte was always there at the back of their minds, spoiling their pleasure.

As they got up to leave Elizabeth said, 'I've loved it here, darling. Thank you for bringing me. You know the nicest places.'

'We'll come again,' he promised her.

'Will we?' She sounded wistful. 'It would be a lovely place to spend our honeymoon — if we ever have a honeymoon, that is. I'm afraid that by the time our chance comes we'll no longer be eligible. We'll probably have been married for years and years.'

'Don't be so gloomy,' he said. And then, realizing that this might be misconstrued, 'You shan't be done out of your honeymoon. Just leave it to me, darling. I'll fix it.'

'You can't fix it while Aunt Charlotte is alive,' she told him. 'Once she gets back it's going to be difficult to see each other, let alone go away for a honeymoon.'

They spent the afternoon in the car, and returned to the Speckled Trout, at Elizabeth's request, for a late tea. But some of the magic had left it, she found. Dusk had blotted out the view, and now it was just another country inn. They ate mostly in silence; Elizabeth sensed that her husband was anxious to be gone, and could guess the reason. The hotel was a busy place on a Saturday and, despite his often casual air, she knew he took a keen interest in it.

As they drove through the dark lanes back to Milford Cross he told her of his plans for the future. His father was old-fashioned, he said, and too content to leave things as they were and always had been. It would be different when he took over. He would modernize the old lounge, install cocktail and snack bars, put in central heating. There would be a new wing to house ballroom and squash court, a swimming-pool in the grounds. 'It's just a hostelry at present,' he said. 'People come to us for a drink, a meal, and a bed for the night, but they don't stay. The place is never full. I want them to look on the hotel as a holiday resort, somewhere to spend a gay week-end; somewhere quite different to the usual run of country pubs. I want to see us booked up for weeks — months ahead. And we will be, once I've got everything fixed. You'll see.'

'It sounds marvellous,' Elizabeth said. 'But won't it cost a lot?'

'Plenty,' he agreed cheerfully. 'We'll have to take it in easy stages.'

She liked that 'we'; it made her feel even closer to him that he should automatically assume she would take an interest in the hotel, be a part of his work as well as his leisure.

'How about the tower room?' she asked. 'Will you leave that as it is?'

The tower room was a feature of the hotel. The tower itself was at the western end of the building, and prior to the First World War the then owner, an elderly German named Goetz, had built into it a room in which he could shut himself away from the imagined dangers that threatened him from the spy-crazy

English. It was still as he had left it, but was never used.

'I think so,' Desmond said. 'Commercially it's more useful that way. The customers lap it up.'

'You promised to take me up there, but you never have.'

'Haven't I? There's nothing much to see, except the view.'

It was just after five-thirty when they reached Milford Cross. Desmond drove direct to the hotel. 'The old man will be wondering where I've got to,' he said. 'I'll take you home after I've made my peace with him. Wait in the car, darling — I shan't be a jiffy.'

The lounge lights were dim as he went in through the swing door; the bar was not yet open. At the far end of the room a little knot of people, Dulcie and his father among them, stood talking. When he saw Desmond Mr Farrel left the others and came to meet him.

'Sorry I'm late,' Desmond said cheerfully, noting the frown on his father's face and omitting an excuse. His father hated excuses.

Mr Farrel glanced up at the clock. 'You must have had an excellent lunch,' he said drily. 'Who was your companion?'

Desmond told him. He was not sure that his father approved of Elizabeth. He could have nothing against the girl herself, but having Charlotte Lane for an aunt was definitely a handicap. 'She's outside in the car. I'm just going to run her home.'

George Farrel looked at him thoughtfully. Desmond was suddenly aware that Dulcie and the others had stopped talking and were watching them intently.

'I think you had better bring Miss Messager in,' his father said quietly.

'Eh?' Desmond was startled. Had the old man discovered already that he and Elizabeth were married? 'What's up, Dad?'

'Her aunt has been murdered,' Mr Farrel said.

'Oh, that!' Desmond grinned. 'That's just a rumour. Elizabeth thinks the gardener and his wife have cooked it up to scare her. We've been discussing it this afternoon. She can't make up her mind whether to confront them with it now or wait until Mrs Lane returns. But either way it seems to me — '

Mr Farrel shook his head.

'This isn't a rumour, Desmond,' he said. 'The police have found her body.'

5

A Bloody Mess

Elizabeth surprised them by her calmness. There were no tears and no hysterics. Her cheeks were a little whiter, her body stiffer; she sat very still, though the hand gripping the brandy they had poured for her was not entirely steady.

When George Farrel complimented her on her control she shook her head.

'It isn't really control, Mr Farrel; it's just that I don't feel anything. Not at the moment. I'm sorry she's dead, that she died like that; but it's an impersonal sorrow, as though she and I had been strangers.' She sighed. 'I don't have to pretend, do I? Every one knows how it was between us.'

The two men nodded, relieved. Desmond, anxious not to betray his close interest in the girl, hovered silently in the background. His father patted her approvingly on the shoulder.

'We understand,' he said kindly.

Elizabeth twisted in her chair to smile nervously up at him, handing him her empty glass. 'Where — how did they find her?' she asked.

'It was young Williams,' Farrel said. 'I gather he had a talk with you this morning' — the girl nodded — 'as a result of which he decided to take a look round the house.'

'But can he do that?' Desmond protested. 'Surely not without a warrant or Elizabeth's permission?'

Elizabeth wrinkled her brows. 'I think I gave him permission,' she said slowly. 'I got so fed up with his questions that I told him he could search the house if he liked. But I never thought he would.'

'Well, he did,' Farrel said. 'And after he'd combed the house he got busy on the yard. The old well was the first place he looked.'

His son glanced at him sharply, opened his mouth to speak, then closed it reluctantly. Elizabeth said quickly, 'You mean she was down the well? Oh, no!'

'So I'm told.' George Farrel's hand was again on her shoulder. 'You mustn't let it distress you, my dear. Let me get you another brandy, eh?'

She shook her head.

'No, thank you. Please — what else? How did she die? Could it have been an accident?'

The pressure on her shoulder tightened.

'I don't know. I understand not — but then I've been told so much by so many different people, and none of them in a position to know the truth. All I can say for certain is that they found her body in the well. The rest is just hearsay.'

She leaned forward, burying her fingers in her hair. Redgold strands gleamed dully in the soft light. The two men looked at each other, the same thought in their minds.

But Elizabeth had not succumbed to tears. She was flushed but dry-eyed when she looked up to ask, 'What ought I to do, Mr Farrel?'

He had already given that some thought.

'The natural thing would be for you to go home, I suppose. But I'm sure you'd rather not. It would be distressing for you, and there's nothing you can do there. So I suggest you stay here. The police will want to see you in due course, but I'll let them know where to find you.'

'Thank you,' she said gratefully. She was surprised at his thoughtfulness. Relieved, too — it augured well for the future. 'I'd prefer that.'

'She can't stay in here,' Desmond said, looking at the clock. 'The place will be full this evening, and it's close on opening time now.' He turned to the girl. 'Go up to my room, Elizabeth. I'll be with you shortly, but I must put a phone call through first.'

They watched her as she crossed the room and went into the hall. The older man was frowning. 'Knight-errantry is a fine thing, Desmond,' he said, 'but don't overdo it. There are rooms other than yours where we could have put her.'

'I know. But a hotel bedroom is a

cheerless place with no fire and no one to talk to. She'll be better off in my room.'

'I dare say. But although I'm sorry for the girl I can't forget who she is.' He looked squarely at his son. 'You may as well know that it's being freely rumoured in the village that she knows more than most about how her aunt came to be in the well.'

'Good God! You believe that?'

'No. But I can't entirely ignore the possibility that it may be true. I suggest that, under the circumstances, ordinary human sympathy would be more circumspect than gushing sentimentality. But suit yourself.'

'I don't gush,' Desmond said, disgusted at such a term being applied to him. 'And I don't rat on my friends.'

Hands thrust deep in his trouser-pockets, head high, he stalked from the room. His father sighed and, after a momentary pause, followed him. Murder was an unpleasant occurrence, but, as Desmond had inferred, it might well be beneficial to trade. He had better prepare for a full house.

Elizabeth did not have to wait long for her husband to join her. He went straight to a cupboard, poured himself a large whisky (Elizabeth refused his offer of brandy for herself; she was past the need for that, she assured him), and rather awkwardly began to offer her his sympathy.

He looked so uncomfortable that Elizabeth felt sorry for him. She knew his rôle was more difficult than hers. 'There's no need for that between you and me, darling,' she said gently. 'But thank you for trying.'

Relieved, he gulped down his whisky and poured another.

'What gets me down,' he said, his eyes fixed on the liquid in his glass, 'is the thought of us joking about her being murdered, and all the time the poor old girl was . . . ' He shook his head. 'Rather grim, that.'

'I know. It doesn't bear thinking about — although I've been thinking about little else since I came up here. I suppose this room reminded me of it.' She shuddered. 'Darling, I think I'll have that drink after all. Not brandy — a gin and tonic.'

He poured it for her.

'It's such an amazing coincidence,' she said. 'Even to the day.' He looked at her oddly at that. 'What's the matter?' she asked.

'Oh, nothing. I was just thinking.'

She sipped her drink. Presently she said, 'How will this affect us, Desmond?'

'You and me? I don't know. It could be sticky.'

'How?'

He put his glass down on the mantelpiece and walked slowly over to her. Balancing himself on the wide arm of her chair, he took her free hand and began to caress it with his own.

'You won't like this, darling,' he said. 'I don't like it myself. But it seems there is already a rumour going the rounds that you had a hand in pushing Aunt Charlotte down the well.'

'I see.' He felt her stiffen. 'Well, that was to be expected, I suppose. Mrs Green hasn't wasted much time, has she?' She sighed. 'Darling, you and your friends have got me into quite a mess, haven't you?'

'We've got ourselves into a mess too,' he said. 'But that's by the way. It's this damned gossip that worries me. How will the county police react to it? Even if they write off Mrs Green they can't ignore Ted Williams. He will have put in an official report, I imagine.'

'About the telegram, you mean, and that note?'

'Yes. And the missing picture.'

'Can't I just tell them the truth — that it was all a joke?'

'The picture wasn't. But the rest — well, I don't know.' He went over to the fireplace, picked up his drink, and switched on the electric fire with his foot. For a few moments he stood staring down at it, watching the element turn from a rusty brown to glowing red. Then he looked up. 'The truth isn't just yours and mine, darling; it belongs to the others as well. They're as much concerned as we are.'

'Well?' Her tone was defiant.

'We've got to consult them before

deciding; we can't simply ditch them out of hand. I rang Alan and asked him to round them up, and I expect they'll be here soon. Then we can sort it all out. But before they come there's something you and I have to settle on our own, my sweet.'

'What's that?'

'Our marriage. Do we or do we not continue to keep it secret?'

Elizabeth smiled faintly. She had forgotten until now that with Aunt Charlotte's death the reason for secrecy had been removed. If good could ever come out of evil this was it. The immediate future, crowded as it would be with policemen and suspicion, would seem less terrifying if Desmond were by her side to share it.

'Oh, let's tell them!' she said eagerly. 'I'm wearing your ring on a ribbon round my neck, but I'd much rather see it on my finger. And then I could stay here with you, couldn't I?'

'It's not quite as simple as that,' he said, steeling his heart against the appeal in her voice. 'I wish it were. I thought the same way as you at first, but now I'm not so sure.'

'Why?'

'One of the first things the police will do will be to get hold of a copy of Aunt Charlotte's will. They'll want to know who benefits by her death. Well, you do. That in itself would make them investigate you fairly thoroughly, even if there were nothing else — as there is, unfortunately. But if the will clearly states — as you say it does — that you don't get a penny of her money if you marry before her death, and if they learn that we were married the day after she was murdered . . . ' He shrugged. 'Well, I know what I would think if I were a policeman.'

'Let's hope they haven't got your nasty suspicious mind, then.' She spoke lightly to hide her disappointment. The logic of his argument was unassailable, yet she wanted to assail it. 'And just because I had a motive for killing Aunt Charlotte it doesn't follow that I did kill her. Even a policeman wouldn't think that, would he? There'd have to be proof.'

'Oh, yes, there'd have to be proof. I'm

not saying they'd arrest you; but it all adds up to a very unpleasant time for you until they discover who *did* kill her. Unpleasant for me, too; apart from worrying about you, I've no doubt I should be suspected as your accomplice.' He smiled faintly. 'Only this afternoon you were resigned to waiting years for our honeymoon. Don't let's ruin everything by being too precipitate now, darling.'

Elbows on knees, her chin cupped in her hands, she eyed him thoughtfully. Eventually she said, 'Is that your only reason?'

He flushed, guessing where her thoughts had led. He would have preferred to say 'yes' and leave it at that; but he suspected that she was still not persuaded of the seriousness of the position, that further argument was needed.

'No, it isn't,' he said slowly. 'You must see, darling, that this would be a most inopportune moment to tell my father we're married.'

'Why? Because he thinks I killed Aunt Charlotte?'

'He doesn't think anything of the sort.' He spoke sharply, angry because she had put him on the defensive. 'But there are these damned rumours, and you could hardly expect him to welcome you as a daughter-in-law while —' He broke off at the sound of hurried footsteps approaching along the corridor. 'Oh, damn! Here come the others. We'll have to sort this out later, darling. But in the meantime remember that I love you, and that I want the old man to feel the same way about you.' He grinned suddenly. 'Hell, no, I don't want that! But I do want you and him to get off to a good start. Understand?'

She had time only for a brief nod before the door burst open and three very frightened and agitated young men piled into the room in a flurry, breathless and confused, firing questions and oaths almost before the door was shut behind them. They had heard the news and some of the rumours connected with it, but the actual facts surrounding the discovery of Charlotte Lane's body were as obscure to them as to Desmond and Elizabeth. 'Alan and I went round to the house to see what was happening,' Michael said, pacing restlessly about the room, the lock of hair tossing backward and forward with each sudden movement of his head. 'Half the village seem to have had the same idea. But we couldn't get near the place — there were policemen everywhere. We tried going down to the river and up through the copse, but it didn't help; all we could see was the glow from the lights they had rigged up round the well. The whole yard was screened off.' He came to an abrupt halt in front of Desmond. 'God, what a mess! And to think the whole bloody scheme was my idea!'

Elizabeth had recoiled from the noise and confusion of their eruption into the room, retreating into her private thoughts. But Michael's last words blended into them, and she said curtly, 'Yes, it's a mess. I'm not blaming you — it's as much my fault as yours for ever agreeing to your suggestion — but it doesn't seem fair that all the onus should fall on me. It's up to you to do something about it.'

Michael stared at her, frowning. Her voice had attracted his attention, but he had paid little heed to her words. He said, speaking not to her alone but to all of them, 'If the police get wind of it we're sunk.'

'We're sunk if they don't,' Elizabeth retorted. 'Or I am. People are already saying I killed her. Did you know that?'

If they did they gave no sign. Desmond, determined to let them have their say before expressing his own opinion, had settled himself on the bed and was absent-mindedly playing some obscure game of his own with interlocked fingers. Bruce's normally rubicund face was white and drawn, and there were dark circles under his eyes (Why the circles? Elizabeth wondered — there had not been time for him to lose any sleep over the murder); Michael was scowling, tiny beads of sweat glistening on his olive skin. Alan nodded sympathetically. He looked more composed than the others, and Elizabeth, hopeful that he, like her husband, could be relied on to recognize the seriousness of her position and to subjugate his own interests to it, addressed herself to him.

'Don't you see, Alan, that the only way I can clear myself of suspicion is to explain that what we did was done in fun?' He had an irritating habit when worried of plucking jerkily at the ends of his close-cropped moustache. He began to do it now, and Elizabeth, exasperated, said sharply, 'Well, don't you?'

'It's a *possible* way,' he said cautiously. 'But there is always the probability that it will prove something of a boomerang. The police may assume there was cause and effect — that the joke got out of hand, as it were, and resulted in murder. In other words, we'd be deliberately inviting them to suspect us. I don't think that would be at all clever.'

'Of course it wouldn't.' Michael was scornful. 'Damned lunacy, if you ask me. Even if they don't think it was a concerted job, they'll certainly believe that one of us took advantage of the situation and killed her. And who's to disprove them?'

Desmond carefully unlocked the little

finger of his left hand from the unnatural position into which it had been forced. As he massaged it gently to restore the circulation he said, 'No one. Because it may very well be true, don't you think?'

Michael stared at him open-mouthed, his lower jaw twitching, unheeded hair almost obscuring his eyes. Bruce drew in his breath sharply, audibly, hunching his shoulders so that his thick neck seemed to concertina into nothing. Elizabeth shrank a little farther into her chair, her lips parted in a faint sigh. But Alan, his blue eyes wide, his head thrown back so that his chin looked unusually aggressive, stuck his hands into his pockets and said, 'Yes, I do. Good for you, Desmond. I'm glad one of us has had the courage to say what all of us must have been thinking.'

'Well, it's the obvious answer, isn't it?' Desmond's tone was mild, almost apologetic. 'I've no wish to insult any of you, but what other explanation is there?'

Michael and Bruce began to protest — Michael vehemently, Bruce half-heartedly. Elizabeth said, 'You know, it never even occurred to me.'

'That's because you have a nicer mind than the rest of us,' Desmond told her, with a warm smile.

'We all disliked her,' Alan said briskly. Dramatics in real life made him feel uncomfortable, and he tried, not always successfully, to avoid them. 'Most of us could be said to have a strong motive for killing her; Elizabeth's would be primarily financial, I suppose, and Michael's and mine the settling of an old grudge. I don't know about you and Bruce, Desmond, but I dare say you've both got one tucked away somewhere.' Desmond made a grimace and glanced across at Elizabeth, but she had turned to look thoughtfully at the flushed, unhappy Bruce. 'We all knew her plans for Thursday, and that a better opportunity was unlikely to present itself. What is more — although I've no doubt some of you will deny it — I wouldn't mind betting that each one of us called at The Elms at some time or another that evening. I did, for one. I didn't kill her — but that's what we'll all say, of course. And one of us could very well be lying.'

Towards the end of this speech his

voice had become more impassioned. He had been carried away by a necessity to make them see the truth of what he said. Now he was suddenly embarrassed. To hide his confusion he added, with a feeble attempt at jocularity which he knew was misplaced, 'That ends the case for the prosecution, your worships.'

In the courtyard below men and women were arriving, by car or on foot, to spend a cheerful and convivial evening in the hotel. Through the half-open window there drifted up to the five young people in the room the sounds of talk and laughter, the slamming of car doors, the crunch of footsteps on gravel. But they did not heed them. They were the sounds of another and a saner world, from which they were temporarily apart.

It was Michael who broke the silence.

'How about the Greens?' His voice was thick, and he cleared his throat noisily. 'Couldn't they have killed her?'

Elizabeth shook her head. 'They went out almost immediately after lunch, and didn't get back until nearly ten o'clock.'

'How do you know? Desmond said you

were out yourself.'

'From five to half-past nine, yes. But I saw them go and I saw them return.'

'That proves nothing,' Michael said. 'They could have come back and killed her while you were out, couldn't they?'

But he said it without conviction, and none of them grasped at the proffered straw.

'There's one important factor to be taken into consideration,' Desmond said. 'The taxi. Aunt Charlotte was catching the six forty-five train, so the taxi wouldn't have called for her later than six-fifteen. That means she must have been killed after five o'clock, when Elizabeth left the house, and before six-fifteen. How does that affect us?'

Alan smiled with his mouth, but there was no humour in his eyes.

'Taken at face value, it affects me nicely. I didn't go to The Elms until after nine.'

'Face value? That means you can't prove it, eh?'

'No, I can't. I was at home on my own that evening. The old man was out.'

Remembering that night, Elizabeth said, 'Were you in the garden when your father brought me home?'

He nodded. 'I had just pushed that cosy little invitation under the front door when you turned up. When I heard his voice I cleared off. I wanted to see you, but not in his company.'

'What did you want to see me about?'

'The safe. I was supposed to make it look as though some one had tried to open it. Remember?'

Yes, she remembered. 'Some one did tamper with it,' she said. 'And removed the picture.'

He flushed. 'It wasn't me,' he said brusquely. 'I was never inside the house.' And added, a trace of bitterness in his voice, 'Not for years.'

'We're getting nowhere,' Michael said impatiently. 'You say yourself you can't *prove* you weren't at The Elms before nine. Incidentally, why did you leave it so late?'

'Because Elizabeth was out,' Alan said, ignoring the suspicion in the other's voice. 'I rang her at six-thirty, and several times after that; but there was no reply. I wouldn't have gone there at all if I hadn't thought of writing that note. At the time it seemed a happy contribution.'

'I heard the telephone,' Bruce said. He was speaking to himself, but at Elizabeth's startled gasp he looked up, his cheeks reddening. 'I — '

Alan interrupted him. 'You mean you were actually in the house at half-past six that evening?'

'Outside, not in. I'd rung the bell, but no one answered. But I could hear the telephone ringing.'

'What were you doing there?'

'I wanted to speak to Elizabeth. Nothing wrong in that, is there?'

'About Aunt Charlotte?'

'No.'

He said it vehemently, explosively. They waited for him to explain further, but he did not. He sat glowering at them truculently, defying them to question him.

They all knew that look of his — they were used to his moods. When Alan spoke again his tone was conciliatory.

'Don't lose your temper, Bruce. No one's accusing you.' He frowned at Michael, who was all set to explode into an accusation. 'Certainly not me. I'm not sure, but I think you've given me an alibi.'

Desmond looked sceptical. 'If I had to rely on an alibi like that I'd skip the country,' he said. 'I'd feel safer.'

'Oh, well, I don't need one. Not yet.' Alan turned again to Bruce. 'Did you see anyone near the house?'

'No. Only Desmond.' His voice was quieter, but sullen. 'He gave me a lift from the corner.'

Three pairs of eyes turned simultaneously towards Desmond, who grinned at them.

'He's right, you know. I'd been into Tanbury, and came back that way; I wanted to give Elizabeth the love note and collect something of Aunt Charlotte's to dump. I met Bruce just as I was turning into the lane. He told me there was no one at home, so we came back here and had a drink.'

Again the silence. Then Michael said, a trifle wildly, 'I seem to have been the only one who didn't go near the place that evening. Nobody can accuse me, thank goodness. I'm in the clear.'

'Not you,' Alan said. 'Don't kid yourself, Michael. We're in this together. All of us.'

Elizabeth flushed. He had not looked at her, and she did not think he meant to include her. But she knew that Michael most certainly would.

'Am I supposed to add my contribution now?' she asked. But her attempt at bravado fell flat, and she added soberly, 'Aunt Charlotte was alive when I left the house at five o'clock. There's not much more I can tell you, is there?'

'Isn't there?' This from Michael. 'Why did you go out that afternoon?'

'Because — ' Remembering, she turned to Alan. 'Was it you who phoned me that afternoon? About Valerie?'

'Me?' He sounded genuinely puzzled. 'Not about Valerie. And not before six-thirty.'

'Then who — ' Bewildered, she looked appealingly at Desmond. 'I don't understand,' she said.

'Neither do I,' he agreed. 'Some one's kidding us.'

Alan looked from one to the other. 'I don't understand either,' he said. 'Suppose one of you explains?'

Briefly Desmond told him. 'Elizabeth thought that one of us had had the bright idea of getting her out of the house before Aunt Charlotte left. She says you suggested it — not the phone call, but that she should be out of the way. Well, I didn't phone her . . . and Bruce and Michael said they didn't . . . so that left you.'

'It doesn't leave me now,' Alan said. 'So what?'

'So one of us could be a liar, and we're back where we started.' Desmond flexed his arms, stretching them languidly. 'Rather a bore, isn't it, to find that one's circle of intimates may include a murderer?'

'Or a murderess,' added Michael.

The blood left the girl's face, so that suddenly her hair seemed to turn a more fiery red. It was the first time any of them had hinted openly at what she had known must be vaguely in their minds. She felt cold and frightened, drained of all vitality, so that the effort to defend herself seemed too great. Yet she knew she must make that effort. If she said nothing . . . if she allowed the accusation to pass unchallenged . . .

'I didn't kill Aunt Charlotte.' Her voice was cold, expressionless. She could not summon indignation to lend conviction to her denial. 'You don't have to believe me, Michael, any more than I have to believe you. But it's the truth.'

Desmond said quickly, 'Nice, friendly type, aren't you, Michael? Any more cracks like that and out you go.'

Alan's comment was so forceful that, having made it, he was suddenly covered with confusion at memory of the words he had used in front of the girl. Bruce nodded approval of their condemnation, frowning angrily at Michael. But Michael merely shrugged. He evinced neither embarrassment nor contrition, and met their frowns with a challenging, 'Well, it's true, isn't it?'

Nobody answered that. Alan said,

'Let's stop bickering and get this thing settled. Do we or do we not tell the police what we had planned to do? Since they don't know about it we shan't have to answer a direct question; but do we volunteer the information?'

'No,' Michael and Desmond said in unison.

'How about you, Bruce?'

Bruce shrugged his large shoulders. 'I'll do what the rest of you think best.'

'Elizabeth?'

She shook her head. 'It's not so easy for me, Alan. I had very little to do with it, yet I'm more involved than any of you.' She told them of her interview that morning with Ted Williams. 'I know he suspects me; I'm going to have a lot of awkward questions to answer. And how can I answer them except by telling the truth? It isn't so much the things that happened, it's the way I reacted to them. How, for instance, can I explain my complete indifference to Aunt Charlotte's fate when that first telegram arrived?'

'Once they discover how it was between you and her — and that won't take them long — it explains itself,' Michael said. 'Anyway, disinterest isn't criminal. They can't arrest you for that.'

'Perhaps not. But they could be very unpleasant about it. And then there's the fact that I went out that afternoon. It looks wrong. In a way I suppose it *was* wrong; if whoever it was telephoned me hadn't stressed the urgency I certainly wouldn't have left Aunt Charlotte to see herself off. Now the police will probably infer that I was trying to fake some kind of an alibi. They may not even believe that there *was* a phone call.' She hesitated. 'Do you?'

'Of course,' Desmond and Alan said hastily. Bruce nodded, but Michael made no sign. He's quite sure I killed her, Elizabeth thought uneasily. Or is he hoping to make a scapegoat out of me?

'That phone call wasn't in the plan,' Alan said. 'I don't know how it fits in, but telling the truth won't explain it. But there's no doubt it's going to be tougher for you than for the rest of us. They can't possibly trace the telegram to Michael, and I seem to be the only other person involved. Well, I'm not worrying; I wrote that note with my left hand, and they won't check it with my handwriting unless I come under suspicion for some other reason.'

'Sit tight and let the police get on with it,' Michael said firmly. 'It's the only thing to do.'

There was a murmur of agreement. Elizabeth said bitterly, 'The chivalry of my male acquaintances overwhelms me. Sit tight and let Elizabeth take the can back! That's what you mean, isn't it?'

'Of course not.' With the others watching, Desmond hesitated to show her affection, but he went over and took one of her hands. It was cold and lifeless, despite the warmth of the room, and he sandwiched it gently between his own. 'But whether we tell the truth or not you're bound to come under suspicion; you inherit the money, and anyone in the village will tell them that you and she didn't get on. Tell 'em the truth, and their questions will be more objective, more searching; they'll hit you harder, so to speak. And there's this to consider. If they suspect us as well as you we can't do so much to help; everything we say in your favour will also be suspect, they'll think we are all in cahoots. Whereas if we're the lily-white boys in the eyes of the law we might be able to pull a few fast ones in your favour. Don't you see that?'

'You make it sound as though you're trying to save me from the gallows,' she said, near to tears. 'I don't need saving. I didn't kill Aunt Charlotte, and nobody can prove I did.'

Desmond looked despairingly at Alan, who shook his head; he could muster no further argument. Michael wisely kept silent. But Bruce surprised them by saying, his voice plaintive, 'If she doesn't want to hush it up you can't make her.' He turned to the girl. 'How about a compromise, Elizabeth? An edited, well-watered version of the truth? Would you agree to that?'

'I wouldn't,' Michael said promptly. 'We'd still be putting ideas into their heads that we don't want there. It's no help at all.'

There was a chorus of agreement

— joined, to their surprise, by Elizabeth.

'Either you tell the truth or you don't,' she said, rubbing her eyes. 'Half the truth is worse than useless and twice as harmful.' She sighed. 'Perhaps you're right; perhaps it would be wiser to say nothing. But — tell me, do you all really believe that one of us must have killed Aunt Charlotte?' In turn she searched their faces for an answer. None was forthcoming, and she said, almost fiercely, 'Well, do you?'

Michael and Bruce shrugged non-committally, uncertain which was the wiser answer. 'It's the only logical explanation,' Desmond said; and Alan added, 'You can quote me on that.'

'You ought to be ashamed of yourselves if you do,' she told them. 'You'd be deliberately planning to shield a murderer. If I thought that way I wouldn't hesitate a moment; I'd tell the truth, no matter what the consequences. But luckily for you I think you're wrong. There are lots of other people who hated Aunt Charlotte and envied her her money, and any one of them could have done it. Her being killed on that particular afternoon may have been sheer coincidence. It doesn't *have* to be one of us.'

The four men looked awkwardly at each other. Desmond knew that none of them shared her belief, however much they might welcome it.

'Does that mean you're with us?' Alan asked, voicing the uncertainty of them all.

'I suppose so.' Her thoughts and opinions, her sense of moral values, were by now thoroughly confused. They were all so sure that they were being sensible, that the course they suggested was in her own best interests as well as theirs. She could place no reliance on Michael; but Desmond would not advise her against his better judgment, and neither, she thought, would Alan. And Bruce? Bruce had said he was in love with her, and that must mean something. 'But what if I'm not a good enough liar? What if they get me into a corner and I can't wriggle out? What then?'

'Tell the truth,' Alan said promptly. 'Only try to warn us first. We mustn't contradict each other.' He smiled at her. 'Okay?'

'I hope so.' She gave him a faint smile in return. 'I'll do my best, anyway, not to let you down. But I warn you' — the smile vanished suddenly — 'if I find out later that I was wrong, that one of you *did* kill Aunt Charlotte, I'll break my promise at once. There won't be any warnings then.'

'Fair enough,' Desmond said. 'I reckon that goes for all of us.'

A light patter of feet along the corridor, and Dulcie Rivers came into the room without knocking. As always, she was dressed to kill. A tight-fitting black woollen jumper emphasized her curves, the full red skirt was designed to flare out with every turn of her slender body, displaying an over-generous length of nylon-encased leg. Her long, pointed finger-nails were blood-red; not a hair of her blonde head was out of place.

'Quite a party,' she said, twirling to look at them all in turn, happily aware of male eyes gazing hungrily at her legs. 'H'm! Cosy — but glum.' She stopped pirouetting to face the girl. 'I'm sorry about your aunt, Elizabeth.' (There was no sorrow in her voice.) 'Mr Farrel asked me to tell you that you can have a room here if you want one.'

Elizabeth thanked her mechanically. She had not hitherto given much thought to the future, but she knew that she could never go back to the house. Not alone, and to sleep.

'It will have to be one facing north,' Dulcie went on cheerfully, taking the drink which Desmond had poured for her. 'The Inspector and the Sergeant have booked the only two vacant rooms on this side.'

That startled them, as she had known it would.

'The police?' Desmond said sharply. 'You mean they're staying here?'

'They are that. Booked in half an hour ago. I didn't take much to the Inspector, but the Sergeant — ' She smiled reflectively. 'He's quite a pet.'

Michael said nervously, 'Are they actually in the building at this moment?'

'No. They've gone back to the scene of

the crime.' She turned again to the girl. 'They want to talk to you, Elizabeth. Mr Farrel told them you were here. The Inspector said he'd like to see you at The Elms just as soon as you can make it.' She shuddered theatrically. 'I don't envy you, my dear. He's positively *grim*!'

6

An Exaggerated Expression of Dislike

'The perfect murderee, eh?' the inspector commented, unconsciously echoing Desmond's words. 'A woman born to be killed.'

'Yes, sir,' Ted Williams said politely.

He was always polite to police inspectors, particularly on meeting them for the first time. And Detective-Inspector Pitt did not look like a man who would take kindly to familiarity from a young constable. He was a long, lean, solemn-looking man, with dull grey hair receding from a high forehead. Ted would have considered him too old for the job (he formed that opinion of most of his superior officers, subconsciously willing them out of his way) had it not been for his soldierly bearing and the alert, watchful eyes.

'And did you collect all this dirt from

Mrs Green?' asked Pitt.

'Not all, sir. Some of it's from my own knowledge, or from what I've heard in the village. There's a lot of gossip in Milford, sir.'

'There is in most villages,' Pitt said.

The glow through the small study window indicated that Watkins and his gang were still busy in the yard. They would be clearing up now. The body had already been removed to the mortuary, and it was unlikely that the well had any further secrets to reveal. If it had they must wait until the morning.

Pitt turned from the window. He took an envelope from his pocket and tipped a small metal object into his upturned palm. 'This glove-fastener,' he said, once more examining it. 'Show me exactly where you found it.'

Williams bent, pointing to the rear of the desk. 'Just about there, sir. It was almost hidden in the fringe of the carpet.'

'And you've no idea where I might find its twin?'

'No, sir. I've been thinking about that.

But it's a common type of fastener, isn't it? I mean, there must be hundreds of them in the district.' His face reddened slightly as he added, 'Matter of fact, I've got fasteners like that on a pair of gloves at home.'

'But neither of them missing, I hope.'

The constable laughed dutifully. Pitt returned the fastener to its envelope, and the envelope to his pocket. 'All right, Williams. I'll see the Greens now. The woman first.'

But as Williams turned to the door it opened from without. A plain-clothes policeman poked his head into the room and announced, 'There's a Miss Messager to see you, sir. The dead woman's niece.'

'Oh! Is Sergeant Watkins still out in the yard?'

'Yes, sir. Do you want him?'

'Not yet. Show Miss Messager in here, will you? And send in that stenographer.' He turned to Williams. 'I'll see the Greens later.'

'Very good, sir. I'll tell them to wait.'

'Wait? Are they going anywhere?'

'They're moving out, sir — back to their cottage.'

'Because of the murder?'

'Partly that, sir.' Williams looked uncomfortable. He had his suspicions about Elizabeth Messager, but it was not for him to discredit her to the Inspector. 'You'll remember I told you about that scene this morning, sir, when Mrs Green brought the coffee in and — '

'Oh, that. Yes, I remember.'

Pitt studied the girl carefully as she came into the room. He usually tried to curb his instinctive likes and dislikes, finding that often he preferred the suspects to the witnesses; and even an elderly policeman could be susceptible to feminine good looks. But he did not consider Elizabeth good-looking. Attractive, perhaps, with that red-gold hair and pointed face and trim figure; but not pretty. He thanked her politely for coming, expressed his sympathy, and placed a chair for her to sit on so that the only light in the room illuminated fully her pale face.

Elizabeth's first impression of the

Inspector was that he needed feeding up. Yet he was no thinner than, for instance, Michael Lane; perhaps it was the long, gaunt face and the hollows in his cheeks that gave her that impression. She was too nervous to study him closely, but she could see what Dulcie had meant when she had described him as grim.

'I want to take you through the events of last Thursday, Miss Messager.' Where he stood his face was partly in shadow, accentuating the hollows. His voice was cool and impersonal. 'I have here some notes made by Constable Williams after your talk with him this morning; they are of no value in themselves, of course, but they give me a line to work on. Correct me if they prove misleading.' She nodded. 'Now, on that day Mrs Lane had intended leaving here to stay with a friend — ' He leaned forward to see more clearly the name written in Williams' notes, and for the first time Elizabeth was aware of his eyes. They were oddly youthful and clear for a man of his age. ' — a Mrs Donelly in Purley. I understand you don't know the exact address.'

'I'm afraid not. There may be some correspondence in the desk which would give it to you. I haven't a key, but I expect you found — '

She paused, shuddering. For the first time she realized in full what murder implied. She had a brief mental picture of Aunt Charlotte's body, dumpy and lifeless, lying grotesquely at the bottom of the well — limbs broken, perhaps, the stupid, too youthful finery torn and filthy and blood-stained. And the face, caked with slime and mud and make-up — how did that look now?

There was a glass of water on the small table beside her. She sipped it eagerly, heedless whether it was there for her use or not. The faintness passed, and she relaxed against the hard back of the chair.

'There were no keys in your aunt's handbag when we recovered it.' He said that more gently, but his voice was again brisk and impersonal as he went on, 'However, this Mrs Donelly should not be hard to find; there can't be many ladies of that name living in Purley.' He referred again to the notebook. 'Mrs Lane was due to catch the six forty-five train from Tanbury to Victoria, and had ordered a taxi to take her to the station. Six miles — say twenty minutes. The taxi should have been here around six-fifteen. You are certain it was ordered?'

'Yes. I heard her on the phone about a week ago. But I don't know where she ordered it from, or whether it arrived. I was out that afternoon.'

'Did she have an account with a car-hire firm?'

'I'm sure she didn't. She always paid cash. She liked handling money.'

He picked up some envelopes from the top of the desk. 'Are these the only letters that have arrived for her since Thursday?'

'Yes.'

'H'm! Personal correspondence only. No bills. Well, it may come on Monday.' He noticed her obvious bewilderment, and smiled. It was a disarming smile, seeming to change the whole expression and structure of his face. It surprised her almost as much as his words. 'I was musing aloud. The point is, you see, that if the taxi had to return without a fare the firm will be sending in a bill. They would still charge for the journey.'

'Yes, I suppose they would.'

'A bill would have given us the name of the firm. But we can't wait until Monday; it means checking with all the car-hire firms in the district. What time did the Greens leave the house on Thursday?'

'Shortly after lunch. I didn't see them go, but it was certainly before half-past two.' She paused. 'Inspector, at what time did my aunt die?'

'Difficult to say. Late afternoon or early evening is as close as the doctor can put it. It's two days, you see, and the conditions — ' He decided not to enumerate the various factors governing the cooling of the body; it might distress her. 'Why, miss?'

'Well, it just occurred to me that if she was killed before the taxi arrived the — the murderer could have gone back to Tanbury in it. The driver wouldn't know there was anything wrong. Or — why, it could even have been the taxi-driver himself, couldn't it?'

He smiled again. I wish he would keep on smiling, she thought. I wouldn't feel so nervous then.

'I congratulate you, Miss Messager. Now you know why I am anxious to trace the taxi.' It sounded sincere; there was no trace of patronage. Then the smile vanished, and a steely ring came into his voice as he said, 'You went out that afternoon about five o'clock, didn't you? In response to a telephone message that turned out to be bogus?'

Elizabeth nodded, suddenly frightened. So far it had been easy, far easier than she had dared to expect. He had not badgered her, he had even smiled at her. But now . . .

'Suppose you tell me about it?'

She told him. It was a rambling, incoherent account with considerable prompting from the Inspector. When it was done he said slowly, 'Didn't Mrs Lane object to your going out that afternoon?'

'Yes. But I couldn't let my friend down.'

'Was it a man or a woman on the phone?'

'A woman, I think. That was what it sounded like; but I suppose it could have been a man. I didn't recognize the voice.'

He wrote down Valerie's address, and that of Henry Torreck; she had told him of the intruder Henry had heard in the garden, and of the unlocked back door. Henry and Mrs Green could be expected to mention those facts if he questioned them later; it would be foolish to omit them now. But she did not mention her telephone call to Desmond — and that was a mistake.

He said, those keen eyes of his intent on her face, seeming to mesmerize her, 'Mrs Green tells me that when she and her husband returned that evening you were talking to some one on the telephone.'

She felt herself flushing. 'Was I? Oh, yes. I'd just rung up a friend to — to ' — her mind groped wildly — 'to tell him I was back.'

'He had expected to see you that evening?'

Had he? She must not go far from the truth; they might question Desmond before she could warn him. 'Lie only when lies are essential,' Desmond had said, before wishing her luck as she left him at the gate. 'Otherwise stick to the truth. It's safer.'

'Yes,' she said. Had she not been out she *would* have seen him; he had intended giving her a note to put in Aunt Charlotte's room. 'And I had promised to meet him the next day. I wanted to check on the time.'

That, too, was true.

He made a note of Desmond's name and address, and she allowed herself to relax a little, hoping he had not noticed the fright he had given her. But fear was still with her. She had known there would be questions against which she must be on her guard, questions for which she had answers ready. But this had not been one of them. Would there be others equally unexpected, and which she might not be able to parry so successfully?

Pitt began to ask her about the Friday. Elizabeth sat up. She knew what was coming; this was something she could deal with.

'You were not worried when the telegram arrived that morning?'

'No,' she said, and braced herself for the expected 'Why?' But it did not come. Instead he said, a hint of laughter in his voice, 'I'm not surprised. It was, of course, quite obviously bogus.'

Lips parted, she stared at him. How could he know that? He couldn't know it. He must be guessing, it wasn't possible that . . .

He was waiting for her to speak. She shook her head, stammering a confused reply. 'I — I'm not sure that . . . '

She stopped. It was safer to say nothing. Let him think what he liked — she wasn't going to grope blindly forward into some unknown trap.

'Don't tell me I overrated your intelligence, Miss Messager,' he said quizzically. 'Mrs Donelly is an elderly lady living, you tell me, in Purley, and anxiously awaiting your aunt's arrival. But the telegram was handed in at Farringdon Street Post Office at eight twenty-five that morning.' He paused, allowing his words to sink in. 'They don't seem to connect up, do they?'

Elizabeth was seized with a wild spasm of anger. How dared they involve her in this ordeal? Wiser! Safer! What did they know about it, sitting in a hotel room arranging everything so calmly, without a policeman in sight? How would they like to be in her place now — fencing, prevaricating, struggling to fool this unpredictable man who was so much more clever than they? At any moment she would be trapped into bursting the silly, swollen bubble, and he would know her for a liar and a . . .

'No!' she said sharply, as much in answer to her thoughts as to his question.

He studied her thoughtfully. Under the scrutiny of those keen eyes she felt her anger and her purpose slowly departing, and she said weakly, 'I didn't see the actual telegram. Mrs Green took the message over the phone.'

'I see. So you believed it to be genuine. Yet you still were not worried?'

That gave her a breather. It was something she had expected, something she knew how to handle. She reeled off the ready-made answer — Aunt Charlotte's selfishness and lack of consideration for others, her anticipated shopping spree — and felt her confidence slowly return. I'm over the worst now, she thought; it was silly of me to panic. There can't be much more to come.

When he mentioned the note that Alan had pushed under the front door she tried to laugh it off as she had tried to laugh it off with Ted Williams. She had no way of telling if she had been successful, for he made no comment and his expression did not change.

'And then you went out?' he said.

'Yes.'

'With Mr Farrel?'

'Yes.'

'Where did you go?'

How on earth could that be important? At least, it *was* important, because they had gone to get married; but what could that matter to him? How could he expect that her actions on Friday might have a connexion with Aunt Charlotte's death the day before?

'To Tanbury. We had lunch there. Then

we went for a spin, and later had dinner at the Tower Hotel. It was after eleven when I got back here.'

'To be told by Mrs Green about the second telegram and the phone call from Mrs Donelly?'

'Yes.'

'You really *were* worried then?'

'Of course.'

'So you decided to inform the police — the next morning?'

It did not need the slight pause after 'police' to convey his meaning. His voice was suddenly stern, and heavy with sarcasm.

Elizabeth flushed. 'It was very late,' she excused herself. And then, remembering, 'And Green told me he had already spoken to Mr Williams.'

Pitt nodded, as though he had anticipated that explanation. Abruptly he switched to the years before — the death of her parents, her life with Aunt Charlotte. It wasn't pleasant for Elizabeth, and he seemed to appreciate that. It was almost apologetically that he said, 'You weren't happy here after your uncle died?'

'No,' she said reluctantly. 'She wasn't an easy person to live with.'

'There was dislike — on both sides?'

'Yes.' It was a damning admission to make, but there was no avoiding it. And she could not tell him of that other side of Aunt Charlotte's character; no one must ever know of that. 'We just didn't hit it off, I suppose. It was probably as much my fault as hers.'

Pitt turned his head and nodded, and Elizabeth realized with surprise that she had completely forgotten the presence of the silent constable in the far corner. It was a measure, she thought, of how her attention had been held.

As the constable left the room Pitt said, 'Constable Drake has been taking note of what you have told me. It will be typed out in the form of a statement, and some time to-morrow afternoon I should like you to call in at the police station and sign it — provided, of course, that you agree with the contents.' He walked over to the safe and stood looking at it. 'You haven't a key to this, I suppose?'

'No.'

'Some one has unsuccessfully tried to force it. Did you know that?'

'Not until Mr Williams pointed it out to me this morning.'

'Not a very hard nut to tackle, I imagine. Anything of value in it?'

'I don't know. Aunt Charlotte drew a lot of money out of the bank this week, but I expect she took most of it — ' She paused, remembering that Aunt Charlotte had never gone on that shopping spree. 'Wasn't there . . . didn't you find . . . ?'

He shook his head. 'No keys, no money. No doubt the killer took those. It may be that Mrs Lane surprised him as he was trying to force the safe and — ' He stopped abruptly. 'Who were her solicitors?'

'I don't know,' she said again. 'I think they were a London firm.'

'Your aunt does not appear to have confided in you overmuch.' It was casually said, but somehow the words had a sinister ring. 'Perhaps with good reason,' was what they seemed to imply. 'We may have to force that desk.'

'I don't mind,' she said.

'Right.' Officialdom seemed suddenly to drop from him like a cloak. 'That's all for to-night, Miss Messager — and thank you. Are you sleeping here?'

She shuddered, appalled by the thought.

'Oh, no! I've got a room at the hotel.'

'Very sensible. So have I. I'll send you back in a car.'

She thanked him for his offer, declining it. 'A friend brought me. He's waiting outside.'

'Mr Farrel?'

She nodded, feeling the blush creeping up her neck. Damn! she thought. Why does Desmond's name keep cropping up? He will begin to think . . .

'I'd like to meet him,' Pitt said.

He went out to the hall, and she heard him talking to some one. When he came back he said, 'You'll be wanting a few things for the night, eh?' Elizabeth hesitated. She wanted them, but she dreaded the thought of going upstairs . . . passing Aunt Charlotte's door. Noting her hesitation, he said gently, 'There's nothing to be afraid of, you know. It is just as it was, you'll see nothing to distress you. But if you're nervous Constable Drake can go with you.'

'Thank you,' she said gratefully, surprised that he could be so genial, so — so fatherly.

'Just the essentials, eh? You can collect the rest to-morrow. You have a key? Good. We'll see the Greens off the premises before we leave — they're not staying either, I'm told — and lock up. No need for you to worry. But I'll keep the back-door key for a day or two if you've no objection.'

He ushered her into the hall. She had a brief glimpse of Desmond staring at her from the sitting-room, and then she was walking behind Constable Drake along the narrow passage. As she passed the kitchen door she noticed that it was slowly opening.

She turned her head and went quickly up the stairs. Mrs Green could do her gloating without her.

Inspector Pitt liked the look of Desmond Farrel. The Inspector was wont to class all young men who wore drainpipe trousers and Edwardian-style jackets as Teddy Boys, and to dismiss them from his esteem forthwith. But this young man looked clean and healthy. His hair, although overlong, was not cut in some preposterous, outlandish fashion. Nor did he wear a string tie.

'This is a nasty business, Mr Farrel,' Pitt said pleasantly. 'Shaken you all up a bit, I dare say.'

'It has indeed.' Desmond smiled faintly. 'It's rather out of our line.'

'It would be. Did you know Mrs Lane well?'

'No, I didn't. Hardly at all, in fact, although I used to see her about the village occasionally.'

'But you are a friend of her niece?'

'Yes.' Desmond tugged nervously at his ear. 'I know it sounds odd, Inspector, but Miss Messager's friends weren't welcome here. I don't think there was anything personal in it; Mrs Lane just didn't like her niece to have friends. She was — well, difficult.'

'So I've gathered,' Pitt said. 'It doesn't seem to have been a happy association.'

'That's putting it mildly. I can't speak from first-hand knowledge, of course, but from what Elizabeth has told me her life must have been absolute hell.'

'It's over now,' Pitt said. 'Did you call at this house Thursday afternoon or evening, Mr Farrel?'

The suddenness of the question took Desmond by surprise — as it was intended to do.

'No. I hardly ever came to the house. I thought I'd explained that.'

'Ah, yes. But you telephoned Miss Messager that evening?'

'Did I?' What had Elizabeth said? He had told her to stick as closely as possible to the truth. 'No, I think it was the other way round. She rang me.'

'Did she mention Mrs Lane at all?'

Desmond shook his head. Safer to be vague. However had this damned telephone call managed to crop up?

'Honestly, Inspector, I can't remember. She may have done. It was just a casual conversation. I think we made a date for the next day. Yesterday.'

There were footsteps on the stairs.

'That'll be Miss Messager,' Pitt said, leading the way out of the room. 'She's been packing. Good night, Mr Farrel, and thank you. I expect I'll be seeing you at the hotel.'

When they had gone he stood for a while in the narrow hall, pulling thoughtfully at his lower lip with finger and thumb.

'I wonder,' he said softly. 'It could be.'

Sergeant Watkins came out from the kitchen, closing the door behind him. He was a square, tough-looking young man with carroty hair and an amiable face smothered in freckles. He played lock forward for the county, and had already collected a Welsh trial cap.

'All ship-shape out back, sir,' he said cheerfully. The 'sir' was accorded more on account of the Inspector's age than his rank. Jim Watkins was no respecter of rank. 'Got rid of your girl friend, I see. Anything doing?'

'Romance,' Pitt said. 'Is that in your line at all, Jim?'

'Not exactly. I work on a less exalted plane.' He grinned. 'Even so, I have my moments. Why?'

'She rang him up Thursday evening as soon as she got back. She was out with him until nearly midnight yesterday, and again to-day. What does that suggest to you?'

'Looks like he's getting it regular,' the Sergeant said coarsely. 'Think they were in it together?'

'I don't know.' Pitt was used to Jim Watkins' one-track mind. He had known him since he was a kid, had pounded a beat with the boy's father. 'But the aunt didn't like him, wouldn't have him in the house.' He snapped his fingers, as though reaching a decision. 'Is the gardener still here?'

'In the kitchen with his missus. They're rarin' to go. The old lady has made so many pots of tea, every time one of 'em moves it sounds like the tide coming in.'

'Tell her to make another. I want a word with her husband.'

* * *

Walter Green was not happy. He had had time for reflection. Charlotte Lane's murder had done more than set his wife's tongue wagging and her ears pricking; it had put paid to his job. The niece wouldn't keep him on; not after that scene this morning. And full-time gardeners weren't much in demand in Milford now; it would mean jobbing work . . . or the council . . . or maybe the building lark. He realized now that he had been well off with Mrs Lane. She had had her tantrums and her funny ways, but often she never came into the garden for days on end. The money had been regular, and he knew where he was. And there'd been pickings.

As a matter of routine Pitt took him through the statement he had previously made to Constable Williams. Then he said casually, 'Were there many visitors to the house?'

Green shook his head. 'Not during the day there wasn't. I wouldn't know about the evenings, not being here.'

'Miss Messager is an attractive young woman.' Pitt forced his face into what he imagined to be a leer. He should have left this to Jim Watkins, he thought regretfully.

'Didn't the lads of the village take her out?'

'They may have took her out, but they didn't come to the house. They didn't dare. Mrs Lane would have sent 'em packing.'

'So you have never seen Miss Messager with a young man?'

'Not as I can think on. Leastways — '

He paused. 'Yes?' prompted Pitt.

'Well, there was a morning last week when she come up from the river through the copse. I reckon she'd been down there with young Mr Farrel. I seen his Wolseley in the lane a few minutes later.'

Farrel again! Concealing his elation, Pitt got rid of the man and sent for his wife.

Mrs Green came into the room bearing a cup of tea in one hand and a tin of biscuits in the other. She was gracious and eager and verbose; this was her day, and she intended not to waste a moment of it. Having delivered herself of her offerings, she settled herself uncomfortably on the edge of a chair and prepared — almost demanded — to be interviewed.

Pitt found it an exhausting business, and was glad of the tea. Mrs Green's replies were far from brief. They wandered here, there, and everywhere; when he brought her up short with a question she listened politely, straining to be off again. And off again she was, almost before he had finished speaking. But through all her verbal meanderings one theme was nakedly obvious — her dislike of Elizabeth Messager.

At last even her tap ran dry. The silence fell like a blessed relief on the Inspector's tortured ears.

'Another cup of tea, sir?' she suggested. 'There's plenty more in the pot.'

He refused hastily, fearful that further refreshment might set her off again. 'It's late,' he said. 'You'll want to be getting home. I'll arrange for a car to take you.'

She thanked him, rose regretfully from her perch, and picked up the cup and saucer and the tin. The certainty that she was actually on her way encouraged Pitt to say, 'One way or another, Mrs Green, you've painted a not very pleasant picture of Miss Messager. I'm surprised. She seems a nice young woman to me.'

'You're a man,' Mrs Green said, as though that bald fact explained everything. 'Mind you, I'm not saying she's down-right wicked' — she had been saying little else for the past half-hour — 'but she's thoughtless and ungrateful. She didn't treat her aunt fair, and that's a fact. Not even after she was dead she didn't.'

Since only a short while before Pitt had seen Elizabeth Messager alive and well, he was able to interpret correctly the intended meaning of this ambiguous last statement.

'How could that be, Mrs Green?' he asked.

'Well, Mrs Lane told me herself as how Miss Elizabeth had given her her word she wouldn't go out of an evening while she was away. And yet no sooner was her poor aunt's back turned — ' Mrs Green paused, flustered, remembering that Charlotte Lane's back had not been turned, it had been dropped down a well. Recovering, she went on, 'That very same evening, sir, she didn't come home till close on ten, it must have been. *And* she left the back door open, which was a wicked thing to do, this house being so far from the village and — '

'How do you know she left it open?'

'Because it was open when me and my husband come in. Miss Elizabeth said it wasn't her as done it, but who else could it have been? I reckon she left it that way when she went out, so's she could get in again. Mrs Lane never would give her a latch-key. She didn't think it right, she said, for a young girl like her to have one.'

'Miss Messager tells me her aunt gave her a latch-key that afternoon, before she left,' Pitt said.

'Give it her, eh?' The woman snorted. 'Well, that's one way of putting it, maybe.'

The Inspector decided that Mrs Green would not make a very reliable witness where the girl was concerned. But he could not refrain from remarking, 'So Miss Messager didn't treat her aunt fairly, eh? But Mrs Lane, I suppose, was kindness itself?'

Sarcasm was wasted on Mrs Green. 'She had her difficult moments,' she admitted. ('Never speak ill of the dead' was an injunction as sacred to Mrs Green's narrow soul as the Ten Commandments.) 'Eggsentrick, you might say. There was them as couldn't abide her.' Forgetful of the cup and saucer in its grip, she extended her right hand impressively towards him in a dramatic gesture. The cup swayed precariously. 'But she was goodness itself to Miss Elizabeth. Doted on her, she did, and that's a fact.'

* * *

It was past midnight when the two detectives returned to the hotel, but they found Desmond waiting up for them. 'I thought you'd be wanting a drink,' he said. 'It must have been quite a day.'

Pitt admitted that he could do with a whisky and water, and they went into the bar. The Sergeant settled for a beer.

'On me,' Desmond said, helping himself to a whisky.

He tried to pump them about the murder, but they evaded his questions.

After ten minutes of desultory conversation Jim Watkins finished his beer, stood up and stretched himself lazily, and said, 'I'm for hitting the hay.'

As they left the bar Desmond said, 'Any news of the picture?'

'What picture?' asked the Sergeant.

'The portrait of Mrs Lane. It used to hang in front of the safe in her study. Miss Messager said it was missing. It seems an odd thing for some one to steal.'

Pitt nodded.

'It wasn't stolen, Mr Farrel,' he said. 'Whoever murdered Mrs Lane obviously hated the sight of her. He couldn't even abide her picture. He threw it down the well after her.'

'Good Lord!'

'It does seem rather an exaggerated expression of dislike, doesn't it?' murmured the Sergeant, yawning.

7

Fear on the Common

Henry Torreck leaned forward to knock the bowl of his pipe against the brick fireplace. A little shower of burnt tobacco fell into the tiled hearth.

'You've been listening to village gossip, Inspector,' he said, reproachfully but without anger.

Inspector Pitt admitted the truth of the accusation.

'I don't like it any more than you do, Mr Torreck, but it's part of the job. And we don't believe all we hear; don't believe any of it unless it has been checked and confirmed. Just occasionally we get something useful from it.' He looked round the untidy, comfortable sitting-room, with its worn armchairs and carpet and the table littered with books and papers and empty teacups; bare of ornament and frills, a room lived in and not fussed over, a room ordered into disorder by men. It had an odour of dust and tobacco and, oddly enough, linseed oil; and through the half-open door came the all-pervading smell of boiling cabbage. 'Just what happened to make you so bitter against Charlotte Lane, Mr Torreck?'

The other sucked strongly at his empty pipe. 'You'll have heard it all in the village,' he said, and sucked again.

'Maybe. But I'd like to hear it from you.'

Torreck shrugged. 'No reason why you shouldn't, if you've time to waste.'

All his working life, he said, had been spent in the employ of William Lane and Son, a firm of timber merchants two miles the other side of Wendingham; from junior clerk he had risen to become general manager and a trusted friend of the boss, Edward Lane. Charlotte West had been Lane's secretary, and a thorn in the manager's side — 'efficient, but a damned sight too bossy; always trying to give me the run-around' — and it had been a blow to Torreck when Edward

Lane had suddenly married her and the couple had gone to live at The Elms. 'I still can't fathom what made him do it,' Torreck confessed. 'She was in her late forties, and no beauty. But he always was an odd chap; suspicious and a bit tight-fisted — but fair, very fair. I got along with him fine. We trusted each other, and if a difference of opinion cropped up we thrashed it out on the spot and promptly forgot it.' He sighed. 'They were good days.'

'His marriage changed him, eh?'

'Not him. He was as much the boss at home as he was at the yard. Charlotte got no change out of him. She liked me no more than I liked her; but she knew Edward looked on me as a friend, and she didn't dare show her dislike in front of him. I spent a lot of time at The Elms. My wife had been dead some years, and Alan was away at boarding-school.

'Some years after their marriage Charlotte's niece came to live with them; the girl's parents had been killed in a road accident. She was a nice kid — she and Alan got on fine together. That was six years ago; Elizabeth was thirteen then, three years younger than Alan. The boy practically lived at The Elms during the holidays. Alan being my son, Charlotte tended to ignore him; but I dare say she was glad to have some one around to keep Elizabeth amused.

'Edward took a fancy to Alan. When the boy left school he offered to send him to Oxford — knowing, of course, that I couldn't afford it.'

'That wasn't the action of a tight-fisted man,' Pitt remarked.

'No. Tight-fisted wasn't the right word,' the other admitted. 'I should have said he was careful with money. He hated to see it wasted, and I guess he didn't think sending Alan to Oxford would be a waste. And he did more. Shortly after that he told me he'd be making me a partner in the firm at the end of the year.' He sighed. 'Two months later he was dead. He was talking to one of the men in the yard, and suddenly collapsed. He died the next day.'

'With nothing sealed or signed, I suppose,' Pitt said. 'You didn't get your partnership?'

'I did not. I got the sack instead. She didn't waste any time over it, either. Some of the men walked out in sympathy; but that didn't worry Charlotte, and it didn't help me.'

'What happened to the business?'

'She sold it. I tried to get a job with the chap who bought it, but there was nothing doing. I've a shrewd idea that Charlotte had taken care of that.'

'But why? What made her so vindictive?'

'She was Edward's wife, but she could never get close to him; he made it plain that he preferred my company to hers. Charlotte hated that; she was the sort of person who had to be first in any relationship. But she wasn't first with Edward, and she blamed me for it.'

Looking at the grizzled, lined face opposite him, Pitt felt sorry for the man. Torreck was fifty-six, but he looked much older. No doubt the events of these last few years had helped to age him.

'How did you make out?' he asked.

The other shrugged. 'Jobs aren't easy to get at fifty, Inspector. Alan had to give up his hopes of Oxford — it hit him hard, poor lad — and with the little money I'd put by he and I started this factory.'

'How's it going?'

'So-so. No luxuries, but it keeps us. With more capital it could be a winner, I fancy. But money's tight these days.'

Pitt nodded vaguely. He was trying to assess the value of what the other had told him — that the Torrecks, father and son, had good cause to hate Charlotte Lane, that they needed money to develop their business. How much money? What did 'more capital' amount to? Could they have expected to find that amount at The Elms? They might have known that the woman had cashed a cheque for her visit to London, but could they have known for what sum?

He was suddenly reminded of a thought that had occurred to puzzle him during the night. As Charlotte Lane's keys were missing, the murderer must have taken them; if he had killed her before tackling the safe why had he tried to force it, why hadn't he used the keys? If, on the other hand, the intruder had been trying to force the safe and the woman had surprised him, why had he not returned to the safe with the keys after he had killed her?

For a moment, forgetful of the immediate problem, he allowed his thoughts to dwell on this. Then he smiled. How did he know the murderer had *not* used the keys? Until the safe was opened there was no way of telling whether it had been rifled or not.

That; then, was the way of it. Odd that he should have wasted sleep over something so obvious.

'When do I start giving myself an alibi for Thursday?' Henry Torreck asked.

Startled out of his reverie, Pitt smiled. 'Any time you like,' he said.

'Well, we knocked off at the factory at five-thirty as usual, but I stayed behind for an hour. I often do. Then I drove over to see a friend the other side of Cosmeston. I'd expected to be home by eight, but I didn't make it.' He explained how he had met Elizabeth and taken her home. 'It was after half-past nine by the time I got back here.'

'You didn't go into the house?'

'No. She didn't even want me to walk up the drive with her, but I insisted.'

Pitt pricked up his ears. 'Didn't want you near the house, eh? Why?'

But Torreck had already regretted the information he had inadvertently given. 'She didn't say, and I didn't ask. No doubt she merely wanted to save me the trouble.'

'But you insisted. Why?'

Torreck told him of the footsteps he had heard. 'But I could have been mistaken, Inspector. Miss Messager heard nothing. Neither did I when I stopped to listen.'

'Did your son also stay late at the factory that evening?' asked Pitt, reluctantly abandoning what had seemed a promising inquiry.

'No. He came home at the usual time.'

'Was he here all the evening?'

'I think so. He had talked of going out to Wendingham — that's a village about two miles from here — but . . . ' He paused. 'Why not ask him yourself? He's in the kitchen.'

Cooking the Sunday lunch, presumably, thought Pitt, as the other left him. The smells of hot food came wafting into the room.

With the smells came Alan Torreck, wiping his hands on a dish-cloth. 'I'm cook for to-day,' he announced unnecessarily. 'We take it in turns.'

'Do you like cooking?' Pitt asked.

'I don't like it, but I'd rather eat my own concoctions than Dad's. He's absolute murder in the kitchen. No feeling for food at all.'

Pitt liked him on sight, and was immediately on guard against that liking. But his voice was more brusque than he intended when he said, 'You didn't like Mrs Lane, did you, Mr Torreck?'

'No. What is more, you try to find some one who did.'

Pitt nodded, acknowledging the thrust. 'Were you at home all Thursday evening?'

The young man hesitated. Then he said, 'Until nine o'clock, yes. I went for a stroll across the common then, just for a breath of air.'

'Meet anyone?'

'No.' Alan grinned. 'They never do, do they? Must make it difficult for you chaps.'

Against his will, Pitt found himself returning the grin.

The telephone rang. 'Excuse me,' Alan said, and picked up the receiver. 'Yes,' he said into the mouthpiece. 'Yes, he's here. Hold on.' He turned to Pitt. 'It's Ted Williams, Inspector. He wants to speak to you.'

The detective took the receiver from him. 'Inspector Pitt here. What is it, Williams?'

'Divisional Headquarters have just been on the phone, sir,' came Williams' precise voice over the wire. 'They've traced that taxi. Burke's Garage, Tanbury. I thought you'd like to know.'

'Yes. Any further information?'

'The Superintendent wants to see you, sir. But he told me to tell you the taxi was never sent. It was cancelled two days before, on the Tuesday.'

Pitt replaced the receiver and stood staring at it, unmindful of Alan Torreck's curious gaze. So that was it. Not unpremeditated, as he had come to suppose, but a cold, calculated murder, carefully planned. What better choice of time than when the woman was known to be going away, when her absence would not be questioned? The taxi cancelled, the niece inveigled out of the house by a trick, the . . .

What about the gardener and his wife? The killer must have known they also would be out? He had known, too, where to cancel the taxi. But the girl had said . . .

Elizabeth Messager!

Pitt was suddenly impatient to be gone. Refusing the Torrecks' invitation to stay to lunch (though not because he doubted the cook's skill; the Inspector was no connoisseur of food), he hurried back to the prim villa that housed Ted Williams and Milford Cross Police Station.

Sergeant Watkins had already returned from Cosmeston, and was awaiting him. 'A very pleasant little assignment,' he told Pitt. 'Who said crime doesn't pay?'

'Any luck?' Pitt asked.

'I made an impression,' Watkins said modestly. 'No more.' And then, becoming serious. 'No doubt about the girl being there on Thursday; but it's a mighty fishy set-up.'

'How?'

'Mrs French thought she seemed upset; nervy and fidgety, as though something momentous had happened or was about to happen. That could have been due to discovering that the phone call was a hoax. But I doubt it.'

'Why?'

'Because she refused to let Mrs French inform the police. Said she could make a good guess at who was responsible, and tried to brush it off as a harmless joke.'

'Anything else?'

'Plenty. Mrs French being her friend, I had to take it easy, of course; she wasn't going to give anything away which she thought might be hurtful to the girl. But I kept on about the aunt, saying what an old devil she must have been, and why had the girl put up with it for so long; and eventually she let slip that, to her way of thinking, our Lizzie would have pulled out long ago if it hadn't been for the aunt's money. She comes into the lot, it seems.'

'Does she, though! Tell me more.'

'Well, it seems Lizzie was reluctant to talk about the aunt while she was there. That could indicate a guilty conscience, couldn't it? And Mrs French confirmed that she had not previously been allowed a latch-key; the girl told her the aunt had given it to her that afternoon.' The Sergeant grimaced. 'Doesn't look too good for our Liz, does it?'

'It looks worse than you think,' Pitt told him. 'Come on, we're going into Tanbury. I have to see a man about a taxi. I'll explain on the way.'

'How about lunch? Don't we get any?'

'No time. We'll grab a sandwich in Tanbury.'

'Sandwich!' Jim Watkins groaned. 'And to think I turned down the offer of a cut off the joint and two veg. And don't misunderstand me, either.'

'I couldn't,' Pitt said.

In the car he tried to sort out the case against Elizabeth Messager. Motive was clear — money, her hatred of her aunt. She was one of the few people who had known that her aunt was going away — date, time, circumstance. She had admitted hearing her aunt ordering the taxi; and, although she had denied hearing the name of the firm, the taxi had certainly been cancelled, and by some one who knew where to phone. Who more likely than Elizabeth Messager to have that knowledge? She, too, would know that the Greens were going out that afternoon; might even have arranged that they should. And, having killed her aunt, she departed for Cosmeston on the strength of an imaginary telephone call.

'Why?' asked Watkins. 'It doesn't give her an alibi for the whole afternoon, which is what she needed.'

'No. But she had to be out of the house at the time her aunt had been due to leave. She must have known the body would be found eventually, that inquiries would be made about the taxi; and she had to be able to plead ignorance. Not only that. Unless she was away from the house for some time during that afternoon there could be no doubt of her guilt.' He frowned. 'It is difficult to see why she should have tampered with the safe, unless it was done to mislead, to make the crime appear as the work of an outsider. That could also have been the reason for the note found by Mrs Green.'

'And the footsteps Torreck heard?' Watkins said. 'Where do they fit in?'

'They don't. He must have imagined them. But the girl's reluctance to allow him near the house was probably because she could not be sure that no incriminating evidence still remained.'

'On top of which we have Mrs French's evidence,' Watkins said. 'Looks solid, doesn't it? What about the telegram? The first one?'

'That beats me. Mrs Donelly didn't send it; the Purley police have confirmed that. But who did? Not the murderer, surely. He wouldn't want to draw attention to the fact that his victim hadn't arrived at her destination.'

'Which brings us to the assumption that it was unconnected with the murder,'

Watkins said. 'Somebody being funny, perhaps. Some one who knew nothing of the murder, but who did know that the old girl was going away.'

'Might be. A damned stupid joke, though. And heartless.'

'It would have to be some one who knew the destination,' the Sergeant said thoughtfully. 'It was signed 'Donelly,' wasn't it? That narrows the field a bit.'

'It does indeed,' Pitt agreed.

Ten minutes later, the Divisional Superintendent in attendance, they were inspecting a ledger at Burke's Garage. 'There you are, Inspector,' the manager said, running his finger down the entries for the 18th. 'Lane, The Elms, Milford Cross. 6.10 P.M. To catch 6.45 train.' The finger moved across to the adjoining column. 'Cancelled 16th.'

'Any idea how it was cancelled?' Pitt asked.

The manager looked inquiringly at one of the two girl clerks who were hovering excitedly around the desk. 'That's your writing, Rosemary, isn't it? How about it?'

‘They cancelled it by phone,’ the girl said decisively. ‘I remember ’specially because the person had such a funny voice. You couldn’t tell if it was a man or a woman. I said so to my friend. Didn’t I, Doris?’

The other girl nodded. ‘Like Herbert Marshall, you said.’

‘Not Herbert Marshall, dear — Arthur Marshall. Herbert Marshall’s the film actor. You know — he walks sort of stiff. He’s got a wooden leg, I think. It’s Arthur Marshall I meant. Usually he impersonates a schoolmistress — haven’t you heard him on the wireless? I don’t think he’s been on lately, but I used to — ’

‘Have you sent taxis to The Elms before?’ Pitt asked.

The two girls looked at each other, uncertain. ‘It’d be in the ledger,’ Doris said, and began thumbing back the pages.

Pitt did not wait for the answer. He left the two girls to their task. Out in the street he said, ‘Not much from that, eh?’

‘It’s another point against Lizzie,’ Watkins said. ‘She’s got a deep voice for a girl. It could have been her who spoke to Rosemary on the phone.'

The Superintendent said, 'Would it interest you to know that this cancellation was phoned through to other garages besides Burke's?'

Startled, Pitt stopped dead to stare at him. A woman bumped into him from behind and then swept round him, glaring at him as she passed. Apologizing, Pitt moved on.

'If you mean what I think you mean it would indeed. Tell me more, sir.'

'When I sent my chaps out to trace this booking for you Burke's wasn't the first garage they tried. At two of the others they were told that some one had rung up to cancel a taxi for Lane at Milford Cross. And in each of these two cases, after the attendant had checked and informed them that there was no such booking, the caller apologized, said he — or she — must have made a mistake, and rang off.'

'He or she?'

The Superintendent nodded. 'In neither case could the attendant say with certainty whether it was a man or a woman.'

On the way back to Milford Cross Pitt said, 'Here's an odd thing, Jim. With one exception every one I have spoken to, the girl included, stresses that Charlotte Lane treated her niece badly; and, since the aunt didn't go visiting or invite the local people to her house, it follows that this information must have been disseminated by the girl. The exception is Mrs Green, who should be in a position to know, and who insists that the Lane woman doted on her niece. So either Elizabeth Messager is inventing a motive for murder against herself, or Mrs Green, who wishes the girl nothing but ill, is denying the motive. It doesn't make sense, does it?' He sighed heavily. 'I wish I knew exactly what *did* go on in that damned house.'

⋆ ⋆ ⋆

Owing to the increased police activity at Milford Cross, a Sergeant had been drafted temporarily to the village to take charge. This had put Constable Williams' nose out of joint; but it was a pleasant surprise for Elizabeth when she called at the police station late that Sunday afternoon to sign her statement. She had not been looking forward to meeting Ted Williams again so soon after her outburst.

As she read through the statement her mind was filled with doubt. The document was fair enough; they had not twisted what she had said, or added to it. It was she who had done the twisting, who had omitted so much. And now she must sign it. Or must she?

'Why, no, miss, there's no compulsion about it,' the Sergeant said, when she put the question to him. 'But it's of no value else. Anything wrong with it, miss?'

She shook her head. 'Signing it makes it seem so — so final,' she said. 'It would be awful if I'd made a mistake, or left out something important.'

He smiled. 'It's not as final as all that,' he said. 'You're not on oath. Don't let it worry you, miss. If you've forgotten something — well, it's not as if you were misleading the police wilfully, is it?'

But it was. They were all misleading the

police, had conspired from the beginning to do so. The whole statement was a mass of deliberate untruths or half-truths.

It did not look like her usual signature when she had written it; she had been too nervous for her hand to control the flow of the pen. But it seemed to satisfy the Sergeant.

It was already dark when she came out of the police station. A keen wind blew down the village street, and Elizabeth hesitated on the steps. Across the street lay the common, and beyond that the hotel; from where she stood she could see the lights in the upper windows. Should she go that way, or round by the road? It was lonely and desolate on the common, and she would catch the full force of the wind. But it was shorter — and would the road be less lonely?

She decided on the common, and set off briskly. She had no torch, but the track, being in constant use, was well defined. A few near stumbles, however, caused her to go more carefully; the common was a favourite parking-place for lovers and picnickers, and their cars had left the ground rutted and uneven. It was no better off the track, for here there were also bushes to contend with.

She thought uneasily of the statement she had just signed. What was the penalty for misleading the police? In addition to making a false statement she had used a false name, she had written 'Elizabeth Messager' when it should have been 'Elizabeth Farrel.' Still more disturbing was the thought that now she had signed she could not deny what she had written. What if she *had* to deny it? What if the police arrested her for murder?

Elizabeth shivered, not entirely because of the wind. She tucked her handbag under one arm and wrapped her coat more closely about her. The track led through trees here, and the night seemed blacker and more threatening. She had a sudden vision of Aunt Charlotte's body, huddled and broken, at the bottom of the well. She had had the same vision the previous evening, when she was talking to the Inspector. But now there was no quiet voice to steady her, to bring her back to reality. Now her thoughts could go on and on until . . .

Terrified, she peered fearfully at the tall trees that shut her in, expecting at any moment to be confronted with the accusing wraith of Aunt Charlotte. She wanted to hurry, to get back to the hotel; but the ground impeded her. It was more uneven here, for many of the tracks that criss-crossed the common were channelled through this gap in the trees.

What if they *did* arrest her? her thoughts went on. What could she say? That the statement was a lie? That she had known, for instance, about the telegram? That even if she had not known she would not have given it a second thought, because Aunt Charlotte could have disappeared into the unknown that day without causing her a pang, for she was going to be married on the morrow and . . .

It was fear of Aunt Charlotte, of her thoughts, that caused her to stop and look quickly over her shoulder. A few lights from the village pricked the darkness, the trees whined and creaked eerily, tossing their branches with abandon as the wind caught them. She was about to turn and go on when, so suddenly that it was upon her even as she screamed, a dark figure rose from the ground and sprang menacingly towards her. A hand grasped her arm, she felt herself pushed violently in the back — and then, still screaming, she fell.

8

Who else is there?

Robert Lane was a small, insignificant-looking man with a receding chin and an expression that seemed to indicate permanent dissatisfaction with life. He had a thin, petulant voice, watery blue eyes that peered suspiciously from above half-glasses, and a mobile lower lip that sucked intermittently and noisily at a dull, drooping moustache. Picture of the eternal pessimist, thought Pitt, ruminating on estate agents in general and this one in particular. How on earth does such a drab individual ever persuade anyone to buy a house?

'Your brother's sudden death must have come as a shock to you, Mr Lane,' he said. 'I dare say it was also a blow to learn that you were not mentioned in his will?'

'Not at all. It was what I had expected.

Edward and I quarrelled shortly after his wedding.'

'You did not approve of it?'

'I said after it, not because of it. What has this to do with my sister-in-law, Inspector? I thought it was her death you were investigating, not my brother's.'

Pitt accepted the rebuff.

'Do you own your present business, sir?'

'No. I'm the manager.'

Pitt was not greatly interested in Robert Lane. The man had a seedy look, and no doubt a slice off Charlotte Lane's generous bank-roll would have been welcome to him. But he had not killed her. His alibi was cast-iron.

He looked across the room to where Mrs Lane sat, firmly wedged in her fireside chair. She was a large, flabby woman with enormous bosom and tree-trunk legs. The legs and bosom so filled the eye that one did not at first notice the sad expression or the slight cast in her eye, the work-roughened hands or the ill-fitting dress.

'I'm sorry your son is out,' he said.

'Gone to the pictures, eh? You know, I'm so out of touch with the cinema that I had forgotten they were open on a Sunday. Does he go regularly?'

'Why, no,' the woman said, with a quick glance at her husband. She sounded short of breath. 'Not really. I've certainly never known him go on a Sunday before. It must have been a film he particularly wanted to see.'

'I had hoped to ask him about last Thursday,' Pitt said, wasting no more time. 'Pure routine, as I said before. Perhaps you can remember what he did that evening?'

'Why, yes.' Again that quick glance at her husband. 'At least — no, I don't think I can.'

The little man has more to him than I gave him credit for, Pitt thought. He certainly has his wife under his thumb. She can't even answer a question without his permission.

'What did you want to know, Inspector?' Lane asked, in his thin voice.

'Well, I suppose your son was at the office until it closed?'

'He was.'

'And after that?'

'I don't know. But he came home in good time for his supper at eight.'

Mrs Lane moved slightly in her chair. 'Oh, but surely, Robert, you remember — '

This time Pitt saw the frown that stopped her. Damn the man! he thought. If I could have sprung it on her alone I might have learned something useful.

He made a last attempt. 'What was it you remembered, Mrs Lane?' he asked.

She moved her hands vaguely. 'Nothing. It — it wasn't important.'

The Inspector knew when he was beaten. He glanced across at the silent Watkins. The Sergeant tucked his elbows in to his sides, spread out his forearms with the palms uppermost, and shrugged his shoulders in a Semitic gesture of resignation.

'That seems to be that,' Pitt said. 'May I use your telephone, Mr Lane? We have another call to make, but I want to check with the police station first.'

Lane nodded, pointing to a small wall

cabinet. He seemed to be in the process of swallowing his moustache, which perhaps accounted for his silence.

The line was engaged. Pitt stood waiting, after telling the operator to keep ringing. The radio was on, as it had been throughout the interview; not loudly, but enough to provide a distracting background of noise. It began to get on the Inspector's nerves.

The ringing tone, then a click. 'Milford Cross Police Station,' came the voice over the wire. 'Can I help you?'

'Sergeant Cole? Pitt here. I should have rung you before, but — ' He broke off, listening. There was a new sharpness to his voice as he said, 'Is she badly hurt?' Another pause. Watkins was all attention. 'Yes, do that. I'll be at the hotel if you want me.'

He put down the receiver, nodded to Watkins, and, with hurried thanks to the Lanes, made for the door. A testy voice stopped him. 'It's fourpence for a local call, Inspector.'

Impatiently Pitt dug his hands into his pockets, explored their emptiness, and looked appealingly at Watkins. The Sergeant handed over the money without a word. But as they climbed into the car he said, 'Some people can be real mean, can't they?'

Pitt let it pass. He might have been referring to Lane.

* * *

Elizabeth awoke to find herself in her bed at the hotel. There was a soft light in the room, but the thumping of her head dissuaded her from turning to look around her. She lay on her back, her eyes half closed, trying to remember. There was a lightly rolled bandage round her forehead, and slowly she raised a hand to feel it. It held a pad in place; she pressed gently and winced at the pain. As she took her fingers away she passed them in front of her eyes; there was no blood on them, they did not feel sticky. Perhaps it isn't broken, she thought. Just bruised.

She closed her eyes, willing herself to remember what had happened. She had gone to the police station to sign the statement; there had been a strange Sergeant there, and she had talked to him, and then — yes, then she had signed. But after that? It must have happened on her way home across the common. It had been dark, and . . .

The click of the door handle made her open her eyes. Dulcie stood there, framed against the brighter light in the corridor. When she saw Elizabeth watching her she came into the room and shut the door, moving to stand beside the bed. But she did not speak. With an effort Elizabeth turned her head to look at her. The expression — or rather the lack of expression — on the other girl's face puzzled her.

'I must have fainted, I think,' she said. Her throat was dry, and she swallowed uncomfortably.

'Perhaps. You also cracked your head against something very solid.' Noticing the swallow, Dulcie picked up a tumbler of water from the table and handed it to her. With difficulty Elizabeth raised her head from the pillow and sipped.

'It feels like quite a bruise,' she said.

'It is.' Dulcie took the glass from her. 'You'll be no beauty when that bandage comes off.'

That isn't important, thought Elizabeth, and wondered that Dulcie should mention it. It couldn't be jealous satisfaction; Dulcie was far prettier than she, and had no cause to fear competition. Who had put the bandage on? But that wasn't important either, and her mind wandered back to the common. She could remember it now. The trees and the darkness — and a figure that had sprung at her from behind, that had pushed her so that she fell and . . .

'What happened?' she asked. 'How did I get here?'

'Some men on the common heard you screaming. They carried you back.'

'But who undressed me and put me to bed?'

'I did,' Dulcie said.

'Thank you.'

The other girl continued to stare at her with that blank expression which seemed to see and yet not see. Elizabeth began to feel uneasy. Why didn't Dulcie ask what had happened, show some interest? It was unlike her to be so silent, so enigmatic.

Then she remembered something that swept Dulcie from her mind. She moved a hand to her neck. Her wedding-ring had gone!

'Is this what you're looking for?' Dulcie asked.

She held the ribbon between finger and thumb — away from her, as though the ring suspended on it were some noisome thing. The look on her face, no longer wooden, intensified that impression.

'You know?' Elizabeth said. It was a formal question; she had already guessed the answer. 'We had hoped to keep it a secret for the present.'

'Obviously. Don't worry, I won't spread the glad news. Do you want to see him?'

Did she? It never occurred to her to query who Dulcie meant by 'him.' But did she want to see him — now, after what had happened, before she had had time in which to consider its implications? Unhappily she realized that what she wanted most was to be left alone. But would Desmond understand?

'Yes, please,' she said.

Her thoughts were not pleasant ones as she waited for him. But he was all solicitude as he knelt beside the bed, his cheek against hers. 'When they carried you in I nearly had a fit,' he said. 'I thought you were dead. What happened, darling? There's an awful bruise on your forehead, and the doctor said you were probably concussed. You just looked at him vaguely when he spoke to you.'

'I was conscious?' she asked, surprised.

'Only just. Neither the doctor nor the Sergeant could get anything sensible out of you.'

'Sergeant Watkins? Was he here?'

'No, the one from the village. Darling, what happened? Can you remember now?'

She told him. When she had finished he said, a puzzled look on his face, 'And is that all?'

'It's enough, thank you.'

'I didn't mean it like that. But to push you down and then clear off — well, what was the point of it?' He moved his cheek from hers and knelt upright, arching his back. 'Sounds like a lunatic to me.'

'It wasn't a lunatic,' she said, a tremor in her voice. 'You know that.'

'I do? How?'

Painfully she turned on her side to face him; her knees were sore, and much of her body still ached. But when Desmond leaned forward to help her she shrank away from him. It was a slight, instinctive action, instantly checked. But Desmond saw it and withdrew his arm.

'Sorry,' he said stiffly. 'Did I hurt you?'

'Oh, no.' She smiled. That too was instinctive; she did not feel like smiling. 'Desmond, you and Alan are convinced, aren't you, that one of — of us must have killed Aunt Charlotte?'

'Eh?' He stared at her. 'What on earth has that to do with it?'

'But you are, aren't you?'

'I suppose so. But it's only an opinion, not a conviction. I'm quite prepared to be persuaded otherwise. Do you want to try?'

She shook her head. 'No. I agree with you and Alan now. And I'm sure that whoever killed Aunt Charlotte tried to kill me this afternoon.'

'But that's absurd!' He was obviously startled. 'For one thing, from what you say there was no attempt to kill you. Goodness knows what was behind the attack, but it certainly wasn't murder.'

'How can you be sure of that? If I hadn't screamed . . . if those men hadn't heard me . . . it might have been very different.'

'All right, he intended to kill you.' He smiled at her. 'What then? Aunt Charlotte was murdered because — well, because she was Aunt Charlotte. You know what I mean. But nobody feels that way about you. So where's the connexion?'

Elizabeth shook her head again, wincing at the pain.

'Aunt Charlotte was killed for her money,' she said. 'Some one tried to force the safe.'

'All right, then, she was killed for her money.' The smile broadened into a grin. 'You see what a docile husband I am? Not an argument in me. But you haven't got any money. So what?'

'I've got hers,' she said, her eyes intent

on his face. 'She left it to me.'

He whistled softly.

'So you have! I'd forgotten that. But who'd benefit by your death? Michael's your only relative, and he's so distant I don't think he'd count. Unless you made a will in his favour he probably wouldn't get a bean.'

'He might expect to.' The palms of her clenched hands were moist with sweat. 'He doesn't know about our marriage.'

'No. But what — oh, I see.' He laughed, his eyelids raised comically. 'I'm the next of kin now, eh? No, he certainly doesn't know that. But Michael wouldn't do that to you, darling. He might conceivably have bumped off Aunt Charlotte — Aunt Charlotte was poison to him, he's firmly convinced she did him and his father out of what he dramatically terms 'their rightful inheritance' — but he doesn't feel like that about you. I know he snaps at you occasionally — you inherited some of the grudge, I suppose — but he'd never harm you physically. And if you eliminate Michael, who else is there?'

'Yes,' she said breathlessly. Her heart

was hammering so hard she thought he must hear it. 'Who else is there?'

'I can't — ' He stopped abruptly, the words ending in a quick intake of breath. With a lithe movement he sprang to his feet, pushing the chair roughly away. 'Good God, Elizabeth! You can't think *I* did it?'

She did not answer. She just looked at him steadily, until her eyes filled with tears and his face became a blur. She heard rather than saw him run from the room . . . heard his hurried steps along the corridor . . . heard him banging down the stairs. Faintly she heard his voice calling; but she was too shaken, too unhappy, to listen.

He was not alone when he returned. He almost pushed the Honourable George into the room, closed the door, and said loudly, not looking at Elizabeth, 'Dad, will you please tell Miss Messager how you and I have been spending the afternoon?'

Embarrassed, his father protested. 'I wish you would explain what all this is about, Desmond. I am quite sure Miss

Messager isn't interested in our domestic pursuits.'

'She will be in this. Tell her, please.'

His father moved a few paces nearer the bed and smiled apologetically at Elizabeth. 'Desmond seems to have gone slightly crazy, my dear. He and I have been going through the accounts this afternoon, and I can only suppose the mental exercise has affected his brain. He isn't used to it.'

'You don't have to be funny,' Desmond said impatiently. 'And be more explicit. It's the time that's important.'

His father looked at him. Then he nodded, and walked over to stand beside the bed. 'So that's it, eh?' he said gravely. 'You think Desmond may have given you that bump on the head?'

There was a lump in her throat. 'No,' she gulped, swallowing hard. 'Not — not really.'

'Good. Because I can assure you he did not. He was in the sitting-room with me all the afternoon — until Tom Carter and his friends staggered in with your unconscious body and deposited you practically in our laps.'

''Staggered' is not very complimentary to the lady,' Desmond said, opening the door. 'But thank you, Dad. That's all I wanted.'

His father did not immediately take the hint.

'I'm sorry about this, Miss Messager,' he said. 'Desmond has many faults, but assault and battery have so far not figured prominently among them. What made you pick on him?'

She could not tell him that. But added to her own unhappiness was the knowledge that she had hurt them both, and she turned her head away, the tears springing to her eyes.

Embarrassed, Farrel leaned over to pat her shoulder gently.

'I'm sorry, my dear. I didn't mean to upbraid you. It's not your fault; concussion does funny things to the imagination. We'll have a good laugh over this when you're well again.'

Wisely, Desmond left her alone after his father had gone. Not until she had dried her eyes and smiled at him guiltily did he come over to her.

'Satisfied?' he asked.

She reached out a hand to take his. 'I'm sorry,' she whispered. 'I didn't really mean it. Your father was right; that bang on the head must have knocked the sense out of me. I wasn't thinking straight.'

'I hope not,' he said. 'If you thought that of me in you right mind you couldn't love me much, could you?'

The sadness in his voice touched her, and she squeezed his hand. But she could not answer him. She *had* been in her right mind, and she *had* suspected him. And she knew, with a sudden clarity of mind that startled and shocked her, that what he had inferred was true. She did not love him.

Thankful for his silence, she lay pondering her problem. She did not love him, and she never had loved him. She had been impressed by his personality and charm, but more than anything it had been the chance he offered to escape from Aunt Charlotte and reality that had attracted her. In her imagination she had built him into something he wasn't, something he never could be; and because of that she had married him.

She squeezed his hand more tightly, appalled by what she had done — not to herself, but to him. Well, at least she could keep that knowledge from him; she had made a bargain and she would keep it.

'Am I forgiven?' she asked.

'Of course.' He sat down beside her, a slight frown on his face. His hand responded only mechanically to her squeeze.

'You don't look forgiving. Are you very far away?'

He smiled then, but the frown quickly returned. 'I was thinking about Michael. Since we're agreed that I wasn't responsible for what happened this afternoon, we're back to him. You know, I've a good mind to check up on him. I don't like this uncertainty.'

She clutched his hand with both her own.

'Oh, no!' she gasped, frightened. 'Don't, Desmond. It would be dreadful if — if — '

'If what?' he asked, surprised. 'We must know where we stand with him. It's a pretty grim situation, not knowing if one can trust one's friends.'

'Yes. But don't you do it. Leave it to the police, darling. Don't let's get mixed up in it.'

'We're mixed up in it already. But just as you say.'

To distract his mind from Michael and in an attempt to show her repentance, she said, 'It's only since I got that bump on the head that I've realized I'm a rich woman now. It's quite a responsibility; I ought to make a will, I suppose.' She smiled wanly. 'Could I do that to-morrow, before anything else happens to me?'

'Nothing will. I'll see to that. But make a will if you want to. I'll ring up old Banner in the morning. He's not much of a lawyer, but he ought to be able to tackle a will.'

'I'll leave it all to you,' she said eagerly. That would certainly help to make amends, she thought, smiling at his sudden grin and the 'thumbs up' sign he gave her with his free hand. 'But I want to give Uncle Henry and Alan something first. They have a right to it, after the way Aunt Charlotte treated them. And it's no good leaving it to them in my will; I want them to have it now.' She hesitated. 'I was going to do the same for Michael and his parents.'

'Trying to unload that inherited guilt, eh? Well, it's your money. I should leave Michael out of it for the present, until all this has been cleared up. But Alan — you know, I don't think he would accept it.'

'Why ever not? I'd only be paying off Aunt Charlotte's debt.'

'I know. But — ' He looked at her oddly. 'Didn't you know that Alan is in love with you?'

'Alan?' She laughed. 'Don't be absurd, Desmond. Of course he isn't.'

'But he is. He told me so — ages ago, in an unusual burst of confidence. That was why I had to rush you off your feet the way I did. I was afraid he'd get in first.'

He took his hand from hers to light a cigarette, and she turned over on her back and lay staring at the ceiling. Alan in love with her! They had played together, gone on holidays together, when they were children; she had looked on him as a brother. Then Uncle Edward had died, and Alan had stopped coming to the house. Later, when she had left school and Alan had gone into business with his father, they had met occasionally. Sometimes he had taken her out. He was cheerful and friendly and kind, and had not followed Michael's example in venting on her his spleen against her aunt. But there was never a hint that he might be in love with her.

'I still don't believe you,' she said. 'Bruce, yes; did you know he asked me to marry him? But not Alan.'

'I suspect that woman's intuition isn't all it's cracked up to be,' Desmond said, smiling. 'Either that, or you happen to be lacking in it. Bruce doesn't love anyone except himself. If he asked you to marry him it was because of Aunt Charlotte's money, and because he'd be stepping up socially. He's an almighty snob.'

It could be true, Elizabeth thought, a little shaken at her apparent lack of perception. There had never been much warmth in Bruce's love-making, despite his emphatic protestations. And he had failed to conceal — or perhaps he had not bothered to conceal — his interest in Dulcie. When Dulcie was around he had eyes only for her.

Dulcie! Wincing at the pain it caused her, she turned quickly to look at her husband.

'Desmond, I clean forgot; Dulcie knows we're married. It was Dulcie who put me to bed, you see.' Elizabeth pulled the ribbon away from her neck. 'She saw the ring.'

'Oh, Lord!' He stared at the ring as though mesmerized by it, his lips forming a soundless whistle. Then he gave a deep breath. 'That's torn everything. How on earth did she know it was me you'd married? Did you tell her?'

'No. I suppose she just guessed. But don't look so worried, darling. She promised to keep it to herself.'

'Dulcie never kept anything to herself,' he told her, frowning.

Footsteps sounded along the corridor

and he stood up, watching the door. 'That'll be the doctor or the police,' he said. 'Damn!'

It was both. And Dulcie. She looked quickly from Elizabeth to Desmond and then away. The doctor went over to the bed and took Elizabeth's hand. He had a paternal air that did not accord with his youthful appearance.

'Feeling better?' he said. 'That's fine. Can you remember now what happened? The Inspector here is anxious for detail.'

Elizabeth told them.

'It might have been worse,' the doctor said, replacing the bandage. 'It's coming out nicely.' As though it were a prize bloom, Elizabeth thought. 'Stay in bed, and I'll pop in tomorrow. We'll have you about in no time. A little swollen-headed, perhaps, but otherwise no ill effects.'

He laughed heartily at his own joke, said goodbye, and made for the door. Pitt hurried after him. They could hear the Inspector's low voice, followed by the doctor's 'No, no. Nothing like that.' When Pitt came back he seated himself on the vacant chair beside the bed and, after some formal words of sympathy, said, 'Did anyone know that you were going to the village this afternoon, Miss Messager?'

'I don't think so. It was after tea that I remembered about the statement you wanted me to sign. But I didn't tell anyone. I just put on my coat and went.'

'Can you describe the man who attacked you?'

'No. It was pitch dark, and he just seemed to materialize from out of the ground. I never saw his face. I couldn't even say if he was tall or short, thin or fat. He was just a figure.'

The Inspector frowned. 'He was probably crouched behind a bush waiting for you. Did he steal anything?'

Her eyes widened. 'I don't know. I never thought about it. But I hadn't any jewellery, and — ' She looked from her husband to Dulcie. 'Do you know where my bag is?'

'You didn't have a bag,' Dulcie said.

'Oh! That's it, then.' She was not greatly concerned. With Aunt Charlotte's money she could buy all the handbags she wanted. 'There was nothing of value in it. Only a few shillings, and my lipstick and compact — things like that.'

But the Inspector was already on his feet.

'And your front-door key to The Elms, eh?'

'Yes. I'd forgotten that.'

Pitt nodded to Watkins. As the Sergeant moved to the door Pitt said, 'I fancy that is what your assailant was after, Miss Messager. But we'll soon find out.'

The two detectives hurried from the hotel and into the waiting car. 'If we hadn't had one-track minds, Jim, we might have guessed something like this would happen,' the Inspector said angrily. The anger was directed against himself. 'We're too late now, of course. All we can hope is that he left his card.'

The Elms was in darkness; there was no sound from within, the front door was locked. They went round to the back and let themselves in, heedless of the noise they made. As Pitt had said, it was too late for that.

In the study the wall safe was open, the

door almost forced off its hinges. Pitt fished out the few documents it contained and studied them thoughtfully.

'Obviously a mercenary type,' Jim Watkins commented. 'Not interested in literature.'

'No,' Pitt said. 'But I wonder if he's interested in the cinema.'

9

Fun for Aunt Charlotte

It was just on ten o'clock that same evening when Desmond, frantically helping the barman to serve the 'last orders' that had already been called for, saw Michael's anxious face watching him from behind the press at the bar. It was obvious that Michael had been trying to attract his attention, for, as Desmond gave him a casual nod of recognition, he pointed upward with head and thumb and left the room.

Desmond was annoyed. Certainly he wanted to see Michael (despite Elizabeth's pleading, it seemed to him imperative to discover whether in fact Michael *had* attacked her that afternoon), but he did not want to be bothered with him yet. So far he had had no opportunity for a private talk with Dulcie; and Dulcie, surely, was a more pressing problem than Michael. Michael must wait his turn.

The bar was as crowded as it had been on the previous evening. Murder, it seemed, was thirst-provoking, and the attack on Elizabeth Messager had no doubt revived any interest that might have been waning. It took longer than usual to clear the bar, despite the urgency with which Desmond applied himself to the task.

Dulcie was not in her room when, receiving no answer to his knock, he peeped inside. Yet there had been no sign of her on the ground floor. Perhaps his father could help.

'She's out,' Mr Farrel told him. 'Went out just before eight.'

'Hell!' The indifference with which Desmond had sought to mask his anxiety could not survive this setback. 'Do you know where she went? Was she meeting some one?'

'It did not occur to me to ask.' Mr Farrel eyed his son with some concern. 'I hope, Desmond, that you are not now involved with *two* young women?'

'I'm not involved with any,' Desmond said quickly, and left him.

Michael was pacing up and down the room like a caged panther; he had a cat-like tread, and the sleek beauty of the cat family. A tumblerful of whisky was disappearing down his gullet at a fast rate.

'I see you've helped yourself,' Desmond said curtly. He was in an unfriendly mood. 'A pity you couldn't get here early enough to buy one in the bar.'

The other did not heed the sarcasm. He drank the remainder of the whisky at a gulp, choked slightly, tossed back the lock of unruly hair, and said excitedly, 'Desmond, you've got to help me. I'm in a hell of a jam.'

'Oh?' Desmond's tone indicated no more than polite curiosity. He shook off Michael's clutching hand and knelt by the cupboard to mix himself a drink. 'What trouble have you managed to get yourself into this evening?'

'This evening?' Michael eased a trembling finger round the inside of his collar. 'Nothing. I'm talking about last Thursday.'

'And I'm talking about this evening. Let's discuss that first, shall we?'

'There's nothing to discuss. I went to the cinema.'

'Really? Have you heard about Elizabeth?'

'Yes. I'm sorry. How is she? All right?'

'She will be.' Desmond perched himself on the edge of the bed and sipped his whisky appreciatively. 'When did you hear the news?'

'What news?' Michael, who had walked over to the curtained window, wheeled quickly. 'Oh, you mean Elizabeth. Why, just now. They were talking about it in the bar.'

Desmond was beginning to feel better. He could see Dulcie when she returned, even if it meant camping outside her door for half the night. Meanwhile this cross-examination gave him quite a kick, an exhilarating sense of power that was just what he needed. If Michael *had* attacked Elizabeth . . .

'Did you go to the cinema alone?' he asked.

'Yes. What the devil is this, Desmond?

Why all these damned questions about this evening?'

'The police will be asking them later, I shouldn't wonder,' Desmond told him grimly. 'You can treat this as a rehearsal.'

'Rehearsal?' Michael stared at him wide-eyed. 'You damned fool, they've asked them already! That's why I'm here.'

'Oh!' It was Desmond's turn to stare. Then he slipped off the bed and went over to the cupboard. 'In that case you certainly *do* need a drink. Here! How's that?'

'Thanks.' Michael sipped greedily. 'Yes, the blighters were waiting for me as I got off the bus.' He shuddered. 'It was hell.'

'What happened?'

'Oh, they were polite enough. Asked me if I'd mind going to the police station with them to answer a few questions. So I went. What else could I do?'

'And then?'

'Well, first they wanted to know where I'd been this evening. The fact that I'd been to the cinema wasn't enough for them; I had to give them the times of the buses, the name of the film — everything.

When they'd got it all down they — '

'Hold it!' Desmond said crisply. 'If I'm to help you I want it in detail too. The whole boiling.'

'But it's not this evening that worries me. It's Thursday.'

'We'll start with this evening.' His glass replenished, Desmond returned to his perch on the bed. What had happened to Elizabeth had not proved fatal, but it was important. To him, anyway. Michael wasn't going to wriggle out of it so easily. 'Come on, get weaving. We haven't got all night.'

Michael scowled, resenting the imperious tone. But it was expedient to reply.

'I caught the four forty-eight bus. I'd been hoping Bruce would come with me, but he was out when I called at his place.' (Bruce had been in the bar around seven-thirty, Desmond remembered. He'd seen him, although he hadn't spoken to him. But where was he earlier?) 'I was in the cinema by twenty past five, came out at ten past eight, and caught the eight twenty-two bus back.'

'What film?'

'"The Searchers." It's a Western. Anything else you'd like to know?'

'You've got it off pat, haven't you?' Desmond said.

He was the cat playing with the mouse; he could goad him with impunity, the mouse would never turn and hit back. That was what he thought. But he had not reckoned on the other's quick temper. Michael's eyes narrowed, his lips parted over clenched teeth. He walked slowly over to the bed and stood squarely in front of his tormentor, one fist raised threateningly.

'What the devil do you mean by that?' he asked.

Desmond was seldom averse to a rough house, despite his languid air. But he did not want one now; he wanted to get the truth out of Michael. He said, smiling, 'Nothing, you idiot. Just pulling your leg.' And, as the other relaxed, 'I never knew you were a film fan.'

'I'm not,' Michael said wearily. 'But Dad was in one of his really filthy moods at tea, and I just couldn't stand it any longer. The cinema was the only place that offered.'

It could be true, Desmond reflected. He would have been willing to accept it had it not been for the guilty look on Michael's face when Elizabeth had been mentioned. Elizabeth had been attacked at around a quarter to five, as near as he could ascertain; if Michael had been the attacker he would have had to run like the wind to catch the four forty-eight bus. But had he caught it? He could have gone into Tanbury by the next bus, and still have seen enough of the film to satisfy any questions the police might have put to him.

Desmond decided on a direct attack.

'Michael, I've got to ask this; some one else will if I don't. Was it you who attacked Elizabeth on the common this evening?'

The effect of this thrust was not easy to assess, since it was directed at Michael's back. But it seemed to Desmond that the back stiffened at the question.

'No, of course I didn't.' He sounded neither surprised nor outraged by the suggestion. It was almost as an afterthought that he turned and added reproachfully, 'I'm sorry you thought it necessary to ask that, Desmond.'

'I'm sorry too.' He eyed Michael steadily, until the other blinked and turned away again. 'All right, forget it. Now, what's all this about last Thursday?'

But now that his opportunity had come at last Michael hesitated to take it. He walked across to the window, fiddled with the curtains, took his time over lighting a cigarette. Then he said slowly, 'It so happens that I didn't go straight home from the office that evening. The police got that information from my father. They asked me where I'd been, and I told them . . . '

He paused, licking his lips. 'You told them what?' Desmond asked, intrigued.

'I told them I'd been with you.'

Desmond stared at him. 'You bloody fool!' he said softly. 'You bloody fool! You think you can get away with that? Why, they'll blow it sky-high in next to no time.' He took a deep breath. 'It didn't occur to you, I suppose, that I might object to being summarily involved in your misdemeanours, whatever they are — that, ethics apart, I might value my liberty rather more than our beautiful friendship? In short, that I might blow the gaff?'

Michael hurried over to him, almost running. 'It's not like that, Desmond,' he said eagerly. 'I wouldn't have done it if I'd thought you'd be in any danger. All I said was that you'd picked me up outside the office some time after half-past five and had given me a lift into Tanbury. I didn't commit you further than that — except to say that, having done our shopping (separately, not together), we had met again shortly after six, when I decided to stay in Tanbury for a drink. I knew you must have left about that time, or you wouldn't have been able to pick Bruce up at half-past six on your way back.'

'I see. And how could you be sure that I didn't go into Tanbury long before five?'

'Because Alan told me on Saturday that he'd seen you in the village at a quarter-past five. I knew I couldn't be far out on time.'

Desmond was startled. 'Alan saw me? What was he doing in the village then? He should have been at the factory — they don't knock off until five-thirty.' A new aspect occurred to him. 'Anyway, why should the fact that he had seen me be of sufficient importance to mention it to you? You weren't checking up on me by any chance, were you?' The guilty look on the other's face answered him. 'I see. Nice couple of friends *you* are.'

'We weren't discussing you in particular,' Michael protested. 'We were trying to sort out where every one was that afternoon, that's all.'

It sounded reasonable. Desmond was still slightly worried about Alan, but that was not something to be discussed with Michael.

'All right. So you were okay on times. But you'd have looked a nice bloody fool, wouldn't you, if, unknown to you, the police had already questioned me before they tackled you? What then?'

That, Michael admitted, was a risk he had had to take — with the odds in his favour. 'Why *should* they question you?

Aunt Charlotte hadn't cheated *you*?' he said bitterly. 'You've no motive, the way Alan and I have. They won't suspect you unless they find out about the joke we'd planned; and if that happens I've now given you an alibi. Back me up in this and we're *both* safe.'

'I don't happen to need an alibi, thank you,' Desmond said. 'What were you doing that evening that you had to keep it secret from the police?'

'I went to see Aunt Charlotte.'

'You *what*?'

'I went to see Aunt Charlotte. Not at the house — at the station.'

'Good Lord! Why? To kiss her good-bye?'

'I borrowed some money from the firm last week,' Michael said. Confession seemed to be coming to him more easily, for he did not boggle at the admission. 'They don't know it yet — but they will if I don't replace it by Wednesday.'

'And you expected Aunt Charlotte to fork out? You must be crazy.'

'I know. But who else could I try? Mother hasn't a bean of her own, and

Dad — well, you know him. Aunt Charlotte was off on a holiday, there was just a faint chance she might be in a generous mood for once.' He spread his arms in a gesture of despair. 'But she never turned up, damn her!'

Desmond studied him with curiosity mixed with contempt.

'You can hardly blame her for that,' he said. 'What did you do then?'

'Caught the next bus home. What else could I do?'

'So you knew from the start that Aunt Charlotte never caught that train,' Desmond said slowly. 'Why didn't you mention it to the rest of us?'

'How the hell could I? You'd have wanted to know how I knew, and I certainly wasn't going to tell you that.' Anger and irritation were overcoming prudence. Question had been piled on question, and it seemed that he was getting nowhere — nowhere, at any rate, that he wanted to go. 'I've had about enough of this, Desmond. If you're not going to help me, then say so. I want to know where I stand.'

In it up to the neck, Desmond thought to himself; that's where you stand. But Michael in trouble could mean trouble for them all. He was a fool and a menace, but if possible he had to be helped.

'All right, I'll back you up,' he said. 'But next time I suggest you consult me first.'

Michael began to stammer his thanks. His relief was so great that it acted like a purge. His bowels and his knees felt weak, and he sat down abruptly. The hand that reached for the whisky Desmond offered him was shaking.

But the whisky helped to steady him, and presently he said, 'What about Bruce? I didn't mention that you'd picked him up on the way back. Will you?'

'Not unless they ask me. Why should I?'

'No.' Michael took another drink and lit a cigarette. He said slowly, 'Bruce was at the house around the time Aunt Charlotte was due to leave. He wouldn't be too keen for the police to know that, would he?'

'If you are suggesting he killed her

think again,' Desmond said impatiently. He wanted to be rid of Michael. The problem posed by Dulcie's knowledge of his marriage was still unsolved, and it could not be shelved. 'What motive would he have had?'

'I fancy he wants to marry Elizabeth,' Michael said. 'Aunt Charlotte would have put a stop to that.'

'Maybe. Look here, do you mind if we call it a day? It's late.'

'Of course.' As he reached the door Michael hesitated. 'I still have to find that money by Wednesday,' he said diffidently. 'I suppose it's no use asking you to lend me fifty quid?'

Desmond was shaken by the question. Despite the other's denial, he had been certain that it was Michael who had attacked Elizabeth that afternoon. It had seemed so obvious. Yet if he had done that — had stolen her key in order to get into the house and force the safe — why did he now need this money? It didn't make sense.

'And how do you expect me to lay my hands on that amount of money?' he demanded, angry because of this new uncertainty. 'I haven't got fifty shillings.'

Michael nodded. The answer did not surprise him. 'I just thought I'd ask,' he said. 'I'm getting desperate.'

He turned to go. There was a hang-dog air about him, a lack of spirit, that spoke more eloquently than words of his despondency. Desmond watched him thoughtfully. Then he said, 'All right, Michael, I'll scrape it together for you somehow. Not now — to-morrow. But for God's sake watch your step from now on. Friendship is a beautiful thing, but you're putting a damned heavy strain on it.'

Michael went, profuse of thanks, a new buoyancy in his step.

The door to Dulcie's room was locked, but a slit of light showed along the bottom. Desmond knocked softly.

'What is it?' came the girl's voice.

'It's me — Desmond,' he said urgently. 'I want to talk to you.'

There was a pause. Then she said, as coldly as distance would permit, 'Well, I don't want to talk to you. Not tonight.'

'But this is important, Dulcie. It won't keep.'

'It will have to. Good night.'

There was the click of a switch, and the slit of light below the door disappeared. Angrily he rattled the handle.

'Dulcie, you — '

Footsteps on the stairs reminded him of the proprieties. He hurried down the corridor, not wishing to be found by his father in the vicinity of Dulcie's room. But it was not his father. It was Inspector Pitt.

'Good evening, Mr Farrel,' Pitt said. He looked tired. 'I was told you had gone to bed, but I'm glad to see they were wrong. Can you spare me a minute?'

'I suppose so,' Desmond said, not very graciously. By the time he was through with the Inspector Dulcie would probably be asleep. 'Come along to my room.'

Pitt followed him. 'It's about last Thursday, sir,' he explained, declining the proffered drink. 'Mr Michael Lane tells me he was with you that evening.'

'Part of it,' Desmond cautiously agreed. 'I had to go into Tanbury, and picked him up on the way. That would be just after half-past five, I suppose. He was waiting for a bus near his office, about a mile this side of the town, and I happened to see him as I was passing.'

'And then?'

'We drove into Tanbury, and separated to do our shopping. I had expected him to come back to Milford with me, but when I met him again shortly after six he said he wasn't coming. I think he wanted to have a pint or two at the George. So I left him. I had to be here by six-thirty.'

'And were you?'

'Near enough,' Desmond said. He felt no qualms about the result of the interview. Only curiosity. A pity one couldn't read the other fellow's thoughts, achieve the satisfaction of knowing how convincing one had sounded.

'Can you name any of the shops you visited?' Pitt asked.

'The official mind at its most suspicious.' Desmond smiled, taking the sting out of the words. 'Yes, I can name them all.' He did so. 'If you want to check I suggest you try the tobacconist. He's our wholesaler.'

Pitt thanked him, wrote in his notebook, bade him goodnight, and made to leave.

'Have I helped in any way?' Desmond asked.

The Inspector smiled wearily. 'It depends on your point of view, doesn't it?' he said. 'Good night, sir.'

* * *

One of the documents Pitt had taken from the rifled safe was a copy of Charlotte Lane's will. In it, as Valerie French had told the Sergeant, Elizabeth Messager was named as the sole beneficiary; but as the will was nearly three years old there was the possibility that it had since been altered or amended. The arrival on Monday morning of Mr Crumley, Charlotte Lane's lawyer, was therefore welcomed by the police. The certainty that the girl was the only person to have a pecuniary interest in the woman's death might help — though not,

Pitt suspected, very considerably.

Since Elizabeth was still confined to her bed, Pitt and the lawyer came to her room at the hotel. Elizabeth welcomed them warmly; she had lost most of her fear of the Inspector, and was tired of her own society. Her husband had spent what time he could with her, but murder had proved to be thirsty work, and trade was brisk. She had thought that Bruce, who had so often protested his love for her, would be certain to pay her a visit. But although, according to the chambermaid, he had been in the hotel he had not tried to see her — had not even, so far as Elizabeth knew, left a message or asked after her.

But Alan had come. He had called early that morning, bringing with him a large bunch of chrysanthemums and a message of condolence from his father. Remembering what Desmond had said the previous evening, she had regarded him with new interest. But if Alan was in love with her he gave no sign; he was friendly and cheerful, but there was no trace of sentiment. Of the two, Elizabeth was the only one to betray embarrassment. She had no illusions about her looks, but it piqued her that that morning she was not looking her best.

He did not stay long, but Elizabeth continued to wonder about him until Mr Crumley swept him out of her mind with his talk of Aunt Charlotte's will. 'To my knowledge it is the only one she ever made,' he said. 'The copy you have there is quite in order, Inspector.' He turned to the girl. 'Do you wish me to read it to you, Miss Messager?'

Elizabeth assured him that she did not. She had no desire to be bored with legal jargon; the substance was all that mattered. 'How much did Aunt Charlotte leave?' she asked.

'The exact figures are not yet available,' he told her. 'But I fear it will be less than you have perhaps anticipated.'

'You mean death duties will take a lot?'

Mr Crumley shook his head sorrowfully. 'I doubt whether there will be any death duties to pay.'

Pitt was as perplexed as the girl. 'I

understood she was a wealthy woman,' he said.

'Wealth is relative, isn't it?' the lawyer said. 'But I fancy 'was' is the operative word here, Inspector. After she had disposed of the business Mrs Lane was worth somewhere in the neighbourhood of twenty-five thousand pounds.'

That was four years ago, thought Elizabeth. And Aunt Charlotte was extravagant, she would have made quite a hole in it. Even so, there should be more than enough for her needs. She would be able to travel, to have an income of her own, to be independent of Desmond. That last thought cheered her more than the others.

'Mrs Lane was extravagant.' Mr Crumley echoed her thoughts. 'Recklessly extravagant. If she had been allowed to proceed unchecked there would have been no provision for the future.' He looked somewhat guiltily at Elizabeth. 'Fortunately — or perhaps I should now say unfortunately — I was able to persuade her to make that provision.'

'How?' Pitt asked bluntly.

'By buying her an immediate annuity of eight hundred and fifty pounds,' the lawyer said. 'It was an uneconomic investment, and one which I was most reluctant to make. But Mrs Lane had no sense of proportion where money was concerned, and it seemed the only solution.' He looked at the Inspector. 'Oddly enough, once I had explained to her the provisions and limitations of the investment, she welcomed it. I had expected opposition, but she was almost childishly delighted and amused by it.' He shook his head. 'A most difficult and incomprehensible woman.'

'I'm not very well up in annuities myself,' Elizabeth said, smiling. 'But I gather I shall have an income of eight hundred and fifty pounds a year. And there'll be the house too, won't there? And whatever Aunt Charlotte had in the bank?'

'The house is still heavily mortgaged,' Mr Crumley said apologetically. 'But — and this, I'm afraid, will come as a shock to you, Miss Messager — the annuity ceased with Mrs Lane's death.

You do not benefit in any way from it.'

'You mean — there's no money at all?'

'There is, I believe, about twelve hundred pounds still invested. But that is all — apart from the house.'

Oblivious of what the two men might think, Elizabeth turned her back on them and lay staring sightlessly at the wall. She was filled with self-pity. For years she had endured life with Aunt Charlotte, had suffered her tantrums and her domineering ways, her selfishness and her often obscene affection. And for what? A thousand pounds, and a house she could never afford to live in. True, she had had no thought of reward when she had given her promise to Uncle Edward. But Aunt Charlotte had made promises too — promises, Elizabeth knew now, which her aunt had had no intention of fulfilling.

There were footsteps on the carpet, a murmured goodbye from Mr Crumley. A door closed. But Elizabeth took no heed. She was remembering what the lawyer had said — that Aunt Charlotte had been amused by the provisions and limitations of the annuity. Of course she had been amused! It was in keeping with her warped sense of humour, her cunning, to bind Elizabeth to her with the glittering prospect of future wealth, to fend off would-be husbands with the threat of disinheritance — and to hug to herself the secret knowledge that the prospect was a myth, the threat empty.

10

A Domestic Issue

'I'm going out, Michael,' Mr Lane said, shrugging his frail body into an overcoat. 'Back in about half an hour.'

Michael nodded, concealing his relief. It was half-past four, three hours since Desmond had given him the money; for all that time it had been burning a hole in his pocket. Now was his chance to return it to the safe.

He went through to the outer office with his father, watched him go out into the dusk, heard the car start up and move off from the gravel front. Then, after assuring himself that the clerks were busy and unlikely to disturb him, he returned to the inner office. Closing the door behind him, he went over to the desk, pulled two bulky envelopes from his breast pocket, tore one of them open, and took from it a wad of one-pound notes.

Carefully he counted them; he had had no opportunity to do this before, they were as Desmond had handed them to him. He placed the last note on top of the pile with a sigh of relief. They were all there — fifty of them. Then he slit open the second envelope, revealing a further bundle of notes. These he left in the envelope; he had counted them before, twice over.

He reached into his pocket for the leather case which, fastened by a slender chain to a trouser button, contained his keys. But as he snapped back the catch he gave a grunt of dismay, allowing the case to slip from his hand. He remembered now; the key wasn't there. His father had borrowed it on the Saturday and had forgotten to return it.

The telephone began to ring. For a moment he did not heed it, but stood frowning at the money on the desk. Then, as he reached for the receiver, a voice behind him said, 'Quite a tidy little sum you've got there, Mr Lane.'

He turned sharply. Inspector Pitt stood by the door, the ginger-haired Sergeant beside him. 'Hadn't you better answer that?' Pitt said, nodding at the receiver.

Michael walked round to the other side of the desk and lifted the receiver. The caller was demanding particulars of a sale; but the file was in the outer office, and he did not want to send for a clerk. He gave what information he could, aware all the time of the bundles of notes on the desk and the inquisitive eyes of the two detectives.

As he replaced the receiver he said, scowling to hide his unease, 'Do you usually walk into private offices unannounced?'

'Not usually.' Pitt strolled across to the desk, picked up the bundle of loose notes, and began riffling them idly. Michael's uneasiness increased as he watched him; there was something disturbing about the Inspector's calm assurance. 'Hard up for a few quid, Inspector?' he asked, his voice a little too sharp. 'Sorry I can't slip you one or two of those. They belong to the firm.'

'So I imagined, sir.' Pitt put down the notes and picked up the full envelope, peering into it. 'Would it be convenient for you to come back to Milford Cross with us now, sir? There are one or two matters we'd like to discuss with you.'

'It wouldn't be at all convenient,' Michael said, his heart beating a shade faster. What the devil was up now? 'My father is out, and I can't leave the office until he returns. Either we talk here, or you'll have to wait.'

Pitt put down the envelope and walked over to the electric fire. 'That's all right, sir,' he said pleasantly. 'We'll wait.'

No, thought Michael, that you *won't* do. Not if you intend waiting in here. That was something he hadn't bargained for, and he had been a fool to suggest it. He shuddered, involuntarily conjuring up a vision of his father walking into the office, with the money still on the table and himself under the surveillance of two detectives. That would put the lid on it.

'My father may be some time,' he said. 'But I don't suppose anything is likely to crop up now that the clerks can't deal with. I'll come with you now, Inspector. The Law mustn't be kept waiting, eh?'

He forced a smile. 'If you'll wait outside for a few minutes I'll be right with you. I just want to tidy up these papers and put the money in the safe.'

'Thank you,' Pitt said. 'But if you don't mind we'll wait in here.'

He did mind, but it would look odd to protest. Nor would it be wise to prevaricate further. His father had said half an hour, but he might well be back before that. He had to get them away quickly.

'As you wish,' he said casually, and began to sort the papers. It was the money that presented the difficulty; he could not put it in the safe, and to pocket it would certainly rouse their suspicion. Yet he could not leave it on the desk. Or — why not pretend to leave it there? Go out with them to the car, and then, on the pretext that he had forgotten something, dash back into the office and stuff the notes in his pocket? He was not under arrest; they would not restrain him forcibly.

He put on his overcoat and walked to the door. 'Ready?' he said.

Pitt nodded. As he passed the desk he tapped the bundle of notes with the back of his hand. 'Forgotten this, haven't you?' he said.

'No.' Damn them! Why did they have to be so bloody officious? What business was it of theirs what he did with the money? 'I don't forget that much money, Inspector.'

Sergeant Watkins was examining the envelope containing the rest of the notes. 'Looks like these have been carried about in a breast pocket,' he said to no one in particular. 'They've got that bent, creased appearance.' He handed them to Michael with a sly smile. 'We have to show off occasionally,' he apologized. 'Gives the public confidence.'

Michael almost snatched them from him. He picked up the money from the table and stowed the lot away in his pocket. 'I'm taking it with me,' he said curtly, aware of their curiosity. 'My father has the key to the safe.'

Angry at the way in which fate had contrived to trap him, he followed them out to the car.

They did not talk on the journey to Milford Cross. Michael accepted their silence with relief; it gave him time to think. But thinking, he found, was profitless; he could plan no defence against the unknown.

At the little police station Pitt said, 'I have a typescript here, Mr Lane, of the statement you made last night. Do you wish to sign it?'

'Why not?' Michael felt in his pocket for a pen. If this was all he had been a fool to panic.

'I'll read it to you,' Pitt said. When he had done so he asked, 'You don't wish to make any alteration?'

'I don't think so. Why? Is my grammar faulty?'

'You say here, Mr Lane, that you caught the four forty-eight bus to Tanbury last night. Is that correct?' And, as Michael hesitated, 'We have a witness who says you didn't — who says you were on the five-eighteen. Do you still dispute that?'

Michael shrugged. He knew when he was beaten.

‘The conductor, I suppose. All right, Inspector, I was on the five-eighteen. So what? Not important, is it?’

‘You left home at four-thirty, sir, or shortly after. How did you fill in the time between then and five-eighteen? That’s what is important.’

‘Oh, I just mooched around. It was nearer four forty-five than four-thirty when I left home. That’s how I came to miss the four forty-eight.’

‘Did you meet anyone you know?’ Michael shook his head. ‘That’s rather odd, isn’t it? Milford Cross is a small place, and I understand you’ve lived here all your life.’

‘Yes. There just didn’t happen to be anyone around.’

The Inspector seemed to accept that. ‘What made you lie about the time, Mr Lane?’ he asked.

Michael sighed with relief. At least one hurdle had been successfully negotiated. He said, with more spirit than hitherto, ‘I should have thought that was obvious. I had been wandering round the village at the time Miss Messager was attacked. It seemed safer to invent an alibi than to admit that.'

You young fool, Pitt thought. He felt almost sorry for the fly who had walked so carelessly into the web. He enjoyed a battle of wits; but this was no battle, it was a massacre.

'Why should you be suspected of attacking Miss Messager? Had you a motive for doing so?'

'Of course I hadn't. But people do get accused of crimes they haven't committed.'

'And acquitted,' Pitt said. 'Tell me — how did you come to hear of the attack on Miss Messager? In case you don't know, it occurred at approximately four-fifty. While you were waiting for the bus, eh?'

With a sinking heart, Michael realized his mistake. 'I heard some one talking about it,' he said lamely, after vainly searching for a way out.

'One of those people who didn't happen to be around, I suppose?'

Michael flushed angrily at the blatant sarcasm. 'No, you' — 'bloody fool' he had been about to say. 'On the bus.'

It was too easy. 'No one but you boarded that bus at Milford Cross,' Pitt said mildly, almost gently.

Michael shrugged helplessly. There was no come-back to that, and he did not attempt one. They had him neatly sewn up. Why struggle against the inevitable?

'Lying does not seem to be one of your major accomplishments, Mr Lane,' Pitt said. 'How did you come by that money?'

The sudden switch in the attack took him off guard. He made a feeble attempt to bluster. 'It belongs to the firm,' he said. 'Nothing to do with you.'

'So you said before, sir. But where did it come from? Not the safe — your father has the key.' Michael glared at him, muttering something about minding his own business. 'Shall we stop beating about the bush, Mr Lane? I am suggesting that you attacked Miss Messager on the common yesterday evening, took the key from her handbag, and with it entered The Elms and then forced the safe in the study. And I suggest that the money now in your pocket was stolen by you from that safe.'

'It's a lie,' Michael said, without any great show of indignation. 'You try and prove it.'

'I will,' Pitt said. 'If that money belongs to the firm your father will have knowledge of it.' He turned to Watkins. 'Get Mr Lane on the phone, Sergeant.'

Michael shook his head. 'You needn't bother,' he said sullenly. 'Dad wouldn't know about it. It's mine. I borrowed it from a friend.'

'Ah!' The Inspector permitted himself a smile of satisfaction. 'Now we're getting somewhere. Who was the friend, Mr Lane?' But his victim only glared at him stonily, and he said solemnly, 'You are behaving very foolishly, you know. Perhaps you don't quite appreciate the serious position you are in? For it *is* serious. Unless you can give me a satisfactory explanation of how you came to be in possession of that money I shall have no alternative but to arrest you on a charge of robbery with assault.'

He did appreciate it. And he knew that only Desmond could save him. But

Desmond had insisted that the loan should remain a secret. Secret from whom? From every one, presumably. Yet Desmond could never have contemplated this predicament when he made that condition.

'Desmond Farrel lent it to me,' he said. 'At lunch today.' He saw the look of incredulity on the Inspector's face, and added, 'If you don't believe me ring up and ask him.'

'A very sensible suggestion,' Pitt said. 'I'll do that.'

* * *

Elizabeth got up that afternoon, but she did not go downstairs. The unsteadiness of her legs and the still painful bruise on her forehead provided a sound excuse for staying in her room, but they were not the main reason. The bandage was off, and she was well aware of the stares and sympathy that would greet her. More telling still, she considered that she looked a fright.

Desmond had tea with her in her room.

He had called in for a few minutes before lunch, and had then rushed off to see Michael. She had expected him to question her about Mr Crumley's visit, and was relieved when he did not. It would not be easy to tell him. However much he loved her, he was unlikely to receive with equanimity the news that the anticipated fortune was not to materialize.

Some of the despondency which had possessed her that morning had evaporated by tea-time. She was even a little ashamed of her behaviour — like a spoilt child, she thought, and wondered what the Inspector and Mr Crumley had thought of her. She was not the heiress she had expected to be, but she certainly was not destitute. She had a thousand pounds, plus whatever the sale of the house and furniture might bring; and she was a married woman with a husband to provide for her. That money could give her the extras, the occasional fling; it could even satisfy, in a not too ambitious style, her longing to travel. Only when she recalled how Aunt

Charlotte had deliberately tricked and cheated her did her chagrin return.

Desmond exerting his charm was difficult to resist, and that afternoon he was in a cheerful and attentive mood. By the time the last of the buttered toast had been eaten Elizabeth was beginning to wonder if she had not been mistaken in thinking she did not love him.

I'm a fickle person, she thought ruefully. It's time I grew up.

'Did old Banner call?' he asked. And added, at her look of bewilderment, 'The lawyer. You said you wanted to make a will. I rang his office this morning. He was out, but a clerk took the message.'

'No,' Elizabeth said. She had forgotten Mr Banner.

'No matter. There's no hurry, is there?' He helped himself to a cake and stood up, smiling down at her where she lay propped against the pillows. 'You look good enough to eat in that get-up. Move over, darling; I think I want to sit on the bed.'

She obeyed, blushing. He leaned across to kiss her.

After some minutes had passed — 'Not during meals,' Elizabeth said firmly, pushing him away, herself aroused by his caresses. Even if I don't love him, she thought, I don't think being married to him will prove a terrible hardship. Not if he's always as attentive as this.

Desmond said, 'Meals don't last for ever, thank goodness,' and bit into an éclair. 'Did you tell Alan of your design for enriching him?'

Alan! She had forgotten Alan. He and Uncle Henry would suffer as much as she, although they would not have to bear the same disappointment.

'No,' she said, once more depressed. 'I didn't, luckily.'

'Why 'luckily'? Changed your mind? Darling, you've gone all dismal on me. Have an éclair to cheer yourself up. Real cream.'

She shook her head. She did not want an éclair, she wanted sympathy. There was so much she could have done with that money — for Desmond, for Alan, even for Michael. Well, Alan and Michael would never know what they had missed;

but Desmond would. Should she tell him now, while he was in this happy mood? Sooner or later he would have to know, and her own disappointment would be easier to bear if she had some one to share it with her.

'Desmond, I — I want to talk to you. Seriously.' He grinned at her, and her heart sank; it seemed such a shame to spoil his happiness. 'About Aunt Charlotte's will.'

'I'm all ears,' he assured her, and turned back to his teacup. 'How much are we worth?'

She said with a rush, knowing it was the only way she would ever get the words out, 'There isn't any money. Aunt Charlotte did the dirty on me. She bought an annuity with what Uncle Edward left her — I think she did it on purpose, to spite me — and now there's nothing. Or practically nothing. About a thousand pounds, Mr Crumley said, and the house. But that's all.'

He did not turn round. He sat very still, the tea-cup poised at his lips. Then he sipped once . . . twice . . . and put the cup carefully back on its saucer.

Elizabeth felt herself trembling.

'Dear me, what a bore!' Desmond said. 'Perhaps it's as well that some one has already seen fit to murder Aunt Charlotte. I might otherwise have been tempted to do it myself.'

The illogicality of this statement was lost on Elizabeth. 'I'm so sorry, Desmond,' she said in a small voice. 'I feel I've cheated you. You thought you were marrying an heiress, and — and now — '

She began to cry. Desmond turned swiftly, gripping both her arms.

'You little fool,' he said, shaking her gently. 'If I'm angry — and I am — it's on your account, not mine. Of course I wanted you to have her money; I kept thinking of what we could do with it together, you and I. But that doesn't mean I didn't want you without it. When I asked you to marry me I said there were no strings attached, and that's as true now as it was then.' He bent to kiss her wet eyes, her trembling mouth. 'Do you believe that?'

She blinked and nodded. 'Thank you,

darling,' she whispered, pulling the sheet up to her eyes to dry them. Then she sighed. 'Now I feel better. It's such a blessed relief to know that you're not angry, that you don't mind.'

'Wait a minute!' he said. 'Don't get me wrong. I do mind, and I am angry. But not with you. When I think of that damned woman — ' He slapped his thigh heavily. 'Oh, well. Have some more tea and then tell me all the details.'

She told him. When she had finished she added, 'That's why I said it was lucky I hadn't said anything to Alan. But I did so want to help them.'

'I know.' He stared thoughtfully at the tea-pot. 'A pity. Not that Aunt Charlotte would think so. She'd be delighted.'

'I suppose she would. How dreadful to get fun out of being unkind; one ought to pity her, really. Desmond, I'm not telling anyone else about the will. Not yet, anyway. They would either feel sorry for me or think me a poor fish to have been fooled so easily. Either way I'd feel humiliated. So keep it to yourself, darling, will you?'

‘Denying Aunt Charlotte the last laugh, eh? Okay by me, if that’s the way you want it.’ He jumped up and began to pace the room. ‘Oh, to hell with the old so-and-so. Let’s forget her.’

‘It’s not easy,’ she said. ‘Even now she’s dead she still seems to dominate my life. I’d give anything to get away from her.’

‘I bet you would.’ He had been looking aimlessly out of the window as he spoke. The curtains had not yet been drawn; but there was little to see, for already it was dark. Suddenly he turned and came back to the bed, a sparkle in his eye. ‘Well, why not? Why shouldn’t we start our honeymoon next weekend? I can wangle it, and so can you; Aunt Charlotte can’t stop you now. How about it? We could try the Speckled Trout, as you suggested.’

She sat up eagerly. ‘Oh, yes!’ Then reality returned, and her face clouded. ‘But we can’t, can we? If we went away together every one would know we were married.’

Desmond laughed. ‘Not necessarily. It does happen otherwise. Still, I’m hoping that by then the police will have got this mess cleared up and we can let the cat out. If not — oh, we'll fix it somehow.'

'You're always fixing things,' she said, smiling. Picking up a compact from the table, she anxiously surveyed herself in the small mirror. 'I look an awful sight for a new bride. People will think you beat me.'

'Any more spanners and I will. Right, then that's settled. I'll book a room to-night.' He exhaled loudly. 'My, but it's good to have something to look forward to. All these policemen are getting on my nerves.'

'Me too.' She patted the bed invitingly. 'Come and sit down, darling, the meal is over.' And blushed at her own forwardness.

'Now that,' said Desmond, 'is — '

The door opened, and Dulcie came in without knocking. After one brief glance at the confused look on their faces she said to Desmond, 'Inspector Pitt has been on the phone. He wants you to ring him back at once.'

She's terribly attractive, Elizabeth thought with envy; no wonder the men all fall for her. There's no need for her to flaunt herself the way she does, she could get them without that.

'Hell!' Desmond said, when Dulcie had gone. '*Now* what have I been up to?'

His dismay was so expressively registered that Elizabeth laughed. 'Go and find out,' she suggested. 'I'll keep. Did you talk to Dulcie about us?'

'Yes.'

'Why has she got her knife into me?' He began to protest, but she shook her head firmly. 'She has, you know. She won't even speak to me now unless she has to. Do you think she's jealous?'

He laughed at that. 'Of us? Perhaps. Maybe she's worried about being left on the shelf.'

'That'll never happen to Dulcie. She's far too beautiful.'

'Yes, I suppose she is. Darling, I'd better go and talk to the Inspector. Be seeing you.'

He used the office phone. As he lifted the receiver and gave the operator the number he was aware that his father had entered the room behind him. Putting his hand over the mouthpiece, he said, 'The police. They want — ' A voice came over the wire. 'Hello! Is that you, Inspector? Desmond Farrel here. I was told you wanted me to ring you.'

Inspector Pitt's voice was formally precise. Even after a lifetime of police work he was never at ease on the telephone.

'Yes, sir. I want to know if you lent — er — anyone a sum of money to-day?'

Desmond swore under his breath. 'Yes,' he said. 'What of it?'

'How much was it, sir?'

Desmond hesitated. That was a question he did not want to answer in his father's hearing. And it might be followed by others, equally embarrassing. 'I think I had better come over, Inspector,' he said. 'This looks like being tricky on the phone.'

'I agree, sir. Can you come now?'

'Right away,' Desmond promised, and rang off.

'What was that in aid of?' George Farrel asked suspiciously.

'I'm not sure. Let you know when I get back.' By then he should be able to concoct an explanation that would satisfy his father. 'Is the car out at the front? I'll have to hurry.'

'You'll have to hurry on foot, then. Bill has taken the car into Tanbury.'

Bill was the bartender. 'Feet it is, then,' Desmond said. 'Lend me your torch, Dad, will you? I'll beat it over the common.'

'Hang on to your handbag,' Mr Farrel advised, with unusual levity.

His son's thoughts were far from mirthful. What the hell has Michael been up to? he wondered angrily. Still more to the point — what has he been saying about me? I told him to keep his mouth shut; if he's been fool enough to chance his arm again I'm damned if I'm going to let him involve me this time. Once is enough where a lunatic like Michael is concerned.

The four men already in the little police station — the Inspector, the two Sergeants, and Michael — made it seem over-crowded. Michael nodded to him guiltily. Desmond returned the nod, unsure of the right attitude to adopt.

Sympathy, bewilderment, annoyance — what was expected of him?

Pitt gave him no time to find out. 'Sorry to trouble you, Mr Farrel,' he said. 'But Mr Lane here says he borrowed some money from you this afternoon. That's correct, is it?'

'Quite correct, Inspector. Did you think he'd pinched it?'

'How much did you lend him, sir?'

From the appeal in Michael's eyes he knew at once that this was important. But how was it important? Was he supposed to increase or decrease the amount? He had to be specific; to feign ignorance of the exact sum would merely confirm any suspicions that Michael had already aroused.

'Fifty pounds,' he said. The truth was safer than a wild guess.

'Exactly fifty pounds?'

'Yes.'

'You wouldn't know the numbers, of course? No. When did you draw the money from the bank, sir?'

Desmond smiled genially. 'I didn't draw it from the bank, Inspector. Not in a lump sum, which is what I presume you mean. That was a little nest-egg I've been saving up. Mr Lane was temporarily embarrassed financially — I believe that is the correct expression — so I let it loose to earn its keep, as it were. But it'll be back — I hope!'

'I see. Did Mr Lane say why he needed the money?'

'No.'

'H'm! I take it you and he are very close friends?'

'We're friends, yes.'

There was a short silence. Jim Watkins hastily reviewed in his mind which of his own friends would lend him fifty quid and no questions asked, and decided that the aristocracy were more trusting than the common run. Then Pitt said, 'That seems to be all, sir. No need to keep you any longer, thank you. You'll want to be getting back to the hotel.'

Was that a hint? What he really wanted was to talk to Michael, to find out what had gone wrong. But had they finished with Michael? Was he free to leave?

'Not just yet,' Pitt said, when the

question was put to him. 'I don't think I should wait if I were you, Mr Farrel.'

Desmond nodded awkwardly to Michael, and left the room. Pitt went with him to the front door, and stood watching him as he crossed the road and disappeared into the darkness of the common. Then he walked thoughtfully back into the station.

Michael had maintained a gloomy silence during the Inspector's short absence. He sat hunched forward on a hard chair, the lock of hair over his face, and greeted the Inspector's return with a scowl.

'Fifty pounds, Mr Lane,' Pitt said. 'Well, that accounts for part of the money. Where did the rest come from?'

But Michael had taken his cue from Desmond.

'That happens to be my own, Inspector. It wasn't enough for — for what I needed, so I borrowed the rest from Mr Farrel. I'd have explained that at the office if Mr Farrel had not asked me to keep it to myself.'

'H'm! Mr Farrel is obviously a

gentleman who likes to do good by stealth. What did you want the money for, sir?'

'That's my business,' Michael said firmly.

Pitt admitted that it was, though he did not say so. After a few more questions they let him go, albeit reluctantly. 'He's the boy, all right,' Pitt said when, some minutes later, he and Jim Watkins came out of the police station. 'But there's not enough evidence yet to charge him. We couldn't have made it stick.'

The Sergeant agreed, shivering at the sudden blast of cold air that greeted them. 'There was about thirty quid in the envelope,' he said. 'If that's his own, and he *did* bust open the safe at The Elms, then — Hey! What's that?'

'That' was the sound of shouting that came from the direction of the common. 'Could be trouble,' Pitt said, breaking into a run. 'Come on, Jim. Let's see you move.'

Jim moved, streaking ahead of his superior officer. But they found, as Elizabeth had found on the previous night, that it was not easy to hurry over the uneven, rutted ground. The shouting had ceased, but they stumbled on, their torches flashing erratically as they went — until a beam of light shone suddenly, and behind it they glimpsed the figure of Desmond Farrel.

He looked and sounded angry. His hair was tousled, his upper lip was already beginning to swell. The string of oaths with which he greeted their arrival caused Jim Watkins to revise his views on the aristocracy and gaze at him in admiration mixed with envy.

'What happened?' asked Pitt, flashing his torch in a circle over the common.

'Some bastard cantered up to me out of the dark and socked me on the mouth. Never gave me a chance, blast him.' He bent to dust his knees. 'Thanks for coming to the rescue. But don't waste your time looking for him. He's well away by now.'

'Who was it?' asked the Sergeant.

'Damned if I know. I never got a proper squint at him. Dropped the torch in the first round.'

'You mean he waltzed up to you, exchanged a few blows, and then cleared off? Just like that?' Pitt said sceptically.

'Yes. And exchanged is right, Inspector. He didn't have it all his own way; I fancy he'll have a black eye to-morrow. If you see one knocking around let me know. I'd like to black the other.'

'Who did the shouting?'

'I did.' Desmond touched his lip gingerly. 'That's going to be sore to-night, damn it!' A cautious grin spread over his face. 'It was good of you chaps to join the party, but I rather fancy it's a private one. A domestic issue, you might say.'

He said goodnight and stalked off jauntily into the darkness. In silence the two detectives watched the beam of his torch until it vanished.

'Becoming quite a battleground, the common,' Watkins said.

'It is indeed.' Pitt sounded thoughtful. 'How long after Farrel left the station did we hear him shout?'

'Seven or eight minutes, I'd say.'

'H'm. And three minutes at the most to get this far. What was he doing after that?'

'A little light sparring, according to him.'

'For four minutes? Not him. A little argument first, I fancy. The sparring came later.'

'So he's lying, eh?'

'So he's lying. He knows damned well who his assailant was. But why deny it?'

'There's a school of thought,' Watkins said, 'which believes in a man fighting his own battles. I admit it's out of fashion these days, but maybe Farrel is old-fashioned enough to belong to it.'

'Perhaps,' Pitt admitted. 'He seems a self-reliant young man. All the same, I'd like to know just how domestic the issue was.'

* * *

Ted Williams was a man with a grievance. The murder of Charlotte Lane had erupted into his life like a bright and shining star promising untold glory. He it was who had first suspected that a crime had been committed (that Walter and Mrs Green might justly claim this distinction was of no account); he it was who had made the first inquiries, had taken upon himself to search the house; he it was who had actually found the body. Yet where was the expected praise, the hints at preferment? A Sergeant had usurped his charge, and he himself was back with the drunks and the motorists, pedalling the lanes as if nothing had occurred to break the law-abiding monotony of Milford Cross.

At that moment he was not pedalling, but pushing; his bicycle had developed a puncture. The dark lane that bordered the west side of the common was as gloomy as his thoughts. But two hundred yards ahead of him, at the corner of Bells Lane, was the first street-lamp, and beyond that the village. He would be able to dump the useless cycle at the station, and perhaps warm himself with a cup of tea.

A man crossed the road hurriedly from the common and paused under the lamp to fumble in his raincoat pockets. Williams recognized him as Michael Lane; and, because everything and everybody connected with Charlotte Lane was of interest to the constable, he quickened his step. Something fell from the young man's pocket, there was the flare of a match as he lit a cigarette; and then he was off down Bells Lane towards his home.

Reaching the corner, Williams propped his cycle against the lamp-post and picked up the object which Michael had dropped. It was a glove. He put it in his pocket; the young man would be almost home by now, and the constable had no intention of making a detour to return his property. That could be done in the morning.

He had already resumed his plodding when memory jolted him into activity. Almost dropping the cycle in his haste, he whipped the glove from his pocket and examined it by the light of his torch.

The fastener was missing.

No longer plodding, the light of battle in his eye, Constable Williams made for the police station. If that glove didn't demonstrate his worth to his superior officers nothing ever would.

11

A Nice Choice in Lies

As he went down the corridor Desmond saw his father come out of Elizabeth's room. Surprised, he slipped hastily into his own; he did not wish to meet his father just then. With his ear to the door, he stood listening to the receding footsteps. Not until they were well down the stairs did he come out.

Elizabeth was up and dressed. She exclaimed in dismay when she saw him.

'What have you done to your lip, Desmond? It's all swollen.'

He told her what he had told the Inspector; he had considered being more explicit, but had rejected it as unwise. Elizabeth would insist on his telling the police all he knew — might even, if he refused, tell them herself — and this was something he had to handle alone.

'You don't think it was the same man

who attacked me, do you?' she asked, troubled.

'Could be.' He did not want to discuss it. 'What did the old man want?'

'He didn't want anything.' Elizabeth looked pleased. 'He's really rather a pet, darling, when you get to know him. That sounds silly, doesn't it — me telling you, I mean? But he always used to scare me, and now he doesn't. He was sweet this afternoon. He came in to see how I was, and we chatted for ages. You know, I think he's beginning to like me.'

'So he should. What did you talk about?'

'Oh, all sorts of things. You, him, me, the hotel. I didn't realize he could be so — so human. And considerate.' She picked up a small bottle from the bedside table. 'He gave me these.'

'What are they?'

'Sleeping tablets. I told him I wasn't sleeping well; this wretched bruise keeps me awake half the night.' She touched her forehead gingerly. 'I like to sleep on my tummy. Did you know that?'

'No. That's one of the things I'm

looking forward to discovering. Where did he get the tablets from?'

'They're his. He says they act like magic. The doctor gave them to him for his insomnia.'

'I didn't know he suffered from insomnia,' Desmond said. He wondered how many other things about his father were unknown to him. Theirs was not an intimate relationship.

'Well, he does.' Her expressive face was suddenly troubled. 'Desmond, do you think some one knows about our being married — some one other than Dulcie, I mean — and that's why you and I have been singled out for attack? Otherwise — well, why should it just be us and not the others?'

'Their turn may come,' he said. And then, again heading her off, 'Why are you all dressed up? Expecting visitors?'

She laughed. 'Only you. Don't you approve? I'm a little tired of pyjamas.'

He grinned. 'I saw nothing wrong with them,' he said, kissing her.

Mr Farrel was more polite than Dulcie; he knocked before entering. 'I don't know what you and that Inspector are up to, Desmond,' he said plaintively, 'but he's here again. And young Michael Lane is with him.'

'But it's only about an hour since I left them,' Desmond protested.

Mr Farrel winced at the sight of his swollen lip. 'You apparently had quite an argument with them, too,' he said.

Again Desmond told his story. Then, to forestall further comment, he said quickly, 'What does the Inspector want, Dad?'

'To see you.' Farrel turned to the girl. 'You too, my dear. Do I send them up, or will you come down?'

Elizabeth glanced at her husband. He said, frowning, 'Better send them up. It'll be easier for Elizabeth.'

His father studied them for a moment. Then he nodded and left.

Desmond said quickly, 'I don't know what all this is about, darling, but I do know that Michael seems to be in trouble. That's why the police sent for me earlier. I hoped I'd put him in the clear; but if I didn't — ' He shrugged. 'Well, Michael's not a very stable character, is he? If they really put the wind up him he may have talked out of turn.'

Elizabeth nodded. She knew Michael even better than did Desmond. But to her it did not seem to matter greatly what Michael might tell the police. From the start she had maintained that truth could not hurt them. The truth about their hoax on Aunt Charlotte, that was; she could appreciate the wisdom of saying nothing about her marriage. And that had come later, it could have no connexion with the murder.

And yet — would she have been willing to tell the *whole* truth about Aunt Charlotte?

'Do they think Michael killed Aunt Charlotte?' she asked.

'I don't know. Perhaps.'

Inspector Pitt looked menacingly angry. With him was Michael, wild of eye yet guiltily defiant, and behind them Alan Torreck. At Desmond's and Elizabeth's surprised greetings Alan shook his head. He was as mystified as they.

Pitt gave them no opportunity for

consultation. 'I understand there has been a conspiracy of silence in connexion with Charlotte Lane's murder,' he said, his voice unpleasantly terse. 'Some kind of stupid practical joke, Mr Lane tells me. He has refused to elaborate except in the presence of you all, and so — '

'I *had* to tell them,' Michael burst out. His dark skin looked more grey than olive, there was a desperate appeal in his voice and eyes that Elizabeth, although she had no love for him, found it difficult to resist. 'I know I should have warned you first, but they didn't give me a chance. They found out that I was in Aunt Charlotte's house that night, and . . . and . . . ' He turned fiercely on Desmond and Alan, who were sitting on the bed with Elizabeth. 'Stop looking at me like that I couldn't help it, I tell you. It was that or — '

Pitt said sharply, 'That will do, Mr Lane.'

Michael turned to stare at him. For a moment it looked as though he were about to offer physical violence. Then the wild eyes became dull, and he nodded and sat down abruptly.

The others were stunned; not so much at his treachery as at the guilt his admission seemed to imply. Was he now trying to implicate them?

Alan said, 'If this is to be the showdown, Inspector, one member of the gang is missing. Did you know that?'

Pitt nodded. 'Mr Poulton will be here directly,' he said.

Bruce was. He came in with Sergeant Watkins, looking nervous as well as mystified. His nervousness increased when he saw them. Even Bruce's wits were quick enough to grasp the significance of that assembly.

Pitt was impatient. Scarcely waiting for the door to close, and indifferent to the fact that there were not enough chairs in the room, he said briskly, 'Well, gentlemen, do I get the truth now?'

It was Alan who told him, after a quick glance at Desmond for confirmation. Listening to him, the Inspector studied the five young people in turn. The girl's eyes were fixed intently on the speaker's face, as though she were seeing him for the first time and needed to impress every feature on her memory. She must have heard his voice; but the words he spoke seemed to be of little moment to her, for the soft half-smile on her lips never faded. Desmond Farrel stared fixedly ahead; occasionally he frowned at some particularly damning revelation, but he did not turn his head or his eyes. Bruce Poulton leaned heavily against the wall, obviously uncomfortable in both mind and body. He too watched the speaker's face, nervously anticipating each point, his eyes darting to the Inspector as it was made in an attempt to estimate its effect. Michael Lane sat slumped forward in his chair, staring glassily at the carpet, his head supported by his hands.

Alan spoke quietly and well, attempting neither to minimize the more damaging points nor to stress the redeeming. He dealt only with the plans they had made, and his own part in trying to carry them out. Not once did he refer to the others for confirmation, and not once was he interrupted.

When he had done Pitt said, 'Thank

you, sir,' and was again silent. None of the others spoke. The silence became oppressive; there were protesting squeaks from the bed as the bodies on it moved restlessly, the squeal of Bruce's rubber-shod sole as he shifted his position against the wall. Their breathing seemed suddenly louder.

'Murder never aroused much hilarity in me,' Pitt said grimly. 'I don't see it as a subject for joking. Particularly when, as in this case, the wish appears to have fathered the thought.' Elizabeth was not sure what he meant by this; but he was looking directly at her as he spoke, and she flushed guiltily. 'Fathered the deed as well, apparently,' he added.

It was Alan, not the girl herself, who came to her rescue. 'Miss Messager was against it from the beginning,' he said, with more heat than before. 'It was to please her that we watered it down. Don't start accusing her.'

'I'm not accusing anyone yet,' Pitt said. He turned to Michael, who still sat staring at the floor. 'You sent that telegram, Mr Lane?'

At the sound of his own name Michael started and looked up. 'I got a friend in Town to send it for me,' he said sullenly.

His sullenness seemed to jerk the Inspector into anger.

'As I understand it, that completed your obligations under the conspiracy. You had no occasion to call at The Elms on Thursday evening. Why did you?'

He rapped the question out so sharply that Michael, whose morale had already been sapped by two previous grillings that day, became paralysed by terror. He stared at the Inspector wild-eyed, the lock of flopping hair unheeded. His mouth was working, but the sounds that came from it were unintelligible.

His friends watched him, sickened yet fascinated. For all of them it was their first glimpse of what fear could do to a man. But it was no new spectacle to the two detectives; they waited patiently, unmoved. And presently the shuddering limbs were still, the slack mouth tightened. Haltingly at first, more smoothly as his self-control returned, Michael began to talk.

Up to a point his story was the same as he had told it to Desmond the previous night. Where it differed was in the later stages. After seeing the six forty-five train depart he had caught the six fifty-two bus back to Milford Cross. But he had left it at the outskirts of the village, realizing that, since Aunt Charlotte had not been on the train, she was probably still at home.

'So you got to the house at about ten past seven,' said Watkins, who by now knew most of the local bus timetable by heart.

'Yes.' Michael paused, trying to recapture the thread thus broken. 'The house was in darkness, but I rang the front-door bell just the same. I thought, you see, that Elizabeth must be in; she was expecting some of us. But no one answered the bell.'

'And then?' Pitt asked.

'I went round to the back. I thought she might be in the kitchen. But there were no lights showing at the back either.' He stopped, glanced quickly at the Inspector and away again, and said, 'The back door was open.'

'Open — or unlocked?'

'Well, closed. Not locked. It opened when I pushed it.'

'So you went in. And then?'

'Then' was the hard part, the part he didn't want to tell. He licked his lips furtively and said, 'There was no one in the downstair rooms; I had the house to myself. And when I went into the study and saw Aunt Charlotte's picture — '

He hesitated so long here that Pitt prompted him. 'You knew the safe was behind it?'

'Yes.' Everywhere he looked there were faces, accusing faces. 'I was hard up, and — ' He gulped. 'I dropped the picture when I took it down; the glass broke. I tried to open the safe — I wasn't going to take all the money, only what I needed. And why shouldn't I?' he demanded hysterically, his voice rising. 'She owed it to me; it was mine as much as hers. If she hadn't turned Uncle Edward against us I'd have had my share. She had no right — '

'Did you open the safe?' Pitt said sharply.

'No. I couldn't. There was nothing to force it with.' His voice was lower now. It sank almost to a whisper as he said, 'And then — well, I suppose I panicked. I didn't know when Elizabeth would be back, or — or Aunt Charlotte. I wanted to get away. I picked up the picture and the few pieces of glass, took them out to the yard, and dropped them down the well. Then I went home.'

The whisper faded to a sigh and died.

Pitt said, 'You didn't destroy that picture deliberately, because of your hatred of Mrs Lane?'

'No, I didn't.' Now that he had told them there was more vitality in his voice. He sat up, flicking back the recalcitrant lock of hair with the old impatient gesture. 'And I didn't kill her either. She must have been dead long before I got to the house.'

'Why do you say that?'

'Because she wasn't there, that's why. I tell you, the house was empty.' He turned angrily to Bruce. 'You know that. You were there before me. Why don't you tell them?'

The Inspector's alert eyes shifted to the blond young man leaning uncomfortably against the wall.

'Yes, Mr Poulton,' he said softly. 'Why don't you tell us?'

Bruce stepped away from the wall. His face was flushed. He said stiffly, 'I called at the house just before half-past six. No lights were showing, and no one answered my ring. So I came away.'

'Did you also try the back door?'

'No.'

'And was your visit connected with this so-called practical joke?'

'No.' And, as Pitt continued to regard him expectantly, 'I wanted to see Miss Messager.'

What was it about the girl, Pitt wondered, that set all these young men running after her? Not her looks; the Rivers girl was twice as pretty. But the Rivers girl, of course, wasn't an heiress. Or a presumed heiress.

He wondered if she had told them.

'Anything further to add to that, Mr

Poulton?' he asked. 'Did you see anyone near the house?'

'No.' Bruce hesitated. 'But I thought I heard some one. In the garden.'

'Whereabouts in the garden?'

'Down towards the copse. But the noise could have been made by the wind. It was blowing quite hard that evening.'

Pitt looked inquiringly at Alan, who shook his head. 'Not guilty, Inspector. I paid only the one visit, and that was after nine.'

'That all, Mr Poulton?'

For the first time since he had entered the room Bruce looked at Desmond. But Desmond was still staring hard at the wall, and did not see the look.

Bruce said, 'I heard a car coming from the direction of Tanbury. It turned out to be Desmond Farrel's Wolseley. He pulled up at the corner and gave me a lift back here.'

'Quite right, Inspector,' Desmond said. 'I too was on my way to see Miss Messager — on duty, as it were. I was the chap, you may remember, who was supposed to collect something of Mrs

Lane's and dump it near the river. I was about to turn into the lane when I saw Mr Poulton.'

'You didn't call at the house, then?'

'No.'

'So you phoned Miss Messager later?'

'No, she phoned me. You asked me that before, Inspector. You wouldn't be trying to fool me by any chance, would you? Not that it seems to matter who phoned whom.'

Pitt said sharply, 'Any fooling that's been done, Mr Farrel, has been done by you and your friends. It's because of your irresponsible conduct and your disregard for the truth that I'm now having to waste time going over old ground. For instance, both you and Mr Lane here told me you gave him a lift into Tanbury on Thursday evening. We now know you did no such thing. So what?'

Surprisingly Desmond smiled.

'*Touché*, Inspector. I apologize. But as for Thursday, I did exactly as I said — except that Mr Lane wasn't with me, of course.'

Pitt frowned. There was something

wrong there; what was it? Maybe it would come to him later. He turned to Elizabeth. 'Have you anything to add to this spate of confession?' he asked.

'No, I don't think so,' she said.

'Are you sure, Miss Messager? Perhaps I'm old-fashioned, but your apparent unconcern at your aunt's disappearance shocks me. The first telegram you knew to be a hoax. Good enough. I might even allow you the somewhat crudely worded note pushed under the mat. A little too melodramatic to be real, don't you think, Mr Torreck?' Alan bowed a polite agreement. 'But the second telegram and the phone call — they *had* to be genuine. And yet — still no alarm?'

'It was late,' she said uneasily.

'Yes, miss, it was late. But crime doesn't keep regular hours, and neither do the police. It was not too late to phone. However, you saw Constable Williams the next day — at his request, not yours — and then went off for the day. Where? Urgent business?'

'No,' said Elizabeth, and told him. As she spoke of the lunch she and Desmond had eaten at the Speckled Trout she remembered how happy they had been, that they would soon be going back there for a whole week-end. It cheered her a little to think of it.

'Just an outing, eh?' Pitt grunted. 'I must say I find that a trifle unnatural under the circumstances, miss.'

Of course he found it unnatural, thought the girl. But, even if she were free to tell him the truth, how could she expect a policeman, whose business was crime and who looked only for the criminal in every out-of-the-way incident, to understand her state of mind on that day? It was *her* day, her very first day as a wife. In a way it was her honeymoon. How could there be room in her mind that day for Aunt Charlotte and policemen?

'There was nothing I could do to help,' she said weakly.

He nodded, not in agreement but as though that was the answer he had expected. But he did not smile at her as he had smiled the first time they had met, and she felt vaguely unhappy that he should so obviously think ill of her.

'Well, that seems to be that.' He stood up. 'I don't intend to lecture the lot of you on the stupidity of your behaviour — though I've no doubt others will have plenty to say later. But how five presumably intelligent people — ' He let out a gusty sigh. 'Good night, Miss Messager. Mr Lane, I must ask you to return to the station with us, I'm afraid.'

Fear had come back to Michael in full volume; he believed arrest to be imminent. But he followed the tall figure of the Inspector docilely enough, with the unusually silent Watkins close behind. In the room they had left the four who remained looked at each other askance, each reluctant to be the first to break the silence, to set the tone of the discussion that must follow. The threat implied in the Inspector's parting admonition — that the law had not yet finished with them — was something none could ignore.

Desmond stood irresolute. Then, with no word of explanation, he hurried from the room. The little party of three was outside his own door as he joined it, and he plucked impetuously at the Inspector's sleeve.

'May I have a word with you, Inspector? In private?'

Pitt looked at him, sizing him up. He did not want to be side-tracked by irrelevancies. Then he nodded to the Sergeant and followed Desmond into the latter's room.

'Keep it short, please, Mr Farrel,' he said.

'All right. It's just that I thought you were a little hard on Miss Messager,' Desmond told him.

Pitt's anger broke over him like a storm.

'Good God, man! Is that all you wanted to say? Hard? Why, if I had my way I'd clap the whole damned lot of you into gaol. You concoct some idiotic practical joke, that no one in his right senses could consider even slightly humorous — and then, when it goes sour on you and a woman is murdered, you haven't the guts or the decency to own up. You let the police waste precious time following false trails that never should have been laid, and which a word from you could have prevented. Hard!' He drew a deep breath. 'Good night, Mr Farrel.'

'Please!' Desmond said. 'Give me a chance to explain. I wanted you to understand *why* Miss Messager seemed so — so callous. I thought it might help if you had the right slant on that.'

Pitt had paused with his hand on the door-knob. Now he came back into the room.

'Go on,' he said tersely.

'Well, you know that Miss Messager and her aunt didn't get on; every one in the village must have told you about the rows they had. But it was all second-hand information spread by Mrs Green, and I wouldn't like to guess how much she exaggerated. It's perfectly true that Elizabeth — Miss Messager — disliked her aunt; she's often admitted it. But you can dislike a person without rowing, can't you?'

'I don't see where this is leading,' Pitt said impatiently.

'No,' Desmond admitted. 'I'm rather off the track. That's because you got me flustered. What I was leading up to is that Miss Messager is a pretty forthright person. She speaks and acts as she feels.'

'Are you suggesting that, because she felt like murdering her aunt, she did so?' Pitt asked, astonished. The expected speech for the defence seemed to be turning into a speech for the prosecution.

'Good Heavens, no! I'm saying that she's no hypocrite. Hating Aunt Charlotte the way she did, it wasn't in her nature to assume a concern she didn't in fact feel. That's *one* reason for what you call her unnatural behaviour. The other is that she didn't believe that her aunt *was* missing. Not until the body was found. She thought it was a hoax.'

'At first, yes. But not later. Not after the second telegram.'

'Yes, she did. Even after the second telegram.' Desmond told him of the discussion he had had with Elizabeth at the Speckled Trout, and of her theory that Mrs Green had invented the second telegram and the phone call from Mrs

Donelly. 'We couldn't think of any motive that might have prompted the woman to play such a trick, unless it was that she disliked Elizabeth and wanted to frighten her. But, apart from motive, the idea made sense at the time.'

Pitt was not impressed, and said so. What he did *not* say was that he suspected Desmond must have had a further motive for inveigling him into his room; the one given was too thin. Yet what was this other motive? To separate him from Michael Lane, so that the latter might attempt an escape? If so he didn't know Jim Watkins. But because there was something here that he could not fathom the Inspector was uneasy. He would have waited no longer had he not remembered that previous statement of Desmond's which had puzzled him. Now he had spotted the flaw.

'Last night, Mr Farrel, you stated that you had to be back here by six-thirty on Thursday evening? Was that the truth?'

'Certainly it was. I told you, I just about made it.'

'Yes. But to-night you also told me that

you had intended to call at The Elms on your way back. You were going to lay some sort of false trail by the river, I believe.'

'Yes. So I would have done if Miss Messager had been at home. But she wasn't, and I didn't.' Desmond was puzzled. 'I don't see what you're getting at, Inspector. There's nothing contradictory there, surely?'

'Isn't there? You had to be back by six-thirty — and you were. But you would have been considerably later than that if you had done what you had planned to do. So either you lied about the time you had to be back, or you lied about your plans, or you lied about the times at which you left Tanbury and arrived at The Elms.' Pitt pulled thoughfully at his nose. 'That's a nice choice in lies, Mr Farrel. Take your pick.'

Desmond was silent. He did not want to admit that he had lied at all; however insignificant the lie might be, it remained a lie, it would still be a canker of suspicion in the minds of the police. But which to choose? All except one could be checked — probably had been checked — and that one was the most damning of all. His father would confirm the time he had been due to return, his friends the tasks that had been allotted to him. That left him no choice.

He said, apparently inconsequentially, 'Did the tobacconist confirm that I called in at his place that evening?'

It was not inconsequential to the Inspector.

'He did. You were there some time between five-thirty and five forty-five. Does that help you to make up your mind? Or do I have to point out that, even if we accept the latter time, you could still have been at The Elms shortly after six o'clock?'

Desmond grimaced. 'I know,' he said frankly. 'That's why I was more than willing to supply Mr Lane with the alibi he needed. It gave me one too — though I didn't let him know that. As a matter of fact, Inspector, I had aimed to be at The Elms by six-fifteen. Mrs Lane should have left by then, I thought, and it would give me just enough time to do what I had to do. But I didn't make it. The car died on me.'

The other's eyebrows lifted slightly. 'Where and when?' he asked succinctly.

The reply was equally brief. 'In the car park. It wouldn't start. Ignition trouble.'

Pitt was not mechanically minded. 'Ignition' and 'fuel' were, he knew, the most quoted sources of trouble, and equally vague. But he decided not to press for a more exact diagnosis. It would probably have no meaning for him, and Watkins and Lane were waiting.

He said severely, 'This is the third different account of that journey I have had from you in the space of twenty-four hours, Mr Farrel. I would suggest a stricter adherence to the truth in future, or you'll find yourself in serious trouble. Will you come down to the station to-morrow, please, and sign your statement? And read it carefully first — in your own interests.'

'I'm sorry,' Desmond said humbly — and humility was strange to him. 'Can I offer you a drink before you go? You must need one.'

‘I do, sir. But you and your friends are so fond of wasting my time that you leave me none to spare.’ Again his hand was on the door-knob, and again he paused. ‘By the way, why was it so important that you should be here by six-thirty that evening?’

‘That’s when the bar starts to fill up,’ Desmond said, surprised. ‘And my father was out.’

12

An Evening full of Surprises

It was at Elizabeth's invitation, given when she heard that his father was away in London, that Alan Torreck stayed to dinner at the hotel. Her husband's assertion that Alan was in love with her continued to intrigue Elizabeth; she wanted to discover for herself the truth of that assertion. She even exerted herself, when Bruce had left them and she and Alan were alone in her room, to lure him into declaring his love; perversely, the fact that she was already married and unable to take advantage of any offer he might make served merely to whet her curiosity. But either Desmond had been mistaken or Alan possessed an obstinate determination to remain a bachelor. All her blandishments and wiles failed to draw from him either word or look which might be interpreted as encouragement.

Dinner was not a gay meal. Desmond's attempts at cheerfulness were spasmodic; mainly he ate in silence, or discussed with Alan the possible significance of Michael's impending arrest. They had no doubt about that, and little sympathy for the victim; their main concern lay in how the arrest would affect themselves. Since they had all been partners in the original conspiracy, it seemed unlikely that they would escape unscathed. Elizabeth, still feeling put out by her inability to break down Alan's barrier of reserve, was in a fretful mood. She railed at them for their cold-blooded and selfish attitude towards Michael's probable arrest; and then, when Alan pointed out that arrest did not necessarily imply guilt, that Michael might be the victim of his own stupidity, she perversely insisted that of course he was guilty — if not of murder, then of assault and attempted robbery at the very least. It had to be Michael or Bruce, she said. Who else was there?

'All of us,' Alan declared bluntly. 'Desmond, yourself, myself. We none of us have a watertight alibi; and all of us had good reason, from the police view-point, to wish Aunt Charlotte dead. Well, perhaps not Desmond. But you and I certainly.'

'You needn't leave me out,' Desmond said. 'I disliked her as much as anyone. No, Bruce is the chap who is the enigma here. He was at the house before Michael, by his own admission; and I can't say he looked particularly delighted when I pulled up to offer him a lift. Quite the reverse. At the time I put that down to discomfiture at having been discovered paying court to Elizabeth immediately Aunt Charlotte was out of the way; he had no other reason to be there. If only he had a motive he'd be a very healthy candidate. But he hasn't. He's not even hard up, like the rest of us; he's careful with money, is Bruce. And his father must be doing pretty well; he's collared most of the meat trade round here.'

'Of course Bruce had a motive,' Elizabeth said, impetuously disagreeing once more. 'He hated Aunt Charlotte like poison.'

The two men stared at her in astonishment.

'Bruce did?' said Alan. 'Why?'

Reluctantly Elizabeth told them of the snubs her aunt had delighted in inflicting on Bruce, of the deep wound it had made in his pride. She had not meant to tell them, but having said so much there was no alternative.

'That alters the look of things,' Desmond said thoughtfully. 'Do the police know?'

'I shouldn't think so. I haven't told them.'

'And Bruce isn't likely to,' Alan said. 'Still, now that they know he was there that evening they're going to investigate him rather more closely. It may be they'll unearth a lot more he's said nothing about.'

Only a week or so ago, thought Elizabeth, they had been friends; now they had thrown Michael to the wolves, and were preparing to do the same with Bruce. Or had they never been friends? Were they just people who had come together for companionship, but with no real feeling for one another? How would Desmond react if it seemed that Alan were guilty — or vice versa?

Elizabeth went up to her room immediately after the meal. Desmond and Alan, still at the table, saw her stop to talk to George Farrel on the way. Desmond, although he could not hear what was said, again noted with surprise his father's increased friendliness towards the girl. Dulcie, who was at the same table, completely ignored her.

His eyes intent on his companion's face, Desmond said, 'Michael tells me you saw me in the village Thursday afternoon.'

'Did I?' Alan frowned. 'Yes, that's right. Near the bus stop. Why?'

'I was wondering how you came to be there, that's all. That was at five-fifteen, and you don't usually knock off till five-thirty.'

There was a strained silence. Then Alan said, 'I'd gone out to buy some tobacco for my father. He intended working late that evening.' The frown deepened. 'Are you suggesting there was something fishy in my being there at that time?'

'No, of course not. In fact, I gather the boot's on the other foot. From what Michael said I got the impression that you were suspicious of *me*.'

'Then you've got it wrong. I wasn't suspicious of anyone.'

'Good. Actually, I was there to collect a parcel off the bus. Unfortunately, it didn't turn up — which was why I had to go into Tanbury that evening.'

Alan nodded, and began to draw faint lines on the table-cloth with the prongs of a fork. Presently he said, 'That was the bus Elizabeth said she caught, wasn't it? Did you see her?'

Desmond stared at him. 'No. No, I didn't. Did you?'

'No. But I was too far away to distinguish people inside it.' He pulled absent-mindedly at his moustache. 'There weren't many on it, were there?'

'No. About half a dozen.'

They did not look at each other. Desmond also picked up a fork. He balanced it on one finger, watching it move gently up and down. Then, with an oath, he slapped it down on the table.

'This is damned ridiculous!' he said. 'Any moment now and we'll start suspecting Elizabeth. Of course she was on the bus; I just didn't see her, that's all.' He stood up. 'Come on, let's go into the bar and have a drink.'

There had been few people in the dining-room, but the saloon bar was crowded. Desmond was soon busy behind the bar, and Alan, left to his own devices, debated with himself whether to stay or go home. He could not really afford an evening's drinking, yet the cheerlessness of home without his father did not appeal to him; he wanted company. It was not left to him to decide, however. He was well known and liked in the village, and the crowd in the bar, already cheery, soon swallowed him up.

It was shortly after nine o'clock that he saw Bruce Poulton beckoning to him from the doorway. Excusing himself from the group around him, Alan obeyed the signal.

Bruce's mien was grimly purposeful. 'What's up?' Alan asked. 'Anything wrong? Is it about Michael?'

'I want a word with Desmond,' Bruce said.

Alan gaped at him. 'Is that all? What's stopping you, then? He's in the bar. Why call on me?'

Bruce shook his blond head. 'I'm not going in there,' he said. 'I'll talk to him outside.'

Alan stared at him doubtfully. 'You're not looking for trouble, are you?' he asked, mistrusting the other's demeanour. 'I noticed you weren't exactly matey at our little get-together upstairs this evening. What's biting you, Bruce?'

'I want to talk to Desmond, that's all. Tell him, will you?'

'I'm damned if I will!' And then, relaxing, 'Oh, come off it, you idiot! Desmond can't leave the bar now, he's busy. Stop being so damned mysterious and aloof and come in and have a drink. If you must talk to Desmond in private you'll have to wait until closing time.'

'Then I'll wait.' Bruce's body was as taut as his voice. 'Tell him I'll be out in the front.'

Troubled, Alan returned to the bar. What the hell was wrong now? Bruce was a moody chap at the best of times; give him something big to chew on, like Aunt Charlotte's murder, and he might turn really nasty. Was he turning nasty now? Perhaps Desmond would know what was biting him.

But Desmond did not know. 'Bruce and I have never really hit it off,' he told Alan, when the latter eventually managed to talk with him privately. 'For some reason he's always seemed a bit suspicious of me. Jealous, almost — though the Lord knows why.' I do, Alan reflected; but we won't go into that now. 'Did he seem mad at me? I mean, is he now striding up and down outside with balled fists all set to sock me as soon as I show up? If so I think I'll decline the invitation.' Desmond grinned. 'I reckon if Bruce hits you you stay hit.'

'Shall I tell him that?'

'No. I'd better see him, I suppose; apart from any other reason, I'm curious. But not now; not until the bar closes. Tell him he can wait in the bar, or the lounge, or the drive, or any damned place he pleases. It's all the same to me.' He had spoken seriously; now he smiled. 'And stick around, Alan, will you? I might be glad of your company later. I never did see any sense in challenging the odds.'

Alan went out to the porch, but there was no sign of Bruce in the large area of light thrown by the floodlights. I suppose he doesn't want anyone to see him hanging around, he thought, and is skulking somewhere out there in the dark. Well, let him skulk; I'm damned if I'm going to search for him. If he insists on behaving like a boor he can have the same treatment.

Desmond was in full accord with this sentiment when he heard it. 'Do him good,' he said cheerfully. 'Cool him down.'

But Alan was not so sure. Bruce was not the cooling type; it might be that the enforced wait would serve rather to swell the anger, or irritation, or whatever it was that had motivated his visit.

During the remainder of the evening Alan paid little attention to the talk that went on around him. Every time he saw Desmond leave the bar he experienced an impulse to go after him; there was always the possibility, he thought, that Desmond's curiosity had overcome his caution, that he had gone out alone to discover what had brought Bruce to the hotel. But he restrained his impulse. Desmond's absences were, he knew, connected with the running of the hotel. He could not be permanently in the bar.

Dulcie, who normally sought excuses to be nowhere else, came in only once that evening. She gave Alan the same warm, subtly inviting smile that she reserved for all personable young men, but he knew that it was mainly mechanical and meaningless in his case. He had never been one of Dulcie's favourites — perhaps for the reason that he had never sought that distinction. Desmond, he knew, stood high in her regard. Yet even Desmond was not in favour that evening, for the girl scarcely looked in his direction during the few minutes she was there.

George Farrel too made only a brief

appearance. Alan — who, like most of Desmond's friends, stood much in awe of the Honourable George — thought, as he had often thought before, that Desmond was more likely to make a success of the hotel business than was his father. George Farrel seldom unbent; he took offence too easily, and seemed to resent the necessity of having to earn a livelihood by pandering to the whims and appetites of his fellow-creatures. That evening his back and his mood were even more rigid than usual. Had he any suspicion that his son might be involved in the mystery surrounding the murder? Aunt Charlotte set us all by the ears while she was alive, Alan thought, and she's still doing it after her death.

There was the usual rush to complete the last orders at closing time, the same cheery goodnights, the usual reluctant leavers who had to be tactfully but firmly helped on their way. Alan watched the scene with rising tension. Now for the showdown, he thought, as he and Desmond waited in the hall until the little knots of chattering people on the drive had broken up and departed, until the last car had gone and the big floodlights had been switched off.

'Come on,' Desmond said. 'Let's see what the big bad wolf has in store for us.'

He went through the swing door with Alan close behind him, and for a few moments the two young men stood expectantly at the top of the wide steps. Now that the floodlights were off there was only the light from the hotel windows to illumine the drive. They could not see him, but Bruce might be very near.

'Well, if he wants me here I am,' Desmond said. Into the darkness he called softly, 'Okay, Bruce. What is it?'

They waited. There was no sound or movement except those caused by the blustering wind. 'Perhaps I ought not to be on view,' Alan said doubtfully. 'He was very insistent that he should see you alone.'

'Oh, come off it, Alan!' Desmond protested. 'He can at least show himself, can't he? What am I supposed to do? Go down into the arena and wait for the lion to pounce? Don't be so damned melodramatic.'

'It's not me who's melodramatic, it's Bruce. Don't get stuck into me.'

Desmond swore, but without any great depth of feeling.

'Damn the fellow! I don't intend to hang around half the night waiting for him to say his little piece. Tell you what, Alan. You stay here, and I'll go down the drive and give him a hail from there. If he doesn't come forward then he's had it.'

'And if he does come forward?'

'Keep your ears cocked for the sound of strife,' Desmond said cheerfully. 'If I need reinforcements I'll yell.'

He walked briskly down the steps, paused at the bottom to light a cigarette, and disappeared into the darkness of the drive. The wind drowned the sound of his footsteps on the gravel, but occasionally the glowing end of his cigarette as he drew on it denoted his progress to the watcher on the steps.

'Bruce!' Alan heard him call. A pause, and then again, 'Bruce!'

If there was a reply Alan did not hear it. Presently Desmond reappeared at the steps. 'He's not there,' he said. 'Probably thought better of it and gone home.'

'I can't understand it,' Alan said. 'The way he looked I'd have said he was prepared to wait all night if necessary. Are you quite sure he isn't there?'

Desmond shrugged. 'Look for yourself. Personally, I'm for a large whisky and then bed. It's been quite a day.'

'You've no idea what he wanted?' Alan asked. It seemed an anticlimax.

'Bruce? No idea at all. But he's an odd cuss — odder than ever since Aunt Charlotte's murder. Whether he did her in or not, it has certainly made its mark on him. Now come on in and join me in that drink.'

But as he pushed at the swing door a voice calling from the direction of the road caused them both to turn and stare into the night. There was the sound of running feet — laboured and uneven, as though their owner was in considerable distress. A moment later the unkempt, unhappy figure of Michael Lane staggered into the light surrounding the porch.

'Good Lord!' exclaimed Alan, as the newcomer slowly began to mount the steps. 'What's up, Michael? I thought you — '

He stopped. 'I thought you would be safely tucked away in Tanbury gaol by now' would not, perhaps, have been the kindest of greetings to a man in such obvious distress of mind and body.

Michael muttered something they did not catch. 'He's pretty well done in,' Desmond said. 'Take him into the bar, Alan. I'll nip in and tell Dad we're having a small private party. We don't want him barging in on us.'

Michael looked a mess; hair tousled, tie awry, trousers muddy at the knees, his hands filthy. But his distress was more mental than physical; he was also winded. He slumped wearily into a chair and clutched his bowed head with his hands, heedless of the mud on them. Alan let him be. Not until Desmond had rejoined them and had thrust a large brandy into

Michael's willing grasp, and had poured whiskies for himself and Alan, did they seek to satisfy their curiosity.

'They let you go, then,' Alan said.

Michael took a greedy gulp at the brandy. 'Yes, they let me go,' he said, and coughed. 'Eventually. Surprised, eh?' They hastily denied their surprise. 'Neither am I. I was at first, but now I'm on to their little game. Sort of cat and mouse. They'll pounce again to-morrow — if I'm still around.'

He was still out of breath, but already his manner was calmer. 'How did you get into that state?' Desmond asked, with a glance at Alan. Exactly what, they wondered, had been implied by that final remark?

Michael slowly spread a hand and looked at it. He raised one leg and slapped aimlessly at its muddiness. 'I came a cropper on the common,' he said. 'Hadn't a torch.'

There was silence. It seemed that all had been said. Alan and Desmond were eager for detail, but uncertain how to pose their questions; and Michael was unwilling to anticipate them. He finished his drink, placed the glass reluctantly on the table beside him, and said, 'Can I have a room here for to-night, Desmond?'

The evening, thought Alan, was full of surprises.

'Of course,' Desmond said, as surprised as Alan. 'But why not go home?'

'I haven't a home to go to.' Michael's tone was bitter.

'Not to-night, anyway.'

This time the silence was longer and more strained. At last Alan could curb his curiosity no longer.

'I don't get it, Michael. Or' — as light dawned on him — 'you mean your father has turned you out? Is that it?'

'More correctly, he won't let me in. The front door is barred against me.'

'Aren't you being rather melodramatic?' Desmond asked. 'They may merely have gone to bed. Didn't you try to knock them up?'

'Of course I did. *And* they heard me. But my dear father objects to my close contact with the police, it seems. As for Mother — ' He shrugged. 'She hasn't a will of her own. She can't even open her mouth without his permission.'

'I'm sorry,' Alan said, and meant it. 'Pretty grim, eh? But perhaps he'll have worked off his bile by the morning. Don't let it get you down.'

Michael nodded glumly. 'I'd rather like to go to bed, Desmond,' he said. 'I've had just about enough of this particular Monday.'

'I'll take you up.' Desmond turned to Alan. 'Are you off now, or will you wait until I come down?'

'I'd better go,' Alan said.

But he did not want to go. Michael had depressed him. He thought of the long walk home, the lonely, cheerless cottage. He wanted to stay.

'Are the coppers in yet?' he asked. 'If you have to wait up for them maybe I'll change my mind and keep you company.' He laughed self-consciously. 'I might even follow Michael's lead and stay the night. At least I shan't then have to get my own breakfast in the morning.'

At the reminder that he was about to spend the night under the same roof as the two detectives Michael had already started for the door; he had no wish to meet them again that evening. Desmond gazed thoughtfully at Alan, uncertain of the other's purpose. He noted with some surprise that Alan was blushing. 'Suit yourself,' he said, with no great enthusiasm. 'That's what we're here for.'

As they left the bar the telephone rang in the office. Desmond answered it. When he rejoined them he looked puzzled and worried. 'That was Bruce's father,' he said. 'Bruce hasn't been home, and he wanted to know if he were here.'

Alan looked at his watch. 'It's after eleven. Where the devil can he have got to?'

'Damned if I know. Unless he's wandering round the common working off whatever it was that upset him.'

They were a glum trio as they went up the stairs to the room that was to be Michael's. When Alan and Desmond were alone again Alan said, 'I don't like it, Desmond. Bruce was in an ugly mood, and dead set on seeing you to-night. If he hasn't gone home it's because he still means to do so.'

'What, now? How can he? Once the coppers are in and I've locked up I'm going to bed. Bruce can ring his head off after that.'

'He won't do that,' Alan said. 'He won't have to.' He tugged nervously at his moustache. 'Bruce won't be waiting for you outside, Desmond. He's somewhere in the hotel.'

'Eh? How do you know that?'

'I don't — but I'm damned sure I'm right. He must have slipped in before the bar closed. There are a number of places in which he could hide, aren't there?'

'Yes. But why should he? I didn't refuse to see him.'

'He didn't know that, and he wasn't taking any chances. This way he won't have to. He'll wait until the place is quiet and then come up to your room.' Alan swallowed heavily. 'If I were you, Desmond, I'd lock my door to-night.'

13

Noises in the Night

Elizabeth lay in bed in the dark and listened to the wind. It had a vaguely sinister sound, augmented as it was by the rattling of the open window and the soft shushing of the curtains. She knew that eventually she would have to close the window if she was to have any sleep that night; but it was at the far end of the room from the bed, and for the present she was content to let it rattle.

She had switched off the light at half-past ten; now it was nearly midnight, but she felt no desire to sleep. Later she would take one of Mr Farrel's tablets; but not yet, not until she had settled the problems that troubled her. Desmond had been in to kiss her goodnight; but he had not stayed long, and for that she was glad. There was something furtive about those nocturnal visits of his which worried them both; they were not at their ease together then as they were during the day. Desmond was her husband, yet because of the secrecy surrounding that fact Elizabeth experienced an unpleasant feeling of guilt when he came to her at night. It was even worse when he left. The listening at the door, the slow turning of the handle, the whispered goodnight, filled her with an unreasonable sense of shame.

Most of them have gone to bed now, she thought. She had heard them come upstairs and go to their rooms, and as each door had opened and shut she had tried to place it. But it seemed that there were new guests that night; some of the foot-steps had led, she was sure, to unfamiliar doors. The one on the far side of Desmond's room, for instance; that had hitherto been empty. She had heard Desmond say goodnight to the new occupant, and it had seemed to her that the answering voice had been that of Alan Torreck. But it couldn't have been Alan. Her ears or her imagination had been playing tricks with her.

Or had it been due to her subconscious desire to hear his voice?

She tried to analyse her emotions honestly. After only four days of marriage to Desmond, was she now falling in love with Alan? Surely not. She had known Alan since she was thirteen; if she had been destined to fall in love with him it would have happened before now. Then why had he begun to monopolize her thoughts? There could be two reasons for that, Elizabeth decided; unsatisfied curiosity (she still did not know the truth about his reputed love for her) and the vacuum left in her heart by Desmond's defection from it. She did not blame Desmond for that latter fact, but the result was the same. The vacuum demanded to be filled.

Not for the first time, she regretted the rash impetuosity which had led her into accepting Desmond's proposal. In that she had wronged herself and him. Had she also wronged Alan?

The wind and the curtains and the rattling window had gradually formed a familiar background accompaniment to her musings; now it seemed to Elizabeth that a new sound had intruded itself into the nocturnal symphony. A shuffling sound; not the shuffling of feet, but as though a heavy body were slithering over the ground on its belly. And it came from beneath her window.

Instantly alert, Elizabeth turned on her back, pulled the bedclothes to her chin in an instinctive gesture of self-protection, and listened. The noise had stopped now; noises always did when one wanted to analyse them. She tried to picture what lay beneath her window; she knew the distant view, but had never consciously examined the foreground. The room was at the back of the hotel, overlooking the cricket ground. She had a recollection of out-buildings . . . a cobbled yard . . . the smell of horses . . .

Horses! That was it, of course. That low building to the right, the one with the sloping roof; that was the stables. In the past it had no doubt been well tenanted; but now there was only Gertrude, the elderly mare who pulled the roller. And it must have been

Gertrude, rustling around in her straw, who had produced that alien sound.

Elizabeth relaxed. All the same, she thought, I'll close that window before I go to sleep. There's a drainpipe runs up to the ledge beneath my window. I don't want any visitors that way.

She returned to her thoughts of Alan. Alan wasn't in the same street as Desmond when it came to looks and charm. He was short and stocky, and rather clumsy in his movements; his hands were those of a worker, not of a dilettante, and his clothes appeared to have been chosen for their serviceability rather than with an eye to their æsthetic value. He was not particularly well read, he had no outstanding social graces. But he had solidity and determination and tenacity, and a readiness to see the good rather than the bad.

Drowsily Elizabeth wondered what he would be like as a lover. Rather forthright, she thought; unable to speak fluently of his love, but eager to demonstrate it. Clumsy . . . but intense. Probably jealous and possessive . . . not always understanding . . .

The window continued to rattle, the curtains to murmur. Elizabeth did not heed them. She was asleep.

* * *

Alan was first in the room, with Desmond close behind. Even when she saw them Elizabeth did not stop screaming. She half sat, half lay in the wildly rumpled bed, both hands gripping the bedclothes, her eyes wide with terror — while scream after piercing scream split the silence of the sleeping hotel.

The two men ran to her, one on either side of the bed. 'For God's sake! Elizabeth!' Alan implored, his arm around her shoulders. 'What is it?'

He thought at first that reason had left her. Her eyes stared rigidly at the door, her body when he touched her was taut and hard. Then suddenly she stopped screaming and slumped heavily against him. Her body began to tremble violently; they could see her limbs twitching under the blankets. Her eyes were closed now.

Tears started to chase their way down the white cheeks, the trembling body became racked with loud, convulsive sobs.

Alan held her close as he looked with troubled eyes at Desmond. The latter shook his head in bewilderment. 'It's all right, Elizabeth,' he said, as though soothing a frightened child. 'It's all right.'

There were others in the room now: Inspector Pitt, still looking very much the policeman, despite his tousled hair and the surprisingly gaudy green and purple pyjamas beneath his raincoat; Sergeant Watkins, also in a raincoat, but with pyjamas of a more sober hue; an elderly couple whom Alan did not know. And behind them in the doorway other guests peered curiously into the room at the frightened girl, the ones at the back on tiptoe to see over the heads and shoulders of those in front.

'What happened?' Pitt asked.

Desmond looked up at him. 'We don't know. She hasn't told us.'

The Inspector grunted. His observant eyes travelled quickly round the room, paused for a moment's reflection at the open window, and returned to the bed.

'Tell us what happened, Elizabeth,' Desmond said gently.

'What frightened you?'

Elizabeth opened her eyes. She looked from one to the other without turning her head and sighed deeply, shudderingly. Her lips were bloodless, although there was a faint smear of lipstick at her mouth.

'A man,' she said. 'He — he tried to smother me with a pillow.'

There was a gasp from her audience. The two detectives stepped closer to the bed.

'You mean it really happened?' Desmond said. 'It wasn't just a nightmare?'

'No.' One hand went to her cheek and then moved slowly, tentatively, to her throat. 'It wasn't a nightmare.'

Alan had cramp in his arm. He withdrew it gently, and she lay back on the pillow that Desmond hurriedly pushed beneath her head. For the first time she seemed to be fully aware of them. She smiled at them faintly through the tears, but her body still trembled.

'Can you tell us any more than that,

miss?' Pitt said quietly. His voice sounded official without being officious.

'I don't think so. Something woke me . . . there was a noise . . . I knew there was some one in the room, and as I opened my mouth to scream the . . . the pillow . . . '

She choked, shuddering at the memory. Pitt picked up a pillow from the bedside chair and examined it; its surface was smooth and freshly laundered. He replaced it without comment.

The little knot of people at the door parted, and Dulcie Rivers came in. She looked cool and fresh and provocatively beautiful. Either she hadn't been to bed at all, thought Alan, as she came to stand beside him, or nothing so commonplace as a scream in the night was going to prevent her from dolling herself up before investigating it.

Elizabeth turned to Desmond. She said, forgetful of the fact that their marriage was still a secret, 'Remember, I told you how I sleep on my stomach? I think that's what saved me. I half twisted round when the board creaked, and then . . . ' She shuddered. 'The pressure pushed me back, I suppose, so that my head was in the crook of my arm. I don't know what happened after that. I must have fainted.'

Pitt said, 'Lucky you did, miss. No doubt he felt your body go limp and presumed that — ' He coughed. 'You've no idea who the man was?'

'No.'

The elderly couple had by now advanced to the foot of the bed in their curiosity. Pitt shooed them away. 'This gentleman' — he indicated Jim Watkins — 'and I are police officers, ladies and gentlemen,' he told the cluster at the door, his tone authoritative. 'I want you all to return to your rooms and stay there. If you wish to go back to bed, do so; we may want to question you later, but that can probably wait until day-light. Or is there anyone who can say now that he or she has some information which might have a direct bearing on this unfortunate incident?'

He looked at them in turn, and they looked back at him. One or two shook their heads, the rest stared blankly. Slowly they drifted off to their rooms, talking softly but excitedly as they went.

Pitt turned to the two young men. ‘Can either of you throw any light on this?’ he asked. ‘Which of you was first into the room?’

‘I was,’ Alan said. ‘By a neck. The scream woke me. I tumbled out of bed, grabbed my raincoat, and ran. Desmond came out of his room as I passed the door. And that’s all I can tell you.’

‘Me too,’ Desmond said.

Pitt lifted the pillow from the chair. ‘Is this yours, Miss Messager?’ Elizabeth nodded. ‘Was it on the chair when you went to sleep?’

‘Yes. I put it there. I never have more than one pillow.’

‘And who would know that? Who would expect to find it on the chair?’

Elizabeth was a little shocked at the question. It seemed to imply that a number of men had access to her bedroom.

Dulcie said quietly, ‘I knew. And Mr Farrel. Both Mr Farrels.’

They looked at her in surprise. She had

been so still that for once most of them had forgotten her presence.

'So we did,' Desmond agreed. He turned to Elizabeth in explanation, though more for the benefit of his listeners than for her. 'We've all popped in at one time or another to see how you were.'

But Elizabeth had abandoned the question for its implication. 'You mean that was the pillow he — he used, Inspector?'

Pitt either did not hear or preferred not to answer. He was gazing at the small glass bottle on the bedside table.

'Sleeping tablets?' he asked.

'Yes.'

'Did you take one last night?'

'No.'

'But some one might expect you to take one, eh? They would know you usually do?'

'No,' Elizabeth said firmly. 'I've never taken one in my life.'

The Inspector's eyebrows lifted slightly. 'Then why — '

She hastened to explain. Her nerves

were steadier now. It was a relief to talk, to dispel in talk some of the terror that had been hers. 'Mr Farrel — Mr George Farrel — gave them to me yesterday. They're his. I told him I couldn't sleep because of this bump on my head, and he thought they might help.'

The Inspector pulled thoughtfully at his lower lip. Help whom? he wondered.

Jim Watkins went across to the open window and flashed his torch at the sill and the ledge beneath.

'But you didn't take one?'

'No. I meant to, but I forgot. I was lying here thinking, and I suppose I just drifted off to sleep without it.' A faint tinge of colour came to her cheeks as she recalled those thoughts, and she looked rather shyly at the pensive Alan. 'That was lucky, wasn't it?'

'Very lucky,' Pitt said drily. 'I notice your father isn't here, Mr Farrel. Is his room on this floor?'

'Yes. Near the head of the far stairs.' Desmond frowned. 'I'm surprised he didn't hear the rumpus, though.'

'Perhaps he took one of his sleeping

tablets,' Pitt suggested.

'Yes, perhaps he did.' Desmond had been on his knees by the bedside. Now he scrambled to his feet. 'I'd better wake him. He ought to know what has happened.'

The Inspector stopped him. 'Not yet, Mr Farrel.'

Jim Watkins' large body was half-way through the window now. Alan watched him, fearful that at any moment the pyjama-clad legs might tilt upward and disappear through the window after the body. But the legs remained firmly rooted to the floor. Presently they were joined by the body, and the flushed face of the Sergeant surveyed the group by the bed.

His expression obviously signified something to the Inspector, for the latter went over to him immediately. They talked together in whispers; and then it was Pitt's turn to lean perilously over the window-sill and peer out into the night.

He did not peer for long. He came back into the centre of the room and said, 'You will all stay here with Sergeant Watkins, please, for the present,' and then walked briskly from the room. A moment later he reappeared, looked thoughtfully from one to the other of the two young men, and said, 'I'd like you to come with me, Mr Torreck. I may need help.'

Alan obeyed with alacrity.

There were lights in the corridors, lights on the stairs and in the hall, but no people — although from behind some of the bedroom doors came the sound of excited voices in conversation. 'Know your way around?' asked Pitt. 'How do we reach the rear of the building?'

Alan took him through the dining-room and out by the French windows. The darkness closed in on them as they moved away from the circle of light. Looking up at the building, Alan saw that there were lights in most of the bedrooms on that side.

They'll dine out on this for weeks to come, he thought.

Pitt headed away from the main block, picking his way by the light of his torch. As they rounded the end of the stables, a long, low building jutting out at right angles, Pitt said, 'How did you come to be spending the night here, Mr Torreck?'

Alan was glad of the darkness; it hid the discomfiture which he knew must show plainly on his face. 'I stayed rather late last night, and it didn't seem worth while going home. Didn't fancy it, either; my father's away, and I hate being on my own.'

It sounded weak and somehow rather sissy, but there was nothing he could add to improve it.

Gertrude was restless in her stall, and she neighed loudly as they passed. Alan looked up at the bedrooms again, trying to pick out Elizabeth's; he knew it must be something the police had seen from her window which had prompted this expedition. But he was unsure of his geography, and there was a similarity about the windows that confused him.

He stumbled over uneven paving, righted himself with a muttered oath, and took a few unsteady paces forward. Then he stopped. The Inspector stood slightly to his right, the beam of his torch steady on something that lay close to the wall.

It was the body of a man. He lay

spreadeagled on his back, and his staring eyes eerily reflected the light from the torch. There was blood on his forehead and in his hair.

'Good God!' Alan said. 'It's Bruce!'

14

A Homily on Pillows

Oh, no!' whispered Elizabeth. 'Not Bruce. It couldn't be!'

The room was crowded. George Farrel had joined them, and Sergeant Cole, and outside in the corridor Constable Williams stood on guard. Dulcie had gone very white at the news; they thought, when she slumped limply on to the bed, that she had fainted, but she shook her head when Desmond and Jim Watkins went to her aid. Of the two girls Elizabeth looked the more composed; but her hands gripped the blanket more tightly, and some remnant of the terror which had formerly possessed her was back on her face.

Desmond and Alan seemed the least surprised. 'I knew he was up to some devilry,' the latter said, after he had told Pitt of Bruce's visit the previous evening, and of his own belief that Bruce had hidden somewhere in the hotel. 'But from what he said I thought it was Desmond he was after, not Elizabeth. He was supposed to be fond of Elizabeth. Why, he even wanted to marry her.'

Pitt turned an inquiring eye on the girl. 'Is that true, Miss Messager?'

'Yes.' She remembered what Desmond had said — that Bruce was a snob, that it was money and social prestige that had attracted him to her. She remembered, too, his interest in Dulcie. 'At least, it's true that he asked me to marry him. But I can't be sure, of course, that he was in love with me.'

That was something, thought Pitt, that most girls would be sure of above all else. But he had seen the speculative look she had given Dulcie as she spoke, the way her fingers had tentatively touched her throat and then returned to grip the blanket, and he did not ask her to explain.

'He must have fallen while he was getting out of the window,' Alan said. 'I wonder why he went that way? Perhaps he was still in the room when Elizabeth screamed, and knew he'd be spotted if he tried to escape through the building.'

'He probably came in that way as well,' Desmond said. 'Climbed up the drain-pipe. I never had much faith in your theory that he was inside the hotel.' He turned to the Inspector. 'Wouldn't there be marks on the pipe?'

'There should be if he used it,' Pitt agreed. 'Would you be able to say if he came via the door or the window, Miss Messager?'

'No. I told you, he was already in the room when I woke up.'

'And before you went to sleep? Did anyone try the handle of your door? Did you hear anyone moving about outside in the yard?'

'I don't remember hearing anyone at the door. And outside — well, there was Gertrude. Or I thought it was Gertrude. A kind of slithering noise.'

'What time was that?' Pitt asked.

'Just before I went to sleep. After midnight.'

'Bruce,' Desmond said. 'I bet you that was Bruce trying the drainpipe.' He looked at Alan. 'I knew you were wrong, Alan. I knew he couldn't be in the hotel.'

Sergeant Watkins was at the window again; it seemed to draw him like a magnet. He said, 'What kind of shoes was Poulton wearing, Inspector?'

'Rubbers.' Pitt turned to Desmond. 'Mr Farrel, what was the ostensible purpose of Mr Poulton's visit here yesterday evening?'

'I don't know. He told Alan he wanted to see me, but he didn't give a reason.'

'You knew it wasn't a friendly visit?'

'According to Alan he didn't *seem* particularly friendly,' Desmond said cautiously. 'I can't imagine why.'

'Can't you?'

Pitt's voice was suddenly crisply accusing. He was no longer the polite investigator, he was a prosecutor facing a hostile witness. They were all aware of the change, and the tension in their looks and attitudes reflected their awareness. Dulcie jerked stiffly upright from a half-recumbent position on the bed; George Farrel's eyes narrowed as he looked from the Inspector to his son; Elizabeth, startled at first into rigidity, sank back on to the pillow with a deep sigh, a troubled look in her grey eyes.

Pitt said, 'A woman has been murdered and a man has died, Mr Farrel. It is time you stopped playing games.' He drew in his breath and exhaled loudly. 'Right? For a start, then — it was Bruce Poulton, wasn't it, who attacked you on the common yesterday evening?'

Flushed and unhappy, but still prevaricating, Desmond said, 'It may have been. But I told you at the time, Inspector, it had absolutely nothing to do with Mrs Lane's murder. It was a private quarrel.'

' 'Domestic issue' was the phrase you used then, sir,' Pitt said. 'That was nearer the mark, I fancy.' He looked sharply at Elizabeth, and then back to Desmond. 'Am I right in thinking you were referring to an event that took place in Tanbury on Friday afternoon? That was the issue, wasn't it? That was why Poulton waylaid you on the common, why he tried to see you again in the evening? That was what had aroused his anger against you and — ' He paused. 'And against Miss

Messager also, perhaps? Isn't that so, Mr Farrel?'

To most of those in the room his words, except in that they implied a quarrel between Desmond and Bruce and that Elizabeth was somehow involved, were meaningless; they had no knowledge of this mysterious event to which he had referred. Even Elizabeth did not understand at first. When she did she felt her cheeks go hot, and looked almost accusingly at her husband. She felt no savage pride, as Dulcie might have done, that two men should have fought because of her; to Elizabeth it was a primitive and degrading act. But that Bruce should have tried the ultimate revenge of murder was too horrible to contemplate.

'No!' she said, hysterically shrill. 'No, Desmond, he *couldn't*!'

But Desmond had eyes and ears only for the Inspector. Since the latter knew so much there was no point in further denial.

'That's about it,' he agreed, his voice hoarse.

George Farrel jerked his astonished

frame into action.

'Will you please explain what you're talking about?' he demanded, stepping forward to confront the Inspector. Pitt was silent, and without waiting longer for an answer he rounded on his son. 'What is it, Desmond? What's this about you and Bruce? What have you been up to?'

'Later, Dad. I'll tell you later.' He brushed his father aside impatiently and moved closer to Pitt, so that they stood face to face. 'Anything else, Inspector?'

'Yes.' Pitt stood his ground, his keen eyes fixed unwinkingly on the young man's. 'Why, do you suppose, did nothing happen to you to-night?'

Some of the tension left him at that. His shoulders drooped a little, his feet shuffled an indeterminate pattern on the floor.

'It may have been intended — it probably was — but it so happened that I locked my door when I went to bed. Sounds sissy, I know — but it's true.'

'What prompted you to do that?'

Alan Torreck had listened to this battle of words with growing bewilderment and alarm. It was a relief to be able to take part, to shed his inaction.

'It was my idea, Inspector,' he said eagerly. 'I told you, I thought Bruce was somewhere in the hotel. He was in an ugly mood, and I was afraid he meant mischief.' He turned to Elizabeth. 'I didn't think to warn you, Elizabeth; it never occurred to me that you might also be in danger. I still can't understand it.'

Elizabeth shook her head. She could not understand it either.

'So you advised Mr Farrel to lock his door, eh?' Pitt said.

'Yes. We'd just left — ' He stopped abruptly, his mouth agape. Then it closed with a snap. 'Michael! We've forgotten Michael, Desmond.'

'Michael Lane?' Pitt said sharply. 'How does he come into this?'

Desmond told him. His former antagonism had left him now; the fight was over, and another quarry had been set up. But he expected further fireworks from the Inspector at having withheld this information, and was relieved when they did not materialize.

‘All right,’ Pitt said. ‘Show Sergeant Watkins where his room is.’ And to the Sergeant, ‘Rout him out, Jim, and bring him along.’

When they had gone Farrel said, ‘While we are waiting for young Lane, Inspector, perhaps you will be kind enough to tell me what all that was about? This happens to be my hotel, and I have a right to know what goes on in it.’

Pitt said, not unkindly, ‘Your son was wise in saying that explanations must come later. Don’t be impatient, Mr Farrel; you’ll know soon enough.’ And when he knew how would he react? ‘It might be a good idea, sir, if you and Miss Rivers were to rustle up some tea. I think we could all do with it. Sergeant Cole can go with you.’

Still protesting, Farrel went. Dulcie trailed after him; it seemed that all vitality had left her, so listless was her attitude. But as she reached the door she turned and gave Elizabeth such a look of bitter hate that Elizabeth was appalled. Had Dulcie been in love with Bruce? she wondered. And was she, Elizabeth, now to be blamed for his death?

Pitt said, 'Miss Messager, have you discussed your aunt's will with anyone since Mr Crumley was here?'

The girl hesitated. She did not want to admit in front of Alan that she had discussed it with Desmond and with no one else. Alan would wonder why Desmond should have been singled out. 'Only with one person,' she said — hoping that, having guessed or discovered the secret of her marriage, he would guess that much more.

Pitt nodded and went over to the window, where he stood for a few moments gazing out at the night. Then he turned and walked quickly from the room. They heard him speak briefly to Williams and go off down the corridor.

Alan's immediate thought, when the two of them were alone, was to question Elizabeth about Bruce, to discover the cause of the quarrel between him and Desmond. But, great as was his curiosity, he could not bring himself to do so. She had suffered too much that night to revive a topic that was so obviously painful to her.

Yet something had to be said; they could not remain silent together for long. With the Inspector's parting query fresh in his mind, but with no great interest (the terms, he thought, were a foregone conclusion), he said, 'What was that about Aunt Charlotte's will?'

Elizabeth told him. She had not meant to tell him yet, but she was too defeated, too unhappy, to defend her pride further. It did not matter now what people should think of her.

She had expected him to condole with her in her ill fortune; instead, a look of pleased surprise showed on his face. Strung up as she was, that irritated her.

'Well?' she asked sharply. 'What's funny about that?'

He was instantly embarrassed. 'I — I'm sorry, Elizabeth,' he said. 'It's bad luck on you, of course. Only — '

He paused. 'Only what?' she demanded.

He did not answer. And suddenly she knew she could supply the answer for him, and felt the blood rush to her face.

Desmond had been right — Alan *was* in love with her. He was an honest young man with a conventional outlook on love and marriage, and it had not seemed right to him that he should ask a potentially wealthy young woman to marry him. But now that her fortune had vanished . . .

They were still gazing at each other when Pitt returned, Desmond and the Sergeant with him. Desmond said bluntly, 'Michael's gone,' and sat down on the bed.

'Gone?' Alan jerked his mind back from the castles it had been building in the air. 'Gone where?'

'He didn't leave a forwarding address,' Desmond said. 'He's just gone.'

George Farrel brought the tea himself; with him came Sergeant Cole, and the information that Dulcie had retired to her room. 'I thought that would be all right, sir,' the Sergeant said. 'She didn't look too good.'

Pitt nodded abstractedly; he was thinking of Michael Lane. Lane would have to be found, but the search need not be immediate. He could not be far away.

As they drank their tea he stood beside the bed gazing thoughfully at the pillow on the chair. He said to George Farrel, 'How many pillows do you sleep with, sir?'

'Two. Why?'

Pitt did not answer the question. 'And you, sir?' This to Desmond.

'Two.'

When he looked at Alan the latter said, 'Sometimes two, sometimes one. Depends how the fancy takes me.'

Pitt sipped the hot tea gratefully. 'I'm interested in sleeping habits,' he said. 'One learns a lot from them. Pillows in particular. I once knew a man who used to push his second pillow under the bed, right out of sight against the wall.'

They considered this in silence; it seemed a frivolous anecdote under the circumstances. Desmond said, 'Eccentric but harmless. What happened to him?'

'He was hanged, Mr Farrel.'

This too was received in silence; an uneasy silence this time, for they were beginning to wonder if the apparent frivolity did not have a more sinister background.

'That seems a rather harsh punishment,' George Farrel said.

'It does, doesn't it? But the pillow wasn't as innocent as this one, you see. There were certain marks on it which shouldn't have been there.'

'Blood?'

'No, sir, not blood.' Pitt seemed suddenly to have lost interest in the topic. He put his cup back on the tray and said briskly, 'It's time we found out what's happened to Mr Lane. We'll have to search the hotel.'

'Can I help?' Alan asked quickly. He did not want to stay there with Elizabeth; all he had to say to her now must be said when they were alone.

'Yes. You can team up with Sergeant Cole. Perhaps you'd go with Sergeant Watkins, Mr Farrel?' George Farrel nodded, and Pitt turned to Desmond. 'I've some business to attend to on the phone, but after that you and I will have a look round outside. Wait for me here, will you?'

In the corridor Pitt stopped to talk to Constable Williams. The latter listened stolidly. He had come to the conclusion that he neither liked nor trusted the Inspector; Pitt, he had decided, had not done well by him. Nor was that his only criticism. There had been some queer goings on in the hotel that night, it seemed; he hadn't been able to hear much that was said in the room, but young Mr Poulton was dead and Miss Messager half suffocated. And all because, in Ted Williams' opinion, Michael Lane hadn't been kept under lock and key. They ought never to have let him go once they'd got him.

'And remember this, Williams,' Pitt concluded. 'Your job is to keep an eye on Miss Messager. Young Mr Farrel is in there with her now, but I'll be back for him shortly. I think she's safe enough, but we can't afford to take chances. There's been enough trouble here for one night.'

Pompous old buffer, thought Williams. 'Yes, sir,' he said smartly.

When they had all gone Elizabeth said wearily, 'Pass me my handbag, please,

Desmond. What time is it?'

'Nearly half-past five.' He watched her as she applied lipstick to her mouth. 'I wonder what Michael is up to. Did he have a hand in this also?'

'I don't know. After this I don't think I'll ever trust anyone again. Desmond — it was Bruce you met on the common yesterday, wasn't it?'

'Yes. I didn't tell you because I thought it might worry you.'

'What happened? What did he say?'

'It was what he did, not what he said. But he accused me of taking you away from him.'

'But it isn't true!' she protested — more to her conscience than to Desmond. 'I never gave him the least encouragement. You believe that, don't you?'

'Of course.' He was still on the bed, and reached across to take her hand. 'Forget it, darling. You've no call to reproach yourself.'

But she could not forget it. She doubted if she ever would. 'Did he know we were married?' she asked.

'Yes. He didn't say how. Either Dulcie told him, or you were right about him seeing us on Friday.'

'But why did you have to *fight* him, Desmond? It was so — so degrading.'

'I didn't.' He sounded indignant. 'He just lashed out at me and knocked me down. It wasn't a fight, it was a massacre — with me on the receiving end.'

Instantly she was sorry; he had had a bad enough evening without her contribution to it. She pressed his hand. 'Do you think he meant to kill us both?' she asked.

'Probably. That locked door may have saved me. Not that any of the locks in this place are worth a damn. But Bruce wouldn't know that.'

She shuddered. 'He couldn't ever have loved me,' she said. 'You were right about that, weren't you?' And then, after a pause, 'I wonder how the Inspector knew we were married?'

'They have a way of finding these things out,' he said. Suddenly impatient, he slipped his hand out of hers and stood up. 'What the devil is he up to? Why doesn't he come back? I want to know how Michael fits into all this.'

The door was open. Outside in the corridor Ted Williams heard their voices and occasionally distinguished words and phrases. But he wasn't listening for them; he was still brooding on the incompetence and stupidity of Inspector Pitt. It was just like Pitt, he fumed, to put the youngest member of the Force present on static guard duty and go chasing after suspects himself. And they hadn't even offered him a cup of tea!

Fretting at his inactivity, he walked a few restless paces. He turned to come back — and there at the far end of the corridor was the tall figure of Michael Lane!

For a brief moment the two men eyed each other, each in an agony of indecision. The fugitive was the first to act; he turned and ran for the stairs that led to the next floor. That was too much for Constable Williams. Banging the bedroom door wide open, he yelled, 'Look after Miss Messager, sir. Mr Lane's just gone up the back stairs. I'm going after him.'

As the constable's footsteps receded down the corridor Desmond hurried to the door. For a moment he stood there, undecided. Then he turned and walked slowly over to the bed.

'What the devil is Michael up to?' he said, frowning. 'If he wants to get away why didn't he go down, not up? What is there — ' He snapped his fingers as the solution came to him. 'The tower! He's making for the tower! Why the devil didn't I think of that before?'

'Does he know about the tower room, then?' she asked.

'Of course he does. But Ted Williams doesn't. Sorry, Elizabeth, but I'll have to go. This is a job for yours truly.'

He was already at the door when she called out to stop him. She had no wish to be left on her own. Bruce had tried to kill her, and Bruce was dead; there was no threat to her from him. But somehow that knowledge did not give her the assurance she needed. While Michael was at large in the hotel the sense of danger persisted.

'I'm not staying here by myself,' she said, throwing off the bedclothes. 'Either you stay too, or I'm coming with you.'

Desmond stood irresolute. Then he laughed.

'Come on, then. But make it snappy.' He snatched the dressing-gown from a chair and thrust it at her. 'Here, put that on. And hurry.'

Obediently Elizabeth hurried. She was flustered by his urgency, but could understand it. As she sat on the edge of the bed wiggling her feet into slippers he caught at her hand impatiently and pulled her upright. Together they ran down the corridor and up the stairs; a narrow passage, uncarpeted, led off from the end of the floor above, and down this they hurried, Elizabeth silent in her soft moccasins, Desmond's shoes clattering on the bare boards. The passage culminated in narrow stone steps that spiralled steeply upward into the tower. Desmond almost pulled her up them after him, not resting until they stood at the foot of the frail-looking metal ladder that provided the only means of ascent to the eyrie above.

'Damn!' Desmond said. 'Either I guessed wrong, or he's in such a flap that he forgot to pull the ladder up after him. I'd better investigate. You wait here, darling, while I have a look-see.'

Still panting from her exertions, Elizabeth watched him as he climbed the ladder nimbly and pushed at the heavy door. It opened smoothly, and he disappeared into the room. Then a light was switched on, and a moment later he was back at the opening.

'He's not here,' he said. 'But come on up. You said you wanted to see the place. Well, now's your chance.'

She found it difficult in slippers and dressing-gown, but she managed it. Desmond handed her into the room, and she stood beside him as he hauled up the ladder, broke it into sections, and closed the door.

'Snug as a bug in a rug,' he said, smiling. 'But I wonder what's happened to Michael.'

Elizabeth shivered and pulled the dressing-gown closer about her. 'It's not so snug,' she said. 'It's cold. Is there an electric fire?'

He bent to switch it on.

'All the conveniences,' he told her gaily. 'I believe the old boy even used to keep food and drink up here.'

The room was square, with windows on each side. To the east she could see the glow above the city of Tanbury; a few lights twinkled in the village to the south. The furniture consisted of table and chairs, a cupboard, and a long settee that stretched almost the length of the west wall. A rather thread-bare carpet covered the floor, and in one corner was a large, old-fashioned safe. There were no pictures or ornaments, no curtains at the windows.

'It must be a fascinating spot in daylight,' she said.

'It is. You can see for miles. Now come and sit down and have a cigarette.'

She went over to the settee reluctantly, hoping he wasn't feeling suddenly amorous; but when she sat down beside him he made no attempt to embrace her. 'Don't you want to look for Michael?' she said, after he had lit her cigarette.

'No hurry. I like it here. Always did.'

'What was he afraid of?' Elizabeth asked. 'Old Mr Goetz, I mean.'

'Us.' He laughed. 'Not the Farrels — the whole English nation. The locals weren't very nice to him, I'm told. That was at the start of the First World War; he was of German birth, and every one had spy mania well developed at that time. Old Goetz was sure they were out to get him, so he built this place. Not the tower — that was here originally, of course — but the room. It was the only place he could feel safe in. They say he always slept up here.'

'Poor old man. I think I know how he felt,' Elizabeth said.

Occasional sounds had drifted up to them from the hotel, but they had had no significance. Now, quite unexpectedly, faint and seemingly far away, a voice called, 'Elizabeth, are you there?'

It was Alan. Elizabeth smiled at the tension and anxiety in his voice; it was good to know he could be worried about her. But as she opened her mouth to reply Desmond's hand closed over it. 'Don't answer,' he said. 'Let's keep them guessing.' He smiled. 'That doesn't mean we have to talk in whispers. They can't hear unless we shout.'

Annoyed, she knocked his arm away.

'Then I'm going to shout. Don't be childish, Desmond. This isn't a game, they're really worried. And who wouldn't be, after what has happened here to-night?'

Alan's voice came again, still faint, more urgent than before. 'Can you hear me, Elizabeth? Are you there?'

Once more her husband's hand closed over her mouth; but this time his other arm was about her shoulders, and he held her firmly. Elizabeth struggled fiercely to free herself; she was really angry now. She tried to shout, but his hand blanketed her voice. She had not before realized his strength.

'Miss Messager.' This time it was the Inspector's voice that called. 'We know you are there, but you may not be able to answer. So listen. As soon as we can get to you we will; in the meantime try to keep away from your husband. He killed Charlotte Lane, and to-night he tried to kill you.' A pause. 'Do you understand, Miss Messager? Your husband is a murderer.'

15

Angel on a Ladder

Desmond took his hand away from her mouth, his arm from her shoulders. 'It doesn't matter,' he said. 'I forgot I'd pulled the ladder up. That's how they know we're here.'

Elizabeth stared at him, incredulous of what she had heard. She was not frightened; she made no attempt to scream, to cry for help. It was inconceivable that Desmond could be a murderer, had actually tried to kill her; he was her husband, he was in love with her. He was charming and pleasant and — no, not ordinary; that was a word one could not apply to Desmond, it had been part of his fascination for her. But he wasn't different as she imagined a murderer must be different.

'Don't you want to answer them?' he asked uncertainly. Her silence surprised him.

She shook her head; not in negation, but as a signal of her incredulity. He hadn't changed, he looked exactly as he had always looked. There must be some mistake. Surely the act of murder would leave its mark on the killer?

'You don't believe them?' He smiled faintly. 'You should. It's true, you know. I did kill Aunt Charlotte.'

She was frightened then; not so much at the confirmation of his guilt as at his apparent calmness. He had spoken of murder as though it were of little account. Either he was mad, or human life was no more sacred to him than that of a fly.

And both alternatives implied danger to herself.

Terrified, she edged away from him, her eyes never leaving his face. He made no attempt to stop her; one arm resting lightly along the back of the settee, he lounged in his corner, apparently relaxed and carefree. But there was a glitter in his eyes, a tenseness to his body, that denied the posture. The muscles of his jaw twitched spasmodically.

'Scared?' The attempt at a laugh failed,

and he abandoned it. 'There's no need to be. You're in no danger from me now.'

Still she did not speak; her throat was too dry, and anyway she would not have known what to say. Neither his calmness nor his assurance of her safety could alleviate her fear. Nothing he might say now would have any significance for her. He could lie or tell the truth as it pleased him; she would not know the difference.

He threw the stub of his cigarette into the fire recess. The action startled her out of her stupor, and she became aware of him as a being. She noticed that his hands trembled slightly as he lit another cigarette. Was his calmness a pose, born of bravado? Was he, too, frightened? Frightened of what? His conscience — or of what lay ahead of him?

'You might at least say something, if it's only goodbye.' He sounded irritable. 'That would certainly be appropriate. Aren't you interested? Don't you want to know what happened?'

Elizabeth nodded. She was reluctant to hear more — fear had dulled her natural curiosity — but to keep him talking might delay whatever it was he had in mind to do. She could not believe it was solely a desire for companionship that had prompted him to bring her there.

'I like you, Elizabeth — in a way I suppose I'm quite fond of you — but I was never in love with you. I married you solely to get my hands on Aunt Charlotte's money. Didn't you guess that?' He paused, apparently anticipating a surprised protest. When she made none, but continued to stare at him wide-eyed and in silence, he went on, 'And I needed it quickly, I couldn't wait for her to die a natural death. Not that I'd made up my mind to kill her when I first asked you to marry me; it was Michael's talk of murder, and the joke we planned, that decided me. With all those red herrings, and so many people involved, I thought I could get away with it. I nearly did, too.'

He was not so relaxed now. He kept shifting his position, and his words were punctuated by quick, nervous puffs at his cigarette, so that his arm seemed to be moving up and down continuously.

Occasionally he moistened his lips with his tongue.

'You did your best to balk me, you know,' he said reprovingly, staring at her. 'I expected you to come back from Cosmeston as soon as you discovered my phone-call was a hoax; I hadn't banked on your spending the evening there. That meant fewer red herrings to confuse the police.' The frown deepened. 'And Michael's unrehearsed contribution worried me at first — I couldn't understand how that damned picture came to be missing. Luckily the police were as foxed as I was.'

Memory of that confusion seemed to unsettle him further, for he jumped up quickly and went over to the door, where he stood listening. Then he began to pace restlessly about the room, pausing occasionally to stare out of a window.

To the east a faint lightening of the sky betokened that dawn was not far off.

Elizabeth watched his every move, as a mouse might watch the cat that torments it. When eventually he came to stand directly in front of her she shrank still farther into her corner of the settee.

'Shall I tell you how I did it?' he asked. 'Killed Aunt Charlotte, I mean?'

She shuddered. A faint 'No' escaped her, but he disregarded it. Or perhaps he did not hear.

'The first thing was to cancel the taxi,' he said. 'I had to ring several garages before I hit on the right one. But Thursday itself was easy. I made sure you were on the Cosmeston bus, and then I drove in to Tanbury for an alibi with the tobacconist. On the way back I parked the car in the woods east of your lane, walked up to the house, and told Aunt Charlotte that her taxi was stuck down the road and that I'd give her a lift to the station. It was just after six then — she was all set to go. I followed her into the house as she went to put on her coat, and — ' For the first time he displayed some emotion. His face was pale as he spread his hands before him and looked at them wonderingly. Elizabeth saw that they were trembling. Then he laughed self-consciously. He said, with forced bravado, 'She had a thick neck, didn't she? I could hardly get my hands round it.'

Elizabeth closed her eyes. His apparent callousness sickened her, and she could no longer bear to look at him.

'She had less money on her than I expected,' Desmond went on. 'About two hundred quid. I took her keys in case there might be more in the safe. Then I dragged her out through the back door and dropped her down the well; and what a weight she was, too! I collected her coat and suitcase and threw them after her; and then just as I was going back to try the safe the front-door bell rang.' Small beads of perspiration had gathered on his forehead. It seemed that past danger could be more real to him than the present. 'That really shook me. But I kept my head. Without bothering to lock the back door, I cut down the lawn to the copse, ran across the lane, and up through the woods to the car. Meeting Bruce at the corner was a stroke of luck. It gave me an alibi of sorts.'

'Elizabeth!' Alan's muffled voice startled them both. 'Are you all right, Elizabeth?'

She looked beseechingly at Desmond. To her surprise he nodded.

'Why not? Go ahead, talk to him. Tell him you're all right.'

Slowly she got to her feet. Her legs felt weak, and for a few seconds she had to clutch at the table for support. Then she walked over to the door. She had to be near it — as near as she could get to Alan and safety and sanity.

'I — ' Her voice cracked, and she swallowed hastily. 'It's me, Alan — Elizabeth. I — I'm all right.'

'Thank God!' His voice was fainter, but the relief it expressed was very evident. 'Is Desmond with you?'

'Yes.'

She began to cry. Ever since she had known the truth about her husband all emotions had been one with fear. Now they began to sort themselves out; her head ached, she felt lonely and weak and sick. The walls and the ceiling seemed gradually to be closing in on her, and she started to beat at the door with her fists.

'I'm frightened, Alan,' she cried hysterically. 'Please, please come quickly. Please, Alan!'

Faintly from below came an oath.

Immersed in her own drama, she could not appreciate the suspense, the dreadful sense of inadequacy and helplessness that filled her would-be rescuers.

'Hang on, darling,' came Alan's pleading voice. 'It won't be long. We're doing all we can.'

'That's enough.'

Desmond caught her by the arm and pulled her away from the door. Elizabeth had not realized he was immediately behind her, and she shrank from him instinctively. She knew it was a foolish action, that it might encourage the sadist in him; but she could not help it.

'No call for hysterics,' he said. He led her over to the settee and pushed her, not ungently, on to it. 'I told you I wasn't going to hurt you.'

Encouraged by his lack of anger, she stammered, 'You — you tried to kill me before.'

'Yes. I didn't want to, but I could see no alternative. It was the only solution — then.' The excitement that had seemed to sustain him ebbed, and he said sadly, 'Now it doesn't matter.'

'But why? What had I done?'

'Nothing. It wasn't you, it was Dulcie.'

Elizabeth stared at him. Her eyes were still wet, but she was no longer crying.

'Dulcie? You mean she *made* you do it?' she asked, incredulous.

'Of course not. Dulcie knew nothing about it. But when she found out we were married she refused to have anything more to do with me.' He sighed. 'I couldn't stand that.'

Elizabeth was stunned. That Desmond — fastidious, aristocratic Desmond — should fall in love with Dulcie had never occurred to her as a possibility. Dulcie was beautiful, yes. But she was also vulgar and promiscuous and cheap, she was . . .

'That shakes you, eh?' He smiled crookedly. 'You must think I'm crazy. Well, so I am where Dulcie is concerned. You may be worth two of her, but that makes no difference. It's Dulcie I want.' The smile faded. 'Once I thought money was more important; that was why I asked you to marry me. I thought, too, that she'd understand, that she wouldn't shut me out. But she did. She wasn't sharing me, she said; it would have to be you or her. And when you told me that there was no money, that I'd lost that too — ' He shook his head. 'That was the last straw.'

His voice was thick with emotion. Elizabeth realized how little she had really known him. That a girl like Dulcie . . .

'We could have separated, got divorced,' she said. 'You didn't have to — to — '

'Divorce takes time; I couldn't wait that long. And a separation would have been useless. Dulcie made that quite plain.'

The sky was greyer now; it will soon be dawn, she thought. Despite the warmth of the room, she shivered. Would they never come?

'Besides, there was Bruce,' Desmond said. 'He knew.'

Yes, there was Bruce; she had forgotten him. Bruce too was dead. He had fallen from her window and . . .

'Bruce knew we were married,' Desmond said. 'Dulcie told him on Sunday night; she was mad at us, you see, and out to cause trouble. Personal trouble, not with the police; she wanted to break up our marriage, and she knew how Bruce felt about you, that he'd hoped to marry you himself. And that made Bruce appreciate how strong a motive I'd had for getting rid of Aunt Charlotte. He got to thinking about how he'd met me at the end of the lane that evening, and he remembered that he'd heard the engine start up a few moments before that. He was pretty sure then that I'd killed her.'

He threw away the half-smoked cigarette. It fell on the carpet, and from force of habit he picked it up and mashed it against the stone grate. When he tried to light another his usually agile fingers were clumsy and ineffective, and twice he dropped the lighter before succeeding.

'He told me all this when I met him on the common yesterday evening,' he said. 'I think he hoped to make some sort of a bargain with me. But we never got to discussing it. When he hinted that he and Dulcie — ' Desmond's teeth shut with a snap. 'I hit him then. But he's tough' — unconsciously he used the present tense — 'and it didn't hurt him. He just waded in and knocked me flying.' He fingered his still swollen lip. 'When he heard the police coming he cleared off, after telling me he'd be round to see me later. That'd be my last chance, he said; if I didn't see it his way then he'd go to the police.' A lungful of smoke choked him, and he coughed angrily. 'So when he turned up at the hotel I knew I had to kill him. There was no alternative if I wanted to be safe. Besides, I hated him because of Dulcie.'

Elizabeth was surprised that she experienced little or no revulsion at this further confession. She felt drained of all emotion; nothing he might say now, she thought, could shock her. At first she had thought, How can Desmond be a murderer? He is my husband; I would have known. But now, although still her husband, he was no longer the Desmond she had married. Now he was scarcely human — a strange creature outside her ken, to whom murder was a commonplace.

'And you did?' she said calmly. How grey his face looked. Was that fear? Or was it the stubble on his chin that made it look so? She had never before seen him unshaved.

'Yes. When Alan told me he was waiting outside I knew I had him. I went out to the stables for a crowbar, and then came round to this side of the building and called him. It was dark, and he couldn't see me; as he came level with where I was waiting I jumped out and hit him. I think he must have died with the first blow, but I gave him a couple more to be sure.'

Elizabeth shuddered. It had been one thing to listen calmly to his talk of murder, but less easy when it came to detail and when the victim had been a friend. Yet her revulsion was still not acute. She was becoming so satiated with horror and death that it was difficult to absorb more and still react normally to it.

Desmond walked slowly over to the east window and looked out over the countryside towards Tanbury. Already the dawn was sufficiently advanced to distinguish buildings and roads and trees. But there were no people visible. It was still, most appropriately, a dead world.

'I hid him in the shrubbery,' he said,

opening the window. ‘After what you had told us at dinner — that Bruce had hated Aunt Charlotte, that he had had as strong a motive as any of us for killing her — I knew I could use him. Later, when the hotel was asleep, I went out and dragged him round to the yard and parked him under your window. I thought it would be assumed he had fallen from it after killing you.’

I assumed it, she thought; did the police? She shivered as the cool morning air reached her. Below, faint and seemingly far away, there were voices that had not been audible while the window was closed. Were they the voices of her rescuers, or merely a village awakening?

Desmond shivered also, and shut the window. She wondered if the voices frightened him, if they destroyed the illusion of security and inaccessibility that the tower room had perhaps given him. He came back to the settee, and Elizabeth shrank tightly into her corner of it, once more afraid. She was, she supposed, a problem he still had to solve. How did he intend to solve it?

He made no move to touch her. He knelt on the cushions with his back to the room, staring out of the window to the west. To the girl it seemed a symbolic posture — as though he appreciated that with the coming of that particular dawn his own sun was sinking.

'I never thought I should tell anyone,' he said presently, not looking at her. 'Least of all you.'

For a moment she wondered why she had been thus singled out for particular exclusion. Then she knew. It was because he had not expected her to be alive to listen.

It was an unpleasant thought. She said hastily, 'Why did you — ' and gasped as she realized the probable explanation. She was alive, but he looked on her as one already dead. He had lied to her again. She was a safe confidante, she would be dead before she could pass on her knowledge.

'I may as well tell some one,' he said, not noticing her new fear. 'The police know, you see. I'm not giving away any secrets.'

That calmed her a little, but it did not stop the tears that had welled into her eyes. She had little physical control left.

'How can you be sure of that?' she asked.

'Something the Inspector said. About pillows. Remember?'

Elizabeth fumbled in her dressing-gown pocket for a handkerchief and dabbed at her eyes, wondering if she would ever again feel normal and calm and unafraid. If she lived — and that, despite Desmond's assurance, was something she did not dare to count on — could she go back to being the same person she had been yesterday? Would this long, dreadful night have no lasting effect? It seemed impossible to believe that it would not.

The opening of the window behind her made her jump. Desmond was staring straight ahead of him, a new expression on his face. She turned her head to see what it was that thus held his attention — and there, only a few feet away, was Sergeant Watkins, his red hair glinting in the weak sunlight.

Startled out of the mental and physical torpor into which she had gradually sunk, Elizabeth scrambled to her knees with a little cry of thankfulness, heedless of the presence of Desmond beside her. All the hopes which she had thought were dead were suddenly revived and centred on the miracle that had happened. It seemed to her, in her ecstasy of relief, that an angel had materialized out of thin air to summon her to freedom.

He was a very solid angel. He clung to a tall ladder, and there was nothing angelic about his expression; it was grimly purposeful. She could not bear to look at him on his precarious perch, yet dared not take her eyes away lest, when she looked again, he might have vanished. A quick glance downward showed her that the ladder sprang from a red fire-engine around which a little group of people were clustered, all of them gazing upward, their faces white in the shadow thrown by the hotel. Then her eyes returned to the ladder to feast themselves once more on the man who clung there. On him alone her life seemed to depend.

‘Good morning.’ Desmond opened the window wide. ‘Chilly out there, isn’t it? I envy your head for heights, Sergeant.’

His voice sounded hoarse but cheerful. The Sergeant’s was equally hoarse, but not at all cheerful. ‘I want to take your wife down with me, Farrel,’ he said. ‘How about it?’

Desmond was so long in answering that Elizabeth had to force her knuckles into her mouth to prevent herself from screaming. She feared that any sound from her might affect his decision adversely.

‘Wouldn’t it be simpler,’ he said at last, ‘if I were to open the door and let down the ladder?’

‘Much simpler,’ Watkins agreed. ‘Will you do that?’

Again the dreadful suspense. Then, ‘No,’ Desmond said. ‘It would be an anticlimax. I should hate to deprive you of the fruits of your heroism. Go ahead and rescue her, Sergeant. I won’t interfere.’

For a moment Watkins studied him; then he made a brief signal to the watchers below. Elizabeth waited, her body tense.

'Stand over against the far wall, Farrel,' Watkins said. 'I'll handle this my way.'

For an agonizing moment the girl thought Desmond was going to refuse. Then he withdrew his head from the window and got to his feet. The smile had left his face. He looked grey and tired and considerably older.

'We're not likely to meet again, Elizabeth,' he said, forcing a smile. 'We won't be moving in the same company. Goodbye and good luck — and a safe journey down.'

He walked slowly round the table and leant against the cupboard. But Elizabeth had eyes only for the Sergeant. He was at the window now, his bulk filling it, a hand on the sill.

'Get up here, miss,' he said gently, patting it. 'I'll see you don't fall.'

Only for a brief moment did she hesitate; the thought of climbing out of the window was unnerving, but the fear of her husband was greater. Gingerly she clambered on to the sill, losing her slippers as she did so.

'Don't look down,' Watkins said. He gave a quick glance at Desmond and then bent to put an arm around her. 'I'm taking you down on my shoulder. Once I've got you just close your eyes and relax. Don't worry, I've done this before. I used to be a stunt man on the films before I joined the Force.'

Despite his injunction, she gave a quick glance down; the ground seemed a long way off, and she closed her eyes. She felt herself lifted and borne outward, and clutched desperately at the Sergeant's jacket. The feel of it reassured her slightly, and she opened her eyes for a last glimpse into the room. Desmond had not moved; he was staring at her with that fixed grey smile of his. Then the ladder seemed to sway and move, and after one swift and frightened look at the unstable earth below she shut her eyes tightly and tried to obey the Sergeant's order to relax.

'I'll be back for you,' she heard him say to Desmond. 'Or you may prefer to leave by the door. You'll find some one waiting.'

If Desmond answered she did not hear

him. Her ears were buzzing and she felt dizzy. A jerk at her legs (he was hitching her more snugly to his shoulder) and then they were descending the ladder, the blood singing in her head.

Alan was the first to greet her as the Sergeant deposited her gently on her feet; he put his arms round her and held her close while she burst into a flood of tears. The small crowd of people left them alone, watching sympathetically. But Elizabeth had no eyes for them. She felt desperately tired and sleepy, drained of all energy and purpose. She did not even want Alan. She wanted only to lie in bed and close her eyes, to drift away into a dreamless sleep that would blot out all the terrors of the past night.

There was a cry from the people around her, and she looked up quickly, terror returning at the sound. Sergeant Watkins was once more on the ladder, climbing slowly. But the staring faces were looking beyond him, and Elizabeth followed their gaze.

Desmond was crouched on the window sill; he looked small and lonely and pathetic. Slowly he raised himself to his feet, his hands clutching the window frame. There was a shout from Sergeant Watkins, a horrified gasp from the watching crowd; then his arms shot out and he sprang for the ladder. His fingers touched it lightly, failed to hold — and he fell, arms flailing and legs bicycling, the slight cry that he uttered swept away on the breeze.

Alan caught her to him, burying her face against his raincoat. But her ears were not muffled. She heard the thud as the body hit the ground, and then she fainted.

* * *

'Did you know it was Desmond who killed Aunt Charlotte?' Alan asked curiously.

Inspector Pitt shook his head.

'You and your friends confused the issue. So did Miss Messager — Mrs Farrel, I should say — by concealing her marriage. But even without that confusion we might not have pinned him down if he hadn't overplayed his hand. Suspicion isn't enough. There's more than one man at liberty to-day whom the police know to be a murderer. They just lack the evidence to convict.'

'I don't see how my marriage made all that difference,' Elizabeth said.

She had had her sleep. The police had been impatient to question her on what had transpired in the tower, but the doctor had held them off. She was suffering from severe strain and shock, he said; rest and sleep were essential. He had given her a sedative, and she had slept for over twelve hours. Now it was evening; the doctor had seen her and had given permission for the police to interview her, and she had told them all she could recall of the previous night. Parts of it were vague, as a nightmare is vague in detail the next morning. Yet she had thought that every moment of it would be imprinted indelibly on her memory!

She had been anxious to see them in order to thank Sergeant Watkins for her rescue. Outwardly the Sergeant had been embarrassed by her gratitude, his face as red as his hair. Yet secretly he had been delighted at the praise showered on him by Alan Torreck and others, and would have felt cheated had not Elizabeth added her thanks to theirs.

'It made suspicion stronger, miss,' Pitt told her. 'Your husband knew the terms of your aunt's will, that you would not inherit if you married before her death. Your marriage to Mr Farrel on Friday, however secret, automatically excluded you from inheriting — provided your aunt was alive on that day. Didn't you appreciate that?'

Elizabeth shook her head. She looked very young and pathetic and appealing, Alan thought. He wondered how long it would take her to learn to laugh again.

'I'm afraid I didn't,' she said.

'No? Your husband did. That was why he chose Friday for the wedding; not because it was the day after Mrs Lane was due to leave (which was no doubt the reason he gave you), but because he knew that by then she would be dead and the money as good as yours. Or his,' he added.

'How did you know we were married, Inspector? Who told you?'

'The registrar. We had a talk with the manager of the Speckled Trout after seeing you yesterday, and he mentioned that Mr Farrel had booked a room for you both for next weekend. That didn't confirm a wedding, but it implied it. The Tanbury police got the rest from the registrar.'

Elizabeth sighed. She recalled Desmond's gay mood of the previous afternoon, his suggestion at tea-time that they should take a belated honeymoon. Up to then, at least, he could have had no thought of killing her.

When she put this to the Inspector he seemed puzzled.

'I don't understand,' he said. 'Mr Farrel booked that room last Saturday, not yesterday.'

'Oh, but he didn't, Inspector. It was while we were having tea, after I'd told him about the will, that the idea occurred to him. I think — thought' — how could she think it now, after what had happened since? — 'that he wanted to prove to me that the loss of Aunt Charlotte's money made no difference to his — his love for me.'

Only he hadn't loved her; it had been the money, not love, that had prompted him to marry her. Dulcie had had his love.

'More likely he hoped to lull you into a sense of false security,' Pitt said. 'He booked that room after you'd had lunch there on Saturday — before your aunt's body had been found, before either of you should have known that she was dead. No doubt about that. I checked it carefully, knowing its significance.'

Alan too saw the significance.

'Aunt Charlotte would never have allowed you to go off for a week-end, no matter what reason you gave her,' he said slowly. 'Desmond knew that. So either it was an empty gesture, or he also knew that Aunt Charlotte was dead, that she couldn't interfere.'

'That's about it, Mr Torreck,' Watkins agreed. 'And he couldn't tell Miss

Messager — beg pardon, ma'am, Mrs Farrel — what he had done because she might realize its implication. Not then, of course — but later.'

Elizabeth wondered why she had been so eager to believe that Desmond's decision to kill her had been sudden, not planned from the start. He himself had said that Dulcie had driven him to it. How true was that?

'I don't know, miss,' Pitt said when she asked him. 'Perhaps he wasn't thinking that far ahead when he killed your aunt. He gave me the impression, however, that he was trying to shift his guilt on to you. Right from the start he went out of his way to stress the dissension that had existed between you and your aunt; he was at it even yesterday. When he saw I wasn't buying that one I suppose he looked for another solution; or maybe he found circumstances going his way and just let them ride.'

'What circumstances?'

'Well, those sleeping tablets, for a start; I doubt if he meant to implicate his father, but he must have felt reasonably sure you would sleep soundly that night. Then Michael Lane, already under suspicion for your aunt's death, was in the hotel and available as a suspect. And finally there was Mr Poulton's body to provide mute evidence of his own innocence. It all added up to a first-class opportunity, from his point of view.'

'A nice touch, that, about the body,' Jim Watkins said, a trace of admiration in his voice. 'The snag with most murders is the disposal of the body. Farrel didn't try to hide it, he flaunted it — and to his own advantage.'

'Was it?' Alan said doubtfully. 'I know I was taken in. Were you, Inspector?'

'I had my doubts, sir. The position of the body didn't look quite right to me. Nor did those head wounds; they weren't what I'd have expected from a fall. But I wasn't sticking my neck out on that until I'd had medical opinion.'

'And no marks on the windowsill,' Watkins added.

'So if he'd held his hand after killing Aunt Charlotte he might have got away with it?' Alan said.

'He might.' Pitt sounded cautious. 'I'm not saying he would, but he might. The Speckled Trout isn't cheap, you know, and yesterday he was able to lend Mr Lane fifty pounds. Where did the money come from, if only the week before he had been hard up? He had no alibi, and the fact that he had invented one told against him. He knew that. That was why he had to prevent Mr Poulton from supplying us with the additional and extremely damning evidence of the car. Then there was motive; his marriage couldn't have been kept secret for long. And don't forget that the field was limited; just the five of you, with your relatives as rank outsiders. Yes, I think we'd have got around to him, Mr Torreck. But whether we would have arrested him is another matter.'

Elizabeth was feeling sleepy again, and she had not followed this very closely. But she had heard enough to say, 'Last night, in the tower, he told me you knew. Did you? He said something about a pillow, I remember.'

'I knew — or shall I say I was ninety per cent. sure? — that he'd tried to smother you. You see, while the others were looking for Michael Lane I went into his room; under his bed was a pillow with lipstick on it.' The Inspector smiled wryly. 'Lipstick on a man's pillow doesn't necessarily imply murder, of course. But why hide it under the bed?'

Jim Watkins repressed with regret the retort that immediately sprang to his mind. In the presence of the girl it was better left unsaid.

'So that was what you were getting at with your little homily on pillows,' Alan said. 'But couldn't Desmond have claimed that he knew nothing about it, that some one else must have put it there?'

'Not after he had just told us he had locked his door. It wouldn't have worked, would it?'

'I suppose not. But why broadcast the information? It meant nothing to the rest of us, of course, but Desmond must have known what you were getting at.'

'I hoped he would,' Pitt agreed. 'I hoped to panic him into making a false move. And in a way I succeeded — though not quite as intended,' he added, with an apologetic look at the girl.

'So you knew he was guilty, and yet you didn't arrest him.' Alan's tone was accusing. 'You left him in the room with Elizabeth, knowing that he'd already made one attempt to kill her. Wasn't that an almighty risk to take, Inspector?'

A darkening of the pallor on Pitt's gaunt cheeks indicated that the shaft had struck home.

'I'm a cautious man, Mr Torreck. Many years ago I made the mistake of arresting a man too soon; I was young and eager, and I thought I'd got him on toast. But I was wrong, and he got away with it. Maybe that's made me over-cautious. But remember that the lipstick was not necessarily Mrs Farrel's — it needed an analyst to determine that — and I had yet to refute the evidence of that dead body under the window. Nor did I see any risk in leaving him with Mrs Farrel; if he had tried to kill her he had planned it carefully, taking every possible precaution to avoid detection. He was hardly likely to make a second attempt while the hunt was on, and in full view of Constable Williams.' His expression grew grimmer. 'My final instructions to Williams were explicit; under no circumstances was he to let Mrs Farrel out of his sight. I've had a few words with that young man since; I don't think he'll again disobey orders so lightly.'

For a while there was silence in the room. Elizabeth found her thoughts turning to George Farrel; she had not seen him or Dulcie since the previous night. Alan had told her that he had not seen them either; there was a rumour, he said, gleaned from the barman, that Dulcie was leaving the hotel — had perhaps already left. Elizabeth could find no sympathy in her heart for Dulcie Rivers; everything that had happened the previous night had been due, directly or indirectly, to Dulcie. But for George Farrel she had nothing but pity.

Vaguely to her mind came the thought that she and her father-in-law could perhaps help each other. They had both suffered, he more than she. He had grown to like her, she was sure of that; so long as his son's death, or the knowledge that she had deceived him over the wedding, had not poisoned his mind against her, she might be able to comfort him a little. That might be . . .

Alan cut into her thoughts. He said, 'I wonder what Desmond wanted the money for? Didn't he tell you, Elizabeth?'

She shook her head. 'But it could have been for the hotel; he was always talking about the improvements he intended making. Or perhaps he just wanted it to spend on Dulcie,' she added, without bitterness.

'And Michael?' Alan asked the Inspector. 'What will happen to him?'

'That's for a court of law to decide, sir. He was brought before a magistrate this morning and released on bail.'

'Poor Michael.' Elizabeth could not even now entirely avoid the sense of responsibility she had always felt for her cousin. 'Alan says he has confessed to attacking me on the common on Sunday.'

'That's so, miss.'

'But why did he try to run away last night? He had nothing to do with what happened here.'

'Just panic, Mrs Farrel. He'd had a tough afternoon and evening, his father had turned against him (though it was his father who put up the bail for him this morning), and with his conscience still nagging him over the lies he'd told he was in no condition to stand any more. Your scream just about finished him off. He didn't know what had happened, but instinct told him to beat it before he was accused of whatever it was. He was cowering in the attic when we found him; I've seldom seen a more frightened man. That was when he volunteered the information, without any prompting from us, that he'd snatched your bag on Sunday.'

'Once he discovered he wasn't wanted for murder he was positively anxious to be arrested,' the Sergeant said. 'He lacks guts, does Mr Lane.'

Desmond hadn't lacked guts, Elizabeth reflected. At times when he had been talking to her in the tower he had shown signs of being afraid, but always he had mastered his fear. And at the end — had that been an accident, or had he fallen deliberately? They would never know. But

Desmond was a gambler, and it seemed to her that that was how he had died — in a last despairing gamble with death, knowing that the ladder was probably out of his reach, that the odds were against him.

'We were a nice bunch, weren't we?' Alan said. 'And look at us now. Desmond and Bruce dead, Michael under arrest.' He turned to the girl. 'You and I are the only ones left with life and liberty. Two out of five. Not many, is it?'

'No,' Elizabeth said.

She smiled faintly at his earnestness, the first smile she had managed for many hours. Then the smile faded, to be replaced by a blush that spread up her neck and flamed in her cheeks. There was no mistaking the look in his eyes.

Inspector Pitt nodded to the Sergeant, coughed, and stood up.

'I wouldn't know about your lives,' he said, usurping Jim Watkins' rôle of humorist. 'But if I'm any judge of human nature neither of you is going to be at liberty for long.'

Other titles in the
Linford Mystery Library:

DEATH CALLED AT NIGHT

R. A. Bennett

Jimmy Ellis believes his parents have died in a car crash when as a young boy he is taken to live with relatives in Australia. The years pass happily, then the nightmare comes. Terrifying images flit through his mind in the dark — all through the eyes of a child, a witness to grisly events seventeen years before. He begins to delve into the past, and soon he finds himself on the trail of a double murderer — a murderer who is prepared to kill again.